PRAISE FOR ANDREW HOLLERAN:

"Brilliant passages and observations . . . Mr. Holleran's powers of physical description have not dimmed."
—*The New York Times Book Review*

"A fine, thoughtful novel . . . Holleran's descriptive passages of time and place are written with love and precision; his dialogue is sharp and true."
—*Los Angeles Times*

"A memorable book . . . Anyone who has ever been in a family will find home truths in it."
—*Boston Globe*

"Genuinely affecting . . . Holleran's deceptively cool, collected prose doesn't hide the uneasy longing at the heart of his book."
—*Publishers Weekly*

"Andrew Holleran has outdone even himself. *Nights in Aruba* is probably the best-written 'gay novel' to date."
—*In Print*

NIGHTS
IN ARUBA

ANDREW
HOLLERAN

❉ ❉ ❉

A PLUME BOOK

NEW AMERICAN LIBRARY

A DIVISION OF PENGUIN BOOKS USA INC., NEW YORK
PUBLISHED IN CANADA BY
PENGUIN BOOKS CANADA LIMITED, MARKHAM, ONTARIO

This is an authorized reprint of a hardcover edition
published by William Morrow and Company, Inc.

Original hardcover edition designed by Victoria Hartman.

Library of Congress Cataloging in Publication Data

Holleran, Andrew.
  Nights in Aruba.

  I. Title.
PS 3558.03496N5   1984   813'.54   84-4885
ISBN 0-452-26395-6

PLUME TRADEMARK REG. U.S. PAT. OFF. AND FOREIGN COUNTRIES
REGISTERED TRADEMARK—MARCA REGISTRADA
HECHO EN BRATTLEBORO, VT., U.S.A.

SIGNET, SIGNET CLASSIC, MENTOR, ONYX, PLUME, MERIDIAN and
NAL BOOKS are published *in the United States* by New American Library,
a division of Penguin Books USA Inc., 1633 Broadway,
New York, New York 10019, and *in Canada* by Penguin Books Canada Limited,
2801 John Street, Markham, Ontario L3R 1B4

First Plume Printing, August, 1984

7   8   9   10   11   12   13   14   15

PRINTED IN THE UNITED STATES OF AMERICA

�֎ �֎ ✖

When I first lived in New York my object was to sleep through Sundays in winter—there was nothing to do with them anyway, so we stayed out Saturday night dancing. When I awoke Sunday evening it was pitch-black and I was pleased to have seen not a moment of daylight; it meant I would not spend the entire day waiting for a particular person to call me up on the telephone, which had at that time, black and silent, the capacity to hold me hostage for whole days. Years later I lost this romantic susceptibility of heart. And I refused to go out at all on Saturday night; there was no point. I spent the bright, sunny Sundays in Central Park. When I went to bed at night the wind was rattling the window in its frame, and my mind was absolutely vacant, as if I were living in a country town and had just come home from a walk in the forest. I had—in Central Park, whose hills, ravines, and individual fields were so dear to me now that when I went to the country I found it in need of a landscape architect.

Around me in that scrofulous room were clothes of former lovers: a pair of boots, a green shirt, a blue parka with the yellow lift ticket—from a ski resort we had visited one Sunday as cold as this one—still attached to the zipper. I refused to throw the lift ticket away, because it was proof that I had lived that Sunday with that lover, the one I thought about each November as I put on that parka the first cold day of winter—when one still enjoys the weather, and the early darkness, and the prospect of snow.

Some nights I told myself that even though I was exhausted I should get out of bed and walk up Second Avenue to Stuyvesant Square and find someone standing under a tree and bring him back to the room in which I lay alone, wasting yet one more night of a youth already artificially extended by my failure to find anything more compelling than this experience. And I threw back the covers, put on my pants, crossed the cold wooden floor through rooms by now so familiar to me I could negotiate them in the dark, put on a shirt, shoes, overcoat, scarf, and gloves, and ran downstairs. The street was always empty at that hour. Two drunks sat on the bench at St. Mark's in-the-Bowery arguing about the attempted assassination of the Pope. "Somethin's comin' *down,* man!" one yelled as I broke into a run up the avenue—simultaneously furious with myself and ecstatic to be awake in the depths of this cold, clear night, racing to reach the little park at Fifteenth Street and learn who was standing beneath the trees. Even on nights when I met someone and went to his apartment or brought him to my own, encouraged by success—or simply avaricious— I would return to the park to find someone else. Other nights I found no one, or no one to my liking, and I returned home with my night finally ended by the knowledge that now I could go to bed without that nagging sense of possibilities not taken advantage of. Other nights I stood before my building till someone walked by. The reason I still lived in New York was that someone almost always did, hoping that between himself and his own apartment a lover would spring up out of the pavement and save himself from the dreadful fate of ending his evening alone.

Sometimes it was too late even for that, however, and as I stood there in the cold darkness trying to convince myself that I should go upstairs to bed, I knew I no longer possessed the youthful heart which had made such moments radiant a decade earlier. So the night before I left for Jasper I tried to go to bed early. I bought the next day's *Times* at the drugstore the moment the truck delivered it, and went up to my room. I read a while: the article on the Chinese census, unemployment in Puerto Rico, a man who wrapped furniture in linen, an exposé of white chocolate, and the tiny paragraphs that told—on an obscure page—of murders, stabbings, bodies found in Central Park, the baby thrown out a window in Brooklyn by a mother convinced he was the devil. Then I set the alarm and lay down and composed myself to sleep. But sleep was impossible. And I began preparing myself for the completely different life I would be expected to live down there, like an actor putting on clothes for a part he is tired of playing.

And the wall outside the window eventually turned gray, and then pale red, and finally it was day. When I went out into the kitchen for a drink of water, the friend with whom I shared the apartment sat at the table groggily drinking a glass of herbal tea.

"Going to Jasper?" he said.

"Yes," I said. "How long has it been since you've seen your parents?"

"Nine years."

"Why?" I said.

"Because I never want to see them again," he said.

"Why not?"

"Because they were bad parents," he said calmly, and lifted the glass of tea to his mouth as he stared dully into space, still captive of the sleep that had eluded me, and which I gave up on entirely by returning to my room and taking down a small canvas bag to pack. His family lived across the river from Manhattan and sent him postcards every now and then for some film festival in Tarrytown, or a note saying Aunt Sara was sick and would love to see him. But he did not budge. He had, with a certitude far beyond me, closed the door on them all. How I had come to share a home with someone whose coldness shocked me—like a man who ends up with a wife not at all his type—was a mystery. It was all a mystery, even though as a young man I had thought figuring things out the only task any man of intelligence would bother with—as if, having figured things out, he would only *then* consent to live. But here I had arrived at middle age and realized I had made no progress, that the moment was past—just as I would look up from the book I was reading on a Saturday in summer and realize when I saw the clock that the last decent train to the beach had left already; or race up and just miss it. I was still on the platform. There was nothing to do but turn back and reenter the city, deserted on the August weekend, as if in silence it would give up its secrets to me.

It could not—and the more I thought about my life the more pointless contemplation seemed. By now I was convinced that thinking was a form of laziness, an excuse for inaction. Often I awoke in the middle of the night in New York as if someone had tapped me on the shoulder—the fabric of sleep came undone—and I found myself in bed frowning into the darkness. I came to possess a certain dark place in the middle of the night which I alone knew of: stern, cold, implacable, far from daylight and friendship. I became dependent on a good night's sleep, which I courted as I had once pursued other things. I could not agree to do anything before noon. And the night before I traveled out of New York, I could not stop thinking for a moment—I could not sleep at all.

It was cold whenever I returned to Jasper, so that even though I finally rose sleepless from my bed and caught a bus to the airport, the chilly air kept me awake. The flight to Gainesville has always gone through Atlanta, and as we went south I continued reading the *Times* like a man picking meat off a bone. I read an article on Volkswagen factories in Ohio, the future of the yen, changes in management at Lloyd's of London. I read the temperatures of cities around the world, and the fishing forecast for Long Island Sound. But as I let the sections of the newspaper drop beside me, I was discarding not only the *Times* but the person who read it daily in New York. And just when I had finished a piece called "The Many Moods of Zucchini," I was ready to put down the newspaper and examine my conscience. There was something about the interior of an airplane—the hush, the gentle bells rung to summon the stewardess, the knowledge that one was high above the earth—that imbued me with the same reflective mood I felt in church before going to Confession. Perhaps it was the brief time it afforded me between the two places in which I lived such different lives. Or it might have been the possibility of crashing: the gravity of the risk I had taken, which always caused me to say an Act of Contrition when the plane was roaring down the runway. Or maybe it was merely the chance to rest, the fact that only in the airplane was I momentarily free of the two lives I tried to keep separate on earth. Perhaps it was just a relaxation of the vigilance required to keep the two ignorant of each other—the vigilance a hypocrite can seldom relax. I stared out the window at the clouds. I waited for some insight, some decision, some new resolve, some solution to come to me as I sat there by the window. But none did. Instead I began to listen to the conversation of the people on my right: a youth from New Jersey going to Gainesville to live in an ashram, and a nurse who had left her husband in Miami and come north to start a new life.

The nurse told how her husband had pestered her for years to allow him to hire a prostitute for a *ménage à trois*. Finally in the eighth year of their marriage she gave in. As

a result of the incident, the nurse discovered she was a
lesbian. She now lived with a woman on a farm near
Gainesville and said she was very happy.

I was so engrossed in the nurse's tale that I was shocked
when I glanced out the window to see the flat pinewoods
of northern Florida beneath the wing, mottled by the shadows of the silver clouds moving overhead. And as the plane
began to descend, the mean landscape came closer: the
grazing cattle, immobile in the bleached, pale, flat fields,
the circular lakes, the umbrella pines, gray shacks, and
shabby farms. The wheels touched the ground—so actual,
so real—there, after all. To my chagrin the plane came to
a stop. The nurse and the Buddhist from New Brunswick
stood up and waited for the stewardess to open the door—
among a host of silent strangers who all seemed to me as
tired, apprehensive, lonely, claustrophobic as I: people who
had to resume their identities on earth. I left the plane with
heavy limbs, marveling that when I crossed the runway
and entered the new, solar-powered terminal, behind the
crowd (of basketball players, professors, and squealing children) I would find my father, aureoled in wisps of silver
hair, the collar of his gray windbreaker turned up, dangling
the car keys in one hand, apart from the crowd. We smiled
and shook hands. He said, "Welcome home," and while it
was good to see him I thought as we walked away how
shrunken a family we were: the two of us. Once in the car
driving from the airport there was little to discuss besides
the flight, the weather. Then the silence began, the silence
of that long drive over the hilly wastes of northern Florida,
when it was not necessary to speak (that was a great advantage of my father's composure: we could spend hours in
perfect silence together), and I began to slow to a rural
speed. The familiar landmarks passed as in a dream—I felt
an entire personality within me begin to disappear. The
dusk thickened. Soon it was night. As we arrived in Jasper

the streetlights came on. We stopped at the post office, whose empty lighted lobby glowed so brightly in the chill darkness (reminding me I would get letters), I forgot my sadness until the car turned into the drive and I saw the wreaths, the Santa Claus, the candles in the windows of the house. A smile of happiness raised the corners of my mouth at the same instant I felt a rush of hopelessness.

"I wonder where your mother is," my father said as we stopped in the garage. "She must be at church, or visiting," he said as we entered the house, fragrant with pine, scented candles, the soft languid nights of Christmas week in north Florida. Here the night was dark, the windows covered with condensed dew tinged amber by the electric candles, the rugs clean, the house stretching around us in perfect order into its nethermost dark rooms as I laid my suitcase on my bed. "Mother!" my father called. "I don't know where she is. Probably telling someone you're coming home. Well, I'm going to bed. There's plenty of food in the refrigerator . . ." he said.

"Good night," I said, "and thanks again for meeting me." And I went into my room. The bed was taut with clean sheets which had, when I lay down for a moment, the fragrance of the sunlight and morning air in which they had dried on the clothesline. And I knew that the sleep I could not find in New York would come to me here with little delay. The house was silent except for my father's breathing. A gust of wind scattered dead leaves over the roof, a sound I often mistook for squirrels. As I lay there with the cold and stillness working into my bones, my eyes wandered over the room and I felt that curious anticlimax of the traveler who after moving in one day from winter to spring, an enormous city to a small town, still finds in the end that he has merely exchanged one room for another. But when I sat up and pulled back the curtain above my bed, I saw, to my astonishment, the sky crusted with innumerable stars, all ice-white, burning in the black firmament. A dog was barking down the road—perhaps at my mother, walking home hurriedly from the house of the neighbors she had told about my arrival. In Manhattan I would hear the quaver of a taxi's horn in the street below my window, but here there was only the sound of the dog, barking, and a sky full of stars.

And yet I began to think that in coming to Jasper I never went far enough south—Jasper, with its chill lake and icy stars, its bare trees and lawns turned gold by the first freeze of winter, its slender column of smoke rising from some hunter's fire in the woods, was still a northern town. That was why we were here: for the change of seasons. But I wanted no more change of seasons; I wanted to be lying in bed again on a hot, still night waiting for my mother to finish her drink on the patio and bid me good night. I wondered if only in warm climates was there serenity. I didn't want to be waiting for her as she hurried to this house; I wanted to be waiting for her as she was then, thirty years ago. "You know I can never live here alone," she said to me once as we walked through this house, locking the doors before retiring. But could I live here with her? Would I ever tell her the truth? I got up and looked in the bedroom across the hall. In the glow of the night light my father slept on his bed in the dim corner: the foundation of our days. On my mother's bureau, clustered beside a tall mirror, were the statue of the Blessed Virgin, the silver tray crowded with crystal bottles of perfume she seldom used, the oval portrait of her own mother. Her bed was not even turned down. I walked down the hall, through the dark rooms, turning on the light in each, revealing the framed photographs, the paintings, lamps, carpets, tables, books, which formed the accumulated substance of this family.

I glanced out through the kitchen window at the dark street, the single lamp left burning at the end of our driveway to light her way home, and then I sat down and waited for this woman who was so anxious to see me, mired in the gloom of a middle age that embarrassed us both. It was only seven o'clock. She was probably in church—arranging flowers, or perhaps confessing sins I no longer confessed: our positions reversed. Thirty years ago I was the puritan and she the libertine. Now circumstances had assigned us the opposite roles, and I was the one astonished by the changes. This woman who was so religious now I could not confess to her, but whom I would not have loved so were she not religious, was still a complete mystery to me. Now her days were spent in all those activities which as a child I despaired of her ever doing. Now she visited the sick, cleaned the altar of the church, washed clothes once a day and hung them out on the line to dry as if her own soul, like those drenched sheets, were whitening in the sun and wind as she approached her final destination. How curious was this house with its artifacts from another house in Aruba. The books on the shelf were the same books that had been on the shelves there—an account of travel in China, a history of ships, a life of Churchill. How had the life we shared there turned into the life we shared here? The candles on the windowsill illumined with an amber light the crescents of dew on the glass; through them everything was blurred, even the light shining at the end of the road to guide her home.

We had exchanged places, she and I. The child who sat in judgment on his parents, who would have turned his mother in, no doubt, to some celestial policeman as readily as a Communist zealot his parents to the authorities—was now the one who feared discovery; who locked his papers, letters, in a trunk, like some dissident afraid of being arrested. But we lived in that family under a different authority: the reign of politeness. Seated in that chair by the cold window I could not help reflecting that the only turmoil in that quiet place was occurring in my mind—and nowhere else. The street was empty, the stars fixed in the sky, the night cold and still; my father's breathing regular; the holy pictures in place, tucked behind the corners of the mirror; the dog barking down the road. Yet in my heart and mind all was despair. How could it be so difficult to reconcile the present and the past? What had I done to make myself feel so uneasy? A drop of dew broke from its crescent and zigzagged down the window to the sill. My pain was purely mental, my fears based on speculation; the enigma of this family I would never solve. Nor would I ever understand the love story in which I had been an actor and which—like all love stories—had its foundation in events and people long before it happened. If I were to explain that love, I would have to go back, to Aruba, to the island on which the three of us were confined. But how could I? And I wondered if it was not time now to look out for myself—to go south farther next winter, as if there I would find a self which had disappeared in false fears and the desire to please others during the intervening years. The dog barking in the street was barking, too, outside our bungalow in Aruba; the woman hurrying home, the one I loved as a child. And as I sat there I decided once more to figure things out: to solve the mystery that baffled me so many years ago when she (beautiful, confident, loved) took me to Aruba on ships that no longer existed, but which I remembered in detail; because all those years I'd been watching, without a word, the behavior of these mysterious people.

1

She and I lived alone only once—in a rooming house in Boston when I was seven—and we didn't remain there very long. The day we told our landlady we were going out to see the motorcade in which President Eisenhower passed through Boston was the day the landlady told us—on our return—we had to leave. The landlady said it was because I had stopped up the toilet by throwing Kleenex in it, but as we drove away in the taxi Mother told me that was not the reason at all. She said it was because the landlady was a Democrat like all the Irish, and had watched us that afternoon from the upstairs window as we waved at the President. "Lace-curtain Irish," she said as we drove to the Parker House; when I asked what that meant, she said she would explain it later.

My father was at a business school nearby and it was November and the two of us were very happy putting overcoats and gloves on every day to go out for shopping and lunch at a little coffee shop whose waitress saved an extra bag of fish-shaped crackers for me to have with my clam chowder. The trees were bare, the sky held thin clouds as hard and white as the swan boats tethered to their dock on a pond on the Common, and Mother thought Jordan Marsh a department store almost as satisfying as those in Chicago. But we left. My father gave us a small portfolio that contained our passports, health certificates, and money, and (happy to be a student once again, living with three other middle-aged men in a dormitory in Cambridge) sent us on our way south. We took one of the oil tankers that left Bayonne, New Jersey, to pick up oil in Aruba. The tanker was so narrow that once at sea the waves broke over it and littered the ship with flying fish, until another wave swept them back into the sea. There were no decks to circumnavigate, or games to play, or children to play with —and when at two o'clock the adults retired to their cabins to nap, the tanker turned into a ghost ship. As I lay on my bunk I told my mother I could not sleep. "Relax," she said. "Start with your toes, and your ankles and your feet, and work up and relax each part of your body." But this did not work and when I leaned out to look down at her, lying in her slip and brassiere on the bunk beneath mine, I saw her blue eyes were closed and her chest rising and falling with the slow rhythm of sleep.

We never knew till we got on board who the other passengers would be, but because the journey took more than a week, and because the passengers were few, they were our only company. Women traveling without their husbands, engineers traveling without their wives, were outnumbered by those who were not married: music teachers, librarians, chemical engineers, instructors in English and Accounting. My mother had a certain sympathy for solitary travelers—and if I was so unlucky as to find myself on a ship with no children my age, I was jealous of the time she spent with them. My mother was convivial; I realized she enjoyed the attention of the captain and his officers at our dining table. She enjoyed the poker games, the conversation in the deck chairs with her fellow passengers, despite the fact that each day was drawing us closer to our home in Aruba. When I told her I did not want to return, she said, "I know. But your uncle is coming in November—we have something to look forward to."

The two of us still shared the same passport; in the photograph inside, I sat on the lap of a woman whose magnificent eyes and faint suggestion of a smile exuded a serene happiness I did not feel. One afternoon, worried about the solitary status of the men and women who shared the passage with us, I asked my mother why the uncle coming to visit us had never married. She thought for a moment and said, "Because he loved my mother too much.

"Your grandmother was very independent," she said as we sat watching the flying fish leap from wave to wave, "but he was her favorite. He took care of her when she was sick and old. He was the one who would drive her down to the gangsters' funerals in Cicero, because she liked to see the flowers. After she died, we knew he would never marry."

The reason she gave for this disturbed me: Was it possible to love someone too much? And didn't she and I have the same terrible sympathy? I was no longer displeased to see her surrounded by the officers at dinner, or at poker, or, when we finally reached Aruba, by a crowd of her golf partners who met us at the dock. She was happy to be home. I was crushed. Aruba was exactly as we left it: every baked hill, every cactus-covered bluff, every granite boulder shining in the sun, every goat standing on the ledges watching us pass. Silence and wind, sunlight and shade, were the alternate sensations of Aruba—and a great baking dry heat that sparkled on the ocean and dried the flats at Bushiribana into huge scales that resembled lily pads curled up at the edges in a drought. By the time we reached our bungalow we were stupid with heat. There was no point in asking Inez—who stood on the porch, clasping and unclasping her hands, blushing and damp-eyed as she welcomed us home—for news. A moon floated above the almond tree though it was only four o'clock. The cat had run away. The wind rustled the date palms. It blew across the flat, oiled earth of the Colony as I went searching through the streets for Ruffles—the strange, windswept, lonely landscape of Aruba.

In Aruba, life was so dull even for Mother that after the welcomers left she insisted I stay up with her while she finished her drink on the porch. Her good spirits perplexed me. How could she be happy here? Aruba had not one element of her former life—no seasons, no cities—and as we drove to church in the weeks after our return, it was past palm trees bleached a leprous, spotty gold by the scant rainfall and relentless sun. The plots of land in the country-side were separated by fences composed of cactus, and all vou saw driving through the *cunucu* was the occasional house or pool hall and a face within watching your car go by. The face was often handsome but soured by boredom as it squinted into the brilliant sunlight. The language was Papiamento. The houses were painted with hex signs to ward off evil spirits. The only car dealership and movie theater on the island were both owned by a family of Belgian Jews who had fled Hitler. They had a villa in the countryside, a yacht, and a hotel suite in New York at their disposal; but their success isolated them—the beautiful daughter returned from school in Paris to find no one in Aruba worth marrying, and the brother went crazy and sank the yacht. Although my mother knew them, I never did. For the most part I hardly knew Aruba at all; it was merely the moan of the wind against the wooden louvers, or the scent of rain soaking into them after a brief thunderstorm. Rain was so rare in Aruba it sent us rushing to the windows to put our faces against the closed louvers, to inhale the fragrance of the water in the wood. We wanted the rain to last forever. But Aruba was ignored not only by passenger ships that stopped at other islands—never ours —it was one of the few places in the Caribbean to lie outside the paths of hurricanes.

And though the two prints by Currier and Ives which hung in the main room of our bungalow depicted "A Winter Sleigh-Ride" and "A Skating Party in the Woods," there wasn't the slightest chance that each morning when we awoke there would be anything but a pure blue sky, a garden filled with sunlight, and the moan of the trade wind against the shut wooden louvers. On a remote island twelve degrees from the equator, in a bungalow from which my older sister had been banished in 1951 for defying my mother by smoking cigarettes, drinking beer, and corresponding with a sailor, there was nothing but the four of us: myself, my mother, my father, and Inez. The only visitors who came to Aruba were odd travelers: Dutch royalty inspecting their possessions, the chanteuse Hildegarde, a senator touring the Caribbean, auditors sent from New York to inspect the books of the Esso refinery. Only one flight a week went to and from Miami in those days, and most of our visitors were members of the mysterious families my mother and father had both left behind when they married each other and came to Aruba.

Curious to know what sort of people produced my parents, I examined not only their exotic clothes—mittens, overcoats, undershirts, if they came south in winter—but their own remarks and behavior while staying with us. The visitors belonging to my mother's family and those from my father's were quite different. My father came from a small town in Ohio and was of German stock. His sisters were three placid, slow-spoken, red-cheeked women who knitted, did not smoke cigarettes, and had no desire to go out at night. They disapproved of my mother because she did not cook and because she did like to smoke, drink, and go out at night. The German aunts and I got along quite well. I wasn't happy my mother did these things either. I took them on walks they wished to take: to the natural bridge at Colorado Point, to the lagoon where the sand flushed pink each time a wave receded, to the pet cemetery in a grove of sea grape trees. My mother never took walks herself. When her own sisters visited she gave lunches, dinners, cocktail and poker parties. But whichever side of the family came to stay, their departure diminished us. Most of the time it was my sister whose comings and goings wrenched my heart. There was no moment more horrifying than that which gripped me as we stood at the railing of the airport, watching her walk across the runway—a tall girl with a set of blue matched luggage—to the airplane, which then revved its engines, accelerated, and rose into the blue sky. The three of us then turned to one another wordlessly and walked out of the airport into the hot wind. My mother and father lighted cigarettes and talked calmly to each other as we began driving home, but I found it impossible to speak.

The silence of the bungalow when we returned after my sister's departure was deathly, the fact that she was elsewhere almost impossible to grasp as I moved my clothes from the bedroom I used while she lived with us to the one I used when she was gone. The room vacated by my sister when Mother sent her off to a Catholic school in Massachusetts had two screened windows; one looked out onto the patio and the other onto the garden. Against the second a hedge of hibiscus pressed its blossoms. The room was used for guests and yet it was to me the temple of our family. We were physically sundered—my sister and I, my parents and their past. But it held all the sacred objects. The windows were shaded with awnings so that it was filled with a gentle, warm light, as rosy and luminous as the interior of a conch shell. A carved Chinese chest in one corner held the pale green Irish linen, seldom used by my mother, which reeked of camphor. Carved on the Chinese chest were mandarins crossing tiny bridges over lily ponds. Upon the polished bureau were the silver brushes and hand mirror that my sister used before she was sent to the nuns on a hill outside Wellesley. In the closet of that room were clothes no one used in Aruba, hung in quilted bags seeded with mothballs: gray overcoats, blue wool suits, the cranberry-red jacket and black beret my mother wore when she went to Europe on a lark one winter and we lived several months without her. On the shelves of the closet was booty amassed over the years of birthdays and anniversaries: a tea service and silver place settings wrapped in towels and old sheets: the treasury of our little family. I imagined that were a volcano to erupt and inundate Aruba in ash, they would find our little household, years later, to resemble one in Pompeii.

Each evening before I fell asleep in this room, when I put down my book and turned off the brass lamp beside my bed, I drew back the gazelle-embroidered curtain from the window that looked across the porch to the window beside the bed in which my mother slept. She drew back her curtain on seeing my light extinguished, and we smiled at each other (thrilled by coziness) before letting them fall back into place.

So apprehensive was I about the cosmic empathy I felt with this woman that when the uncle who remained a bachelor because he loved my grandmother too much arrived, I inspected him with care. No one knew a thing about his personal life: He lived in Chicago with another of my aunts, and not only was he known for leaving the house when an argument began, but he was never asked on his return where he had been. We were said to resemble each other in our dispositions; I disliked voices raised in anger too. But when he arrived he surprised me by being an ordinary, friendly man whose reserve my mother respected as much as her older sister in Chicago did. He astonished me further by finding a chore to do every day of his visit—since there were no leaves to rake in our garden, he dredged the fish pond instead—and by having large blue eyes, the only other person whose eyes resembled my mother's.

But if my uncle and I were alike in our maternal obsession, the two weeks we shared the room in the corner of our bungalow convinced me that was our only resemblance. I had no intention of living so orderly a life when I grew up, for one thing. At nine I had no desire to wear golf slacks, polo shirts, or after-shave cologne. I did not want to have a pair of frosted Ray-Bans I would put back neatly in their case when I returned from the golf course, or pale gray and white golf shoes with shirred flaps and perforated tips. I would never sprinkle talcum powder between my toes when I emerged from the bath. I did not intend to come down to the tropics on vacation, have silver sideburns, or ever be middle-aged. I certainly did not intend to take a nap in the afternoon. It was this custom that baffled me above all. It made me think our bungalow was only a ship at anchor in the wastes of an empty ocean. I could no more sleep at home than I could at sea, and if there were any more proof required that my uncle and I were very different, I need only glance over at his bed—my heart racing in the sepulchral stillness—to see him slumbering peacefully in his monogrammed pajamas, beside the carved Chinese chest.

He surprised me one afternoon by remarking, when he came upon me under the date palms reading one of those novels set in ancient Rome or Napoleonic France, that my mother had read a great deal too as a child—until she was fourteen, when all of a sudden she ceased being shy and came out of her room for good. That my mother had ever been shy astonished me. "Oh yes," my uncle said. "Your mother used to sit at the top of the stairs whenever we had visitors and listen to their voices from the landing. She would do that even when it was only her own brothers and sisters downstairs."

This bit of information implied that people could change a great deal in life—but I did not apply it to myself, because it pertained to a family far larger than my own: the enormous family in which my mother and her brother were only two of eight children. This family which we were so distant from eventually reclaimed my uncle. His last morning in Aruba he put on an undershirt, suspenders, cuff links, and folded over his arm the gray herringbone overcoat he would wear in the snowy cold of Chicago when he got home two days later. We watched the airplane that would take him back to Miami disappear in the hard, blue, empty, sunny sky above the baked and cactus-covered hills of Aruba. Then we drove back in the Buick down the low coral coast, past the familiar landmarks (the fishing boats whose nets were drying in the sun, the decomposing automobile, the palms of Bushiribana, the bridge across the fetid Spanish Lagoon, the little house above whose lintel the words GOD IS LOVE were painted). Only the sound of the wind filled the car.

"Why is everyone so quiet?" my father asked.

"Because *I'd* like to be going to Chicago," said my mother.

We fell silent in the hot, windswept car. In the rearview mirror I could see the cream-colored water tower, the low red roofs of the city of Oranjestad clustered around its turquoise harbor behind a string of mangrove islands. A single schooner laden with bananas floated at the dock. The harbor at Oranjestad was too shallow to receive more than sailboats selling fruit. The earth was so hard the dead were buried aboveground in cement houses, and when we left the airport it was sometimes impossible to distinguish between the houses of the living and the houses of the dead in their groves of thorn trees surrounded by cream-colored cement walls.

In fact Aruba was seldom on maps of the Caribbean in 1952, and as we drove home after saying good-bye to my uncle, all those things that would give it touristic value later on—its dry, hot weather, its ceaseless sunshine—I considered regrettable. My mother's auburn hair, her blue eyes and pale complexion had nothing to do with the landscape in which some mysterious decision had left her. As the parched landscape went by I planned when I grew up to live in some soaked region where it never stopped raining, and clouds of mist blew in daily from the sea to drench the dark, primeval forests: Puget Sound, for instance. I thought of the photographs in American magazines of men in yellow slickers beaded with rain, holding bowls of Campbell's soup, or loggers smoking cigarettes in a grove of giant redwoods. Instead, the hot wind that deformed the divi-divi trees (so that the branches all grew horizontally in one direction) filled the car, and I was looking at the old Buick decomposing at the side of the road just before the bridge across the fetid inlet called the Spanish Lagoon. This rotting car was succeeded by the palms of Bushiribana and a yellow house in front of which two children without pants stood among a dog, a hen, and its chicks, waving at us as we went by. Then came a mission church whose open door revealed a dark interior; a soccer field on which the Fanya All-Stars were playing a team from Maracaibo; the village of Sint Nicolaas; a sudden descent from the coral plateau to the coast; a grove of sea grape trees, and then the flat plain that intervened between it and the red roofs of the American colony, sparkling in the sunlight between clusters of palms made green by the water imported here on ships. No one spoke.

When we were finally within the precincts of the neat bungalows and their immaculate walled gardens, the wind died down and with it our spirits. There was nothing now between us and our driveway shaded by two almond trees. When we finally came to a stop, I saw that the bungalow, the garden, were exactly as we left them. A lizard clung to the screen of my bedroom window when I went in to remove my shoes, its throat bloated into a yellow sac. I spent the next hour packing my own suitcase in the bedroom and—taking the bull by the horns—went out onto the porch and said to Mother and Inez: "Take me to Miami!" They both covered their mouths with their hands and shook with laughter.

No one was going anywhere. The sole evidence of motion was hardly that: Walking into the garden, I looked up and saw an oil tanker's silhouette pasted on the horizon of the sea. But the ship hardly moved and an hour later it was still there. A moon floated above the almond tree. The wind rustled the fronds of the date palms; it blew across the flat, oiled earth of the Colony and rustled our hedge of gardenia bushes. The scent of asphalt baking in the heat, of oiled playgrounds, enveloped the garden. We lived with the odor of petroleum products: putting greens, playgrounds, streets, were all composed of some product of the refinery into which the men disappeared every day. The sun glittered on the rooftops of the bungalows, blurred the surface of the sea beyond the reef, and glistened so brightly on the yellowing palm fronds that as they shook in the breeze it looked as if water, not light, were streaming off their tips.

It was only after the sun disappeared beneath the horizon that the objects—palm trees, flowers, fish pond, wrought-iron gate, low yellow wall—that formed the garden around our bungalow assumed any color and ceased to be mere surfaces reflecting light. It was only at dusk that the elephant-ear vine that climbed the trunk of the date palm, the blades of grass in the lawn, the purple water lilies and lily pads curling at their edges on the fish pond, the yellow almonds fallen beneath the boughs of the almond tree, assumed their own hue and shape. Dusk was so welcome after that long white day—and so empty now that our visitor was gone—that we sat on the steps of the bungalow (warm with the hours of blazing light) and watched the world turn blue. First the sea acquired a rough and watery surface. Then this blue deepened, and as the air itself thickened and things faded in the distance, when the wind itself actually seemed to take on a density it did not have during the white afternoons, and turned slightly cool as it came off the sea, the ocean assumed an indigo so dark it was indistinguishable from black, whereupon I felt, even on that warm tropical island as my mother smoked a cigarette beside me, an involuntary shudder pass through my body, for there is nothing so foreboding as the sight of a very deep ocean stretching as far as one can see when night is falling. Men seem lonely indeed, and brave for having sailed it to reach islands like the one on which we found ourselves.

"I'm going in," my mother said, picking up her cigarettes and matches and standing. "Dinner's in ten minutes. I forget what we're having."

Then there was only the wind in the darkness, which seemed full of sound now that we could see nothing: palms thrashing against each other, leaves rustling on the hedge of olive trees. The cement was cool. When I entered the house I saw my father holding my mother's chair out for her. Dinner was very quiet without our guest. We said grace. The wind howled against the louvers. Inez repeatedly sighed in the kitchen, because she had missed the six o'clock bus to the village, the words: "Lord Jesus preserve me." Her sandals slapped against the floor as she brought the pot roast and corn in from the kitchen.

We ate beneath two paintings: one of a duck leading its babies to a pond in Holland, the other of a woman knitting in an apple orchard outside a whitewashed hut while her children played at her feet. "That is how I want my family," my father said as he glanced at the second painting. It was very nearly how he had it. He went to bed early because he rose each day before dawn to sit on the porch and contemplate the problems he must solve at the office; my mother often went out visiting. But when he was awake at home our life was very placid. And sometimes when I lifted my head from the book I was reading beneath the date palm, and heard the slap of Inez's sandals as she crossed the patio to wash the screens leaning against the hedges, and Mother sat on the porch talking with the woman who lived next door, I felt his dream was the sweetest one on earth.

My father was a man of forty years by the time I arrived on earth and his life by then had assumed a certain routine. Before I awoke he had already gone down to the office in a crisp white shirt and dark tie held in place by a silver tiepin. The Colony which surrounded his bungalow—the mica in its red-shingled roofs sparkling in the sun as we waited for him to return home for lunch—was a place as hierarchical as any human community, and I knew exactly his place in it. Enclosed by a fence, entered in the presence of a uniformed guard who examined license plates or asked for identification, it seemed purely middle-class: the reproduction of an American suburb whose children roller-skated, chewed bubble gum, read comic books, worked on jalopies, held bake sales, went to basketball games and Fourth of July picnics. Yet it was neither purely American nor homogenous. Europeans worked there: Beside us lived a Dutch family, in particular, whose children (both my age) were forbidden to play with Americans. Every day I could hear their shrieks as they played kickball behind their garden wall, like children trapped in a cholera zone. The Americans they were protected from came from every social class and circumstance possible—from small towns in Oklahoma, cities in New England, Texas, and California. Yet all these women had maids and gardeners because, on a global scale, an ordinary American was far more prosperous than a Portugese peasant, say, or a woman from Saba. How this was so I had no idea. But I knew the bungalows overlooking the sea were grander than those inland, and that if a man was one of six executives, he drove a company car; and each of these six executives was given a different model appropriate to his position around the large golden conference table my father showed me one evening when I went to the office with him while he retrieved some papers. I knew just what office he left when at noon a whistle blew in the Colony, hotter than the air itself, and he come home to have lunch. After lunch he took a half-hour nap, during which I sat beside the telephone and made sure that if it rang I snatched it up before the noise could rouse him from his sleep. At one o'clock a second whistle sounded, shrill and hot—as if the noonday were not hot enough on that incandescent island—and my father rose from his bed. He slept on his back, and when he came out onto the porch, and put his glasses back on, it was as if he had not been sleeping at all; not even his tie was loose. He said good-bye and walked out the door and returned to his office in the black Buick baking in the drive.

Four hours later he arrived home in that same black car, and got out as starched, as neat, as he was when he left; and as I put my arms around him, having arrived from school an hour earlier, I could smell the odor of his air-conditioned office by pressing my face against his shirt. It was still chill and fragrant.

We were not able to communicate directly with this businessman; we used the medium of my mother. Whenever we had anything bothering us it was to her we went. My father replied in the same fashion. She was an embassy in which two nations who do not recognize each other leave letters. This was odd, since my father (she often told us) loved us—and asked (we knew ourselves) very little in return: I had to wear polished shoes and have neatly cut hair; my sister was forbidden to bite her fingernails. What could have been simpler? Yet we regarded him with awe.

That magisterial body lying in crisp, starched perfection on his bed during the thirty minutes between twelve-thirty and one P.M., when I tiptoed into the bedroom to retrieve a pencil I had left there by mistake, frightened me, and I crept out of the room with my breath held and heart pounding.

My father—like a god—was exempt himself from mortal religion: He never went to church. The rest of us dressed for Mass at a church in the village of Sint Nicolaas. When we left him in bed on Sunday morning, reading one of the paperback westerns he consumed as rapidly as packs of cigarettes, drinking coffee as he turned the pages of *Honcho from Red Hell,* I was torn between the belief that the Church was an enormous privilege and the sense that it was a duty my father was magnificently free of. When we returned from Mass he was no longer in bed reading his western. He was now dressed for golf, sitting in a wicker chair underneath the two date palms in our garden, reading the financial section of the Miami *Herald,* studying the stock market. "My advice to you," he said once, "is to get a degree in law and finance. And you'll be able to write your own ticket."

My father had no vice that I could see—unless it was the compulsive generosity that caused my mother to criticize him for offering me money even when I did not ask for it. When I was ill he brought me brand-new books. But here was the rub: I could not think of a single thing to say to him when we were alone together.

In fact, when I found myself with my father on a Sunday afternoon drive, for instance, I had to rack my brain for topics of conversation I felt might interest him. These, I concluded, could be only two: world events and matters of finance. But though I expressed a curiosity about the gold standard and how it worked, we knew as I sat there beside him that his answer was going in one ear and out the other. Still, the two of us made the effort. Yet when the drive ended I was not sure at all if I bored my father or interested him.

On Saturday afternoon he ate lunch (always the same lunch: fried fish with lemon) and went off to the golf course. On Saturday evening he and my mother went out. My mother asked me to select her necklace and insisted I kiss her as a benediction before sending her into the night. On Sunday, people came to our bungalow and sat in the garden under the date palms and drank. I was seldom alone with my father, and when one evening we were to attend a Father and Son Banquet together, I ran away instead.

My father belonged to the haircut-and-polished-shoes school of fatherhood—I could have blown up a bank as long as my loafers were shined, my sister said—and we saw each other little. The worst time came when we went to get our hair cut together. "Why do you hate so to get a haircut?" he asked me once on our way to the barbershop.

"Because it's so boring!" I said. "Because I hate sitting there waiting for him to finish, and then I have to wait while he puts talcum powder on my neck!" I said, squirming on the car seat at the thought.

"Why, you should relax," he said to me. "It's the most pleasant thing in the world. I still remember the time a man in Havana, Cuba, shaved off a beard I had grown—the smell of the shaving cream, the lotion he slapped on my neck, the sound of the water running in the gutter across the street. It was a beautiful morning."

My father enjoyed the morning. He got up hours before the rest of us, and went out onto the porch and drank coffee and smoked cigarettes and thought. What he thought I was never sure—when asked once about his early life, he simply told me his father died when he was young, he lived in a big house in a small town in Ohio with a barn behind where he would sometimes go to strangle a chicken for dinner, that in summer he worked on surrounding farms, and eventually he moved to Chicago and went to work for Standard Oil. He gave me two pieces of advice: never to save money on shoes, and to treat oneself to a steak dinner now and then. The afternoon I asked him point-blank, "What is your philosophy of life?" he looked up at me with a momentarily confused expression on his face and said: "I guess I'm a fatalist—whatever happens, happens." This was his German side—the same calm his elder sister felt escorting psychiatric patients to hospitals during the Korean War. She told me always to empty my bladder before a plane crash. But I think his real philosophy of life—his opinion of how it was best lived—was expressed, curiously enough, in that epigram he often repeated as he hovered over me on the oily driving range, adjusting my grip, advice that supposedly pertained only to the Titlist at my feet but which summed up better than anything else his pagan, tolerant, humane approach to existence: "Good golf is easy golf." It was my nervousness, my very anxiety to know for sure what life meant, that made me rush through life in a perpetual state of worry.

One afternoon when everyone was out I went through his drawers. They were filled with neatly folded handkerchiefs, starched shirts, dark ties, and numerous pairs of cuff links, including several he seldom wore, in blue boxes. Boxer shorts, socks—maroon, blue, or black—and golf shirts filled the middle region. In the very bottom among the westerns and packs of Camel cigarettes, however, I came upon the photograph of a serious, handsome young man of about fifteen years, with thick hair and thin lips. It took me a few moments before I realized it was my father. There was also rolled up an engraving of a nude woman reclining on a sofa, a Parisian print my father had purchased at one time and which was the subject once, when alluded to, of a smile on my mother's lips. Both of these shocked me, somehow: to realize my father was once as young as I was, and to know naked women were a source of pleasure to him. My poor father! I thought. Once so young and handsome.

I closed the bottom drawer and moved across the room to my mother's polished bureau and opened one of hers. It was a riot of brassieres, stockings, and worn missals she no longer used. This silken chaos perfectly represented this particular woman—who, if she began Sundays in pearls, perfume, and white gloves, almost always ended them seated in a chair in the living room, extracting a cigarette as she told me, "You're not going to bed till I finish this drink." These words horrified me: Puritan that I was, in love with domestic order, I wanted her to be forever sober; but the only time that occurred was during Lent, when she gave up alcohol. Nothing was more touching to me than to visit in the middle of a sunny afternoon a friend whose mother was baking some cake whose recipe was in the latest issue of a women's magazine. But my mother told me more than once that she did not particularly like the company of other women—whose conversation centered on such petty things—much less their magazines.

If I had been forced to look at my mother objectively as she sat in that chair beside the little brass lamp from Indonesia, I would have had to say she was a Catholic woman from Chicago who had met her husband at a lake resort in Wisconsin. She was living with her large family in Oak Park, Illinois, and working as the receptionist in the medical department of the telephone company. Why she left it all for the island on which she now found herself I often wondered, because when I sat on the porch with her through the long evening, she told stories about her previous life that made it seem quite happy. She adored her family. She had on her bureau a tiny oval portrait of her mother: a woman in a high-collared dress, her hair piled high upon her head. Even though mother smoked cigarettes, enjoyed alcohol and poker, horse-races and black-jack, she was but one generation removed from the Victorians, and left the room when anyone began an off-color story. She said once to me: "I think I would have been happiest in the last century, dancing the waltz." In fact she had a reputation in Aruba for standing on her head at parties.

My mother was completely out of my control; she was two women, and which of them would be seated on the porch when I got home from school I never knew beforehand. During the long periods when no visitors from the United States were in our bungalow my mother had little to do. She usually rose late and had tea on the porch and then conferred with Inez about the day ahead of them. On Tuesday she shopped. On Wednesday she played poker with seven other women who met at one of their bungalows. Her duty was to greet my father when he returned from work, at which time he mixed cocktails, took one out to the Portugese gardener, then sat on the porch to talk with my mother. I suspected even as I brought her a tray of tea on the porch in the afternoon that we imprisoned my mother by not allowing her to do any work. She was like one of those purely ceremonial empresses whose existence, while gilded, is completely controlled by those who wait on her. We never allowed her to do the slightest thing for herself—not out of any conspiracy, but rather because there were so many of us (my father, myself, Inez) who volunteered their services. Tea and sandwiches, drinks, ice cream were brought to her on trays; occasionally we collided in the kitchen preparing little morsels for her, embarrassed suitors of the same woman.

When I came home from school and found her sitting on the porch in her blue robe, she seemed as inexplicable to me as the gardenias that fell from the hedge outside my bedroom window and maintained their symmetry even as they decomposed on the lawn, petals detached but in place. Her beauty seemed to me as tragic as the flowers that no one bothered even to cut or put in a vase: nature's superfluity. Her looks I see now were Celtic: her auburn hair (the closest thing I could find to it was the coat of a neighbor's Irish setter), the blue eyes which were so striking they set her apart (in my view) as some heroine captured by tribesmen of a muddy hue. My father, sister, and I had the misfortune to possess brown eyes; the gene that made her eyes blue had been squandered in the blood of my father's family, inundated by the waters of an inferior river. It hardly mattered that the closet and the chest in the pink bedroom were filled with silver tea services wrapped in towels, Irish linen, inlaid cigarette boxes, figurines—her eyes were lost forever. They remained a sign of her superiority. I viewed her—as I did all women, perhaps—as a lady stranded in circumstances beyond her control. She was the princess trapped in the hut of mud and wattles on the Rhine.

Yet this captive woman depended on our love—the three superstitious kisses on alternate cheeks she insisted on when I said good night, the tea I brought her that was not important in itself (some days she hardly touched it) but stood for affection. If there was no symbol there must be an assurance of some sort. "You don't love me," she would say in the middle of those long evenings on the porch when I was her sole audience, forbidden to leave until she finished her drink, "and you never have. You're just like your father." I protested that I did love her but she continued to insist on my indifference. "You'll see," she said with such tragic conviction I began to wonder if she weren't correct, "when I'm dead and gone."

"Mother, don't say that!"

"Why not?" Her cigarette glowed in the gloom, and she stared straight at me as she tapped it against the ashtray and said: "'Tis a fearful thing to see the human soul take wing."

The first time I heard this I was speechless—till I whispered, "What does *that* mean?"

"'Tis a fearful thing to see the human soul take wing," she sighed with the same air of possessing a truth I was not privy to.

This suggested she was dying of a secret disease and I shouted, "What do you mean? What do you mean?"

One night during my sister's visit Mother intoned this line with baleful authority, and my sister stood up and yelled, "That's from a poem by Byron, Mother! We read it last week in English class. It refers to a political prisoner dying in a chateau in Switzerland!"

Mother said in a low, dramatic voice, "Exactly. Exactly."

Silence. Then I blurted, "But you're not our prisoner! We don't keep you in prison!"

"No?" she said. "Think about it." And she stood up, gathered her cigarettes, and without another word went off to bed. I didn't even think she wanted to go to bed, but the line demanded a dramatic exit.

My sister—impervious to Mother's charisma in a way I was not—was seldom there, however. On those afternoons when I came home to find Mother seated serenely on the porch in her blue silk robe, a book on her lap, a cup of tea on the table beside her—the last faithful love I would ever have—I was a fool to suppose that this was the calm, sensible, domestic mother of my dreams. As I came onto the porch she looked up from her book and said, "And whose little boy are you?"

"Yours," I said.

She laughed and said, "No, no, there must be some mistake. Just tell me your name and I'll have Inez walk you home."

"*This* is where I live," I said. "I'm *your* son."

She smiled gently and said, "Where do you really live? Whose are you?"

And not until I was weeping uncontrollably in her lap did she put her book down to comfort me.

On its cover a voluptuous blonde lay in a pool of blood beside a revolver and a broken champagne glass beneath the Venetian blinds of a house in Miami. My mother read murder mysteries as omnivorously as my father devoured westerns, and there was always a small stack of them on the nightstand beside her bed. Sometimes she was reading the lightweight Air Mail Caribbean edition of *Time* magazine which came once a week to our house, with pages thin as onion-skin, or the more substantial *Saturday Evening Post*, with its series by Clarence Budington Kelland which all ended with the words, *To Be Continued*. One afternoon as I lay on the carpet at her feet reading my own volume of the Hardy Boys series, she looked up in the perfect stillness, narrowed her eyes at me, and said, "I wonder how you'll turn out." I did not know what to tell her. I was quite happy as we were and would have consented to time's cessation at that moment. I was always silently thrilled to return from school and find my mother reading—I was apprehensive when I saw her on the patio with other people drinking gin and tonic. When she put her head back to sip her drink, in fact, my mother's upper lip rose and I could see through the glass her front teeth upon the rim; it was the only time she was not beautiful, that moment when the lip drew back to reveal two white teeth on the edge of the glass. She put the glass down, swallowed, and the moment was over. She leaned forward and listened to Belle Ewart confide something to her behind a confidential hand, as if there were spies in the hedge trying to read lips.

Hours later the guests would leave, my father would be in bed, and I would be seated in the living room watching my mother dance impromptu hulas in her bare feet, hands telling a little story that was not clear, a happy smile on her lips as moths beat against the screens to get at the light.

Other evenings she simply sat in her chair and told stories. She liked to tell stories. After a while I began to recognize the staples in her repertoire: the time the steering wheel of the car came off while she was driving down Michigan Avenue, the time she borrowed her older sister's lace dress and ripped it walking on stilts, the time a mysterious man sent her a box of Fanny May's chocolates every Friday when she worked as a medical receptionist at Marshall Field's, the time she flew solo across Lake Michigan. These were good stories but she ruined her performance by repeating them; when one was finished, she would extract another cigarette, sip her drink, look off into space, and then begin the story again from a slightly different angle. I listened because I was afraid of her sarcasm, her moral authority, her declaring my sister and me "selfish." I was determined not to be selfish. But the repetition of the stories drove me slightly mad. I imagined a quick slap across her face—perhaps it was the only way to force her to stop repeating; perhaps she had no control over it. Yet when I did say, "Mother, you're repeating yourself!" she froze, the cigarette at her lips, her other hand about to lift the matchbook. She regarded me with narrow eyes.

"I'm repeating myself," she said. "What should I do: roll over and die?"

In reality the remark wounded her so, she took the unlighted cigarette from her lips, put it down, got up and went to the bedroom door, where she turned with one hand on the knob and said, "Someday when you're a little older, you may realize that repeating yourself is not the worst thing you can do in life. Think about it. There are other things far worse." And she went into the bedroom, leaving me far more devastated than I had been by boredom and frustration; leaving me with head in hands, like a child who wishes to capture a butterfly and ends up killing it instead.

Most times the accusation had no effect on her. She said,

"So what?," struck the match, lighted her cigarette, and said, "Well, what *would* you like to talk about? Give me a topic." Then she picked up her drink and began another story. My father emerged to insist my mother go to bed. She refused. He had to wrestle her against the wall to get her into the bedroom, like a madwoman who refuses her straitjacket, until my mother suddenly looked at us both, during a break in the wrestling match, with an expression so amused I suddenly burst out laughing. And she covered her mouth with one hand and laughed too. "If you haven't got a sense of humor," she said, "forget it. You might as well lie down and *die.*" And after bending down to accept the three superstitious kisses from me on alternate cheeks —left-right-left—she shuffled on into the chilly air-conditioned depths of her bedroom. The door closed, and there was only the sound of the machine shuddering and dripping on the hibiscus hedge beneath their window. I sighed and went around the room collecting the detritus of the long afternoon and evening: the glasses, napkins, ashtrays, bottles.

In the morning I found another woman—so crestfallen that when, during lunch hour, I entered her bedroom, still chilly with a night of air-conditioning, she kept the bedspread across the lower part of her face so that only her beautiful blue eyes regarded me with alarm as I walked across the room. The other woman seemed miles away. Inez was singing "Rock of Ages" in the kitchen, and I brought the inlaid brass tray she prepared on these mornings (a cup of tea, a bowl of milk in which a single piece of peppered toast floated soggily) to her mistress. Mother looked as if I might strike her, however, as if she had never seen such a bowl of milk and toast in her life, although it was as regular a feature of these mornings as my forgiving her. I bent down to kiss her but she pulled the bedspread tight across her mouth, fearful her breath was stale. I stood back. She lowered the bedspread, sat up and said: "Can you ever forgive me?" Then she allowed me to kiss her on the cheek and she accepted the gardenia I had torn off the hedge outside.

"Do you know what you said last night?" I asked her once, after a particularly sarcastic performance shocked me so I concluded it was merely the alcohol that caused her to say such things to whoever happened to be in the room.

"Of course I know what I said last night," she said as her cool blue eyes regarded me. "I always know exactly what I'm saying." In the clear light of day, the dancer of hulas, teller of stories, was another person altogether—so sensible she often seemed to me appallingly cold.

When Lent arrived she gave up alcohol altogether and was completely rational. The puritan in me was finally at peace; our household was perfect. The wind against the louvers, the sunlight blazing on the baked and arid cactus-covered hills, even the sighs of Inez as she sat down to rest on the steps of the maid's quarters, were finally synchronized with the spiritual universe: We were virtuous for forty days. People came to visit but they, not Mother, got drunk. She remained as clear-eyed as Athena, or Mary, a virtuous Hebrew wife in the midst of Babylon, and saw them on their drunken way after I had gone to bed. There were no stories, no melodramatic scenes; and the very sea, the hills, the granite boulders shining in the sun between herds of goats, formed the landscape of those biblical heroes who filled my imagination in both Old and New Testaments. It was Lent in Palestine. It was Lent in Aruba. I returned from school each day to pray, before the altar assembled on my bureau, to induce the Blessed Virgin to appear, or any saint who would care to manifest himself to me, until I heard a knock on the door and my mother's hearty voice saying, "Will you let us in there? Inez wants to clean. She says those things are covered with dust!"

My eyes roamed quickly over the portrait of the Sacred Heart of Jesus, whose immense almond-shaped eyes followed you as you walked past, the large ceramic and small wooden crucifixes, a statue of the Infant of Prague which glowed in the dark, another of the Blessed Virgin on a ceramic cloud ascending to heaven, and I said, "I'll dust them."

"That dresser is the *only* thing in the house Inez is not allowed to touch," my mother continued. "I hope those fronds," she said, referring to the palms blessed on Holy Sunday by the priest which I had taped to the wall above the altar, "are not drawing roaches."

"How can you say that?" I gasped behind the closed bedroom door.

"Well, it's possible," she said in her energetic voice, the voice she used throughout Lent. "Now let us in! You've got plenty of time to pray," and with that she opened the door and I looked up to see the two women, Inez already armed with cloths and a feather duster, ready to ransack my room. I rose from my knees. My mother stood there while the fronds were inspected. The house itself was raised up on short stilts embedded in pots of sticky oil, so that no animal might crawl from the coral ground into our rooms; but now we saw, paralyzed on a wall, a waterbug, and heard a shriek as Mother came to a halt with one fist on her breast and the other arm pointing at the impressive winged cockroach.

"Kill it! Kill it!" she yelled.

Her excitement only made me panic; as I nervously thrust a broom at the roach, the division in my heart (between obedience to her, and obedience to God) caused me to be completely ineffectual. The roach dashed off behind the bureau. She turned on me and roared, "Is something wrong with you that you cannot even kill a bug? God!" she said, with a sneer of contempt. "What am I raising, *a man who cannot even kill a bug*?" She took a cigarette out of the pack in her pocket, lighted it, and crossed her arms. "I'm not sleeping tonight until that bug is killed," she said flatly.

"But, Mother!" I said in despair. "We should not be allowed to destroy what we cannot create, and since we cannot create even a cockroach, since only God can do so, we have no right to kill it!"

"Either that bug is killed," she said calmly, "or I will call your father."

"You are—you are—" I said, speechless at the thought of her calling him to perform the deed in lieu of myself. Her own fear of the bug's appearing again made her leave the room. I thrashed about with the broom, wondering about the contradictions of this woman. After a suitable length of time I went to the living room and found her seated in a chair, with folded arms and a determined set mouth. "I did it," I said. "It's gone."

She removed the cigarette from her mouth and said, "You did not kill that cockroach. Now go back and do it."

I returned to my room, moved the bureau away from the wall, and found the roach, its antennae waving rapidly in an attempt to fix its position in the universe, and killed it. I returned to the living room with its carcass on a paper towel. Like an Oriental empress in one of those biblical tales that colored my imagination, my mother rose with some dignity to inspect the offering. Then she said, "It's time for my poker club," and went to her bedroom to dress. "We'll have to have a thorough cleaning there tomorrow morning, first thing," she said. "I find it very peculiar that you would not kill that bug when I asked you to. I have a lot to think about. A *lot* to think about," she said, and put her cigarette between her lips and disappeared into the air-conditioned depths of her bedroom without even asking for three kisses. I had to think also: Did my distaste at killing an insect mean I was superior or inferior to her conception of manliness?

And when a classmate showed up at our bungalow one

afternoon to settle a grudge, it was Mother who pushed me out the door and then stood on the porch with Inez—like two men at a cockfight—and hollered, "Come on! Come on! Keep fighting!" as we rolled around in the flowerbed trying to push each other's face in the dirt. Women baffled me, my mother in particular. I never asked why during my childhood Mother would, with a little shove, not only propel me out the door to fight my classmate but also out of our pew at St. Therese's toward the Communion rail at Sunday Mass. She never went herself. She insisted we go but she did not budge. On Saturday afternoon she drove us down to the village for Confession, and waited in the car while my sister and I crossed the blazing bright courtyard and went inside the tiled and shadowed church. As I knelt in a pew near the great open doors, where there was a breeze, idly examining my conscience, I could see her smoking cigarettes in the car, or eventually getting out to talk to some other American woman waiting in the shade of the thorn tree. I would see them talking while the nuns in white habits glided down the long arcade behind them. The soft breeze, the holy water drying on my forehead, the murmur of the Aruban widows in black dresses and black scarves who prayed before the statue of St. Therese, surrounded us in a great hush, while my mother lighted her cigarette outside and smiled at something her companion said.

If for some reason I chose not to receive Communion—if I decided on Sunday morning that my soul was spoiled by sins committed since my last Confession—as the pews emptied around us of communicants, she would press my ribs, lean over, and hiss in my ear: "What's wrong with you? Go on!" And I, loyal to Christ, my own standards of sanctity, would shake my head and feel my body stiffen. Afterward she would say impatiently as we drove away from church, "Why didn't you take Communion?"

I would simply say, "Because . . ." and look out the window stubbornly, sad and angry with the knowledge that I had envied others, been jealous, or hated someone, as we drove through the still sleepy village, just coming to life with the sounds of roosters, goats, women emptying pails into the gutters. But why she did not take Communion I did not ask. Did she ever worry that we would? I concluded that in her past she was guilty of a sin, but what that sin was I had no idea. So I let her poke me in the ribs, lean over, and whisper, "Go on, get up there!" I was going in her place.

The Americans and the Europeans always knelt together on Sunday morning in the first ten rows of pews south of the broad aisle that intersected the church. The priest and the nuns were Dutch but the congregation was Caribbean. One was conscious always of being different. The young black women of the village thronged the courtyard whenever an American or British girl got married at St. Therese's. They stood on the steps watching the flower girls and ushers and bridesmaids, and afterward they went to Father de Haas and said they wanted a wedding just like that. I sat with my mother in the front pew of the second section, where the breeze, fragrant with Shalimar and scented holy water, swept through the church. Near the altar, among the women in black dresses and black scarves —the Aruban widows in perpetual mourning who said the Rosary at the foot of the statue of the Blessed Virgin—was an American boy my age who was far more devout than I, and who lived across the street from us, and who always went to Communion on Sunday.

This apprentice saint prayed even in school. I would see him sit up, pale and startled at his desk beside the louvers. when the teacher called on him.

The louvers of our classroom were usually shut against the brilliant sunlight and monotonous trade wind. Sometimes during study hall, that somnolent, silent hour, I would put my face close to the louvers to feel the soft breeze whistling through the slats and then open them just enough to see the brilliant coral plain outside and the chafed ocean.

School let out at three o'clock and Wheatworth and I walked home together because we lived on the same street. During Lent he gave up conversation unless it was absolutely necessary and our walks were silent. His reputation for sanctity had spread among the maids: They knew he had taken all the money he could find in his father's house and gone down to the Community Church and distributed it among the Portugese gardeners there, most of whom refused to take it. He went to Mass in the village every day and they passed him on the road walking home as their bus went by, and when the same bus passed us on its way back to the village, the driver honked the horn and the windows sprouted arms waving handkerchiefs as voices called to him. Lent made Wheatworth happy. On Good Friday he fainted in church because he had not eaten in two days, and was disappointed when told it was not through supernatural causes. He was so grave and kind that my father—who gave an opinion so seldom that when he did it carried weight—said, "There should be more people in the world like Michael." He was kind, and seemed to have no regard for the material wealth that characterized his life. On Easter Sunday he fainted again during the Consecration of the Host. The event only confirmed in the eyes of all the maids that he was a saint. It began with a commotion near the lily-heaped, incense-clouded altar. We looked up from our missals and saw Wheatworth being borne from the church against the tide of communicants, pale as a wax saint, on a bier of native women, to be revived outside.

My own religious quest—as much an attempt to escape my family, perhaps, as anything else, to escape the world itself by following the one road no one could pursue me on —waned. It was impossible for an American, as impatient as I was, to sustain the intense concentration needed to induce the Blessed Virgin to appear. Eventually the bedroom whose louvers were closed against the howling wind ceased to be the gloomy cell of an apprentice saint and became simply a bedroom. Religion deteriorated into art. I abandoned the *Lives of the Saints* and turned to a novel by Lloyd C. Douglas in which the Roman hero went home after his rejection by the beautiful daughter of a Christian senator and had his slaves flogged, so that their groans would make him forget his own pain. Such voluptuous sadomasochistic pleasures were permissible in this work because eventually Marcellus would become a Christian himself, living with his wife and children on a small island (not unlike Aruba) remote from the decadence of the Roman court—in our case, New York. This scheme of things attracted me intensely: sin and reformation, carnival and atonement, debauch and penance. But the only decadence available to a youth my age was the banal rites of passage conducted by classmates—and having seen enough of drinking, smoking cigarettes, I wanted none of them. So when my mother whispered "Go!" as others began to leave their pews to approach the altar and receive the Host, I went as a kind of offering, a hostage to virtue, because no one else in my family was communing. And the awe that stiffened my face as I stood waiting to kneel before the priest was perhaps only partly religious, and partly that of the child who senses that in a secular world of conspicuous sinners, the most rebellious thing he can do is to take religion seriously.

Driving back to the American colony after Mass on Sunday, my duty discharged, I hardly spoke to my mother. There we were, prosperous Americans moving in a Buick through a town composed partly of shacks with corrugated tin roofs and walls of cardboard, in front of which women inexplicably stood sweeping the coral ground with a broom. We passed a few chickens, dogs, a woman watching the street from the window cut into the cardboard panel that constituted the wall of the house, young men in yellow hats on their way to a soccer match at the stadium. Wheatworth (who went to all three Masses on Sunday and hitched a ride after the last one) stared with dark, narrowed eyes at the passing poverty—his greatest desire, to live among the impecunious in Saavaneta, in a hut with an earthen floor. Going back to the Colony was for him merely to test his faith. He believed it really was harder for a rich man to enter Heaven, and saw in the faces of these women in black scarves, scattering chickens as they swept the oily ground, the women who followed Christ through Galilee. I watched his eyes dampen and fill with sympathy as the wind ruffled his black hair on this Sunday morning which seemed (now that Mass was behind us) so cheerful to me, with a rooster crowing, a radio playing, the fresh breeze coming in off a sunlit sea. His face stiffened when, leaving the poorer quarters behind, we came to the new part of town in which the men congregated outside pool halls and cement-block bars in short-sleeved electric-blue shirts and tight-fitting tops and straw hats with plaid bands around the brim tilted back over their sun-bronzed faces. The music that blared from the shadowy rooms behind them consisted of trumpets, blurting fast merengues, or unfolding the long sexual complaint of a bolero. This sound—or the sight of these men lounging outside the Caribe Bar—caused Wheatworth to murmur, as he sat by the window in the back seat squinting at the passing scene, "How can people forget that even now Christ is dying for them on the Cross?"

It was a question there was no answer for. Mother turned to me and said, "Get me a cigarette, will you?" The men meanwhile stood inside every bar we passed. On the veranda of the Strand Hotel the Dutch sailors sat with bottles of Heineken in hand. They combed their hair straight back from their foreheads with Vitalis, and rolled up the sleeves of their shirts (a masculine style my sister insisted I adopt whenever she took me anywhere in public) to reveal the tattoos on their triceps. Then they waited for women to pass by on the sidewalk like my friends in the theater waiting for the movie to start. "The world is divided into two kinds of societies," my father said: "those that tolerate flies, and those that do not." The former apparently outnumbered the latter near the equator but we belonged to the second kind. We drove through this Caribbean town no more than five minutes—that was all I saw of it—before the houses grew sparse, and then as we felt the breeze from the ocean fill the car we passed its last home, a cement building on which the owner had painted the words GOD IS LOVE above the lintel. The road went down a hill, through a grove of sea grape trees, passed the guard, and then traversed the flat, windy coral plain to the Colony.

Once we reached the Colony—if it was Lent—we stopped at the Hunts', a childless couple who liked to cook breakfast on Sunday morning for their friends' children. This visit had a virtue in my eyes: I imagined it was kind on my mother's part to stop there at all. "Life is pointless without children," my mother said one afternoon. So I supposed she was sharing her children with the Hunts on these sober Sunday mornings when—because she gave up alcohol for Lent—blueberry pancakes took the place of whiskey sours. Lent made me happy: She was in her robe every evening at seven o'clock.

Our own household was as sober those forty days as that of a Roman family during the reign of Augustus. If guests filled the garden when we arrived home, my mother made sure their drinks were fresh and drank soda water herself, and in the evening thrilled me by reading a book in the lighted living room across the carpet from my father and me. If there were no guests in the garden, my father went to the golf course, my sister was ordered to take me to the movies, and my mother protested—in the voice of that sensible, cool, detached woman who reigned supreme all of March—when he gave us more money than necessary for our excursion: "You spoil these kids rotten," she said. "You're always giving them money. They'll have nothing to want when they grow up." Her words haunted me all afternoon even in the midst of pleasure, as I watched pirates with oiled chests leap onto burning decks to rescue Rhonda Fleming, and the Blessed Virgin appear above a bush to three children in a field in Portugal. On our return I mentioned the letter the Pope had been given by the children at Fatima which, when opened, would reveal the future of the world.

"What letter?" said my mother, looking up from the book she sat reading in bed, where we found her already in her nightgown.

"The letter the children who saw Our Lady at Fatima were given," I said. "A letter which when opened will reveal the future of the world."

My sister said nothing.

"It's all true," I said. "She made the sun stand still. Thousands of people saw it. The Pope has the letter now."

"So why hasn't he opened it?" my sister said.

"Because he's not supposed to, until 1980," I said.

"That's ridiculous," she said confidently. "No one can predict the future, there is no such letter, and if there were the Pope would have opened it by now. Wouldn't he, Mother?" And we both turned to her for confirmation of our beliefs.

"I'm sure the Pope is a gentleman," she said calmly, already turning back to her book—this sober woman seemed at times completely uninterested in us; that was the only disadvantage of this state—"and I don't have to tell you that if someone tells you not to look at a letter, you don't. Do you?" she said.

"Well," said my sister, "it would depend on what was in it. If it held the future of the world, I sure as hell would." And she left the room.

I looked at my mother but she was deep in a paperback book called *The Vermilion Corpse*, no urgency to know the future of the world in her lighting of a cigarette and turning of a page. The unaccustomed peace throughout the bungalow was so pleasing that I left the room and sat on the dark porch to listen to the silence.

All of this ended on Easter, however. For most of the year the character of Sunday evenings was quite different. She and I went our separate ways after Mass and when I came home in the evening the guests were just leaving. My father went to bed, and my mother insisted I go visiting with her.

I did not always want to go but she refused to visit without me. If I said no, she said, "Then I'm not going," and sat down in the chair opposite mine and folded her arms. She looked so stubborn—so forlorn—sitting there, I could not bear to condemn her to the fate that was mine so many Saturday mornings: no one to play with. Other nights she stood up after watching me read my book without a change of heart, took the car keys, went to the door and said, "It is sad but true that we never appreciate what we have when we have it. I'm afraid we have raised two very selfish children. Think about that, when your mother is dead and gone." Then she departed. The wind moaned in the louvers. The screen door on the porch banged. I was so convinced she would not leave without her companion that I was amazed to hear the car engine start and the Buick drive off with a spurt of gravel in the driveway. It now was clear to me she planned to wrap the car around the white-washed base of one of those solitary streetlights whose brilliance only made the darkness of the tropic night seem more forlorn. I ran out of the bungalow in bare feet and chased after her, up and down moonlit hills past quiet bungalows, asking: Why must she go out? Why did she do this? Why couldn't she stay at home, bake pies, knit socks, supervise a Girl Scout meeting? Rage subsided in gratitude to God when finally I came to rest on the bright gravel outside some bungalow on the Lower Road, and I laid my head on the Buick's still-warm hood and waited for her to come out. It was my responsibility: We were linked somehow. It was understood that I was my mother's and my sister was my father's; and whenever someone had to go out and get Mother to bed, I was chosen.

"You're the only one she'll listen to," my sister said, more bored than ever with such behavior when she visited us on vacation from her school in New England.

"Me?" I said in a protesting voice. "Why me?"

"Because you're her pride and joy," my sister said matter-of-factly as she turned the page of the fashion magazine she was reading (a new interest which had replaced Perez Prado records and basketball, to my amazement; my sister was going to be a woman, after all).

And some evenings I felt my power when I went out to tell her she must go to bed, and she stood up, silently accepted the three superstitious kisses, and obeyed me without a word. I belonged to her, just as my sister belonged to my father. On a business trip to New York while she was a senior in boarding school, he took her around to theaters, restaurants, nightclubs, and jewelry stores, and bought her an aquamarine bracelet simply as a reward for not biting her nails. I heard my mother's sarcastic comments (like those of a lover who has a rival) when he returned. So that when I sat in the movies Mother never went to, watching Danny Kaye tap-dance out of a flying saucer onto the promenade in Cannes, or Fred Astaire saunter down Fifth Avenue in a top hat, I wanted only to take my mother around New York and give her furs, jewels, penthouses, and bouquets of gladiolas as big as palm trees.

Instead she sent me to boarding school in New England. "Did I do the right thing?" she asked plaintively one evening, touching me with her willingness to appear in doubt before me. I could not say. Just when boys my age were finally entering the world so long denied them, the world in which I had lived unquestioned all my life—the harem —I found myself in the company of men whose beauty on the soccer field at twilight, whose smooth chests glowing in the light of study lamps, startled me. When I confessed the fact to a nurse at Student Health she made the small noises of regret my mother made when hearing the news of some plane crash or a family wiped out in a tenement fire. The psychiatrist said it was a groundless fear. Through those crisp autumn nights I remained as pure and cold as the water in the mug on my desk beside the study lamp and the letter I was writing my parents. They left Aruba when my father retired and, after driving around the country, finally came to a small town in northern Florida, where—tired of living out of suitcases, I suspect— they bought a house on a lake. Having by now formed friendships at school, which, no matter how much I disliked it, was clearly now my home, I was touched when she described the lake, the motorboat, the wide beach, in the obvious hope that we, her children, would like the place— and I thought she must know something about the selfishness of the human heart if she was worried we would not visit her unless there were water skis.

When they first lived in Jasper my parents celebrated their freedom in their Florentine gold convertible; in jaunty caps and tweed coats, beside a leather case filled with

bottles of Scotch, gin, and vermouth, they set off on trips
west and north to see the national parks. On some of these
trips between school years I was taken along; as silent as a
pet dog, I sat in the back seat of that huge car beneath the
boxes of Kleenex, the road maps, the tiny bars of soap
wrapped by the Holiday Inns we were leaving in our wake.
In the grip of that dreadful realization of the adolescent—
that he must make his own way in the world, and separate
himself from the creatures who have brought him this far
—I began to view everything with a critical eye. When the
light waned and my father suggested my mother select a
motel, for instance, she could never make up her mind.
Each time we drove past one she had not found worthy as
we approached, she said plaintively as it receded, "That
one looked nice." It was this spirit that corrupted her entire
conception of life, I began to think: Driving through the
suburbs of Houston, San Antonio, Denver, she exclaimed
over the imposing houses whose bay windows and chim-
neys seemed exactly what she had in mind. "I've always
wanted a house with a fireplace in every room!" she would
say. But like the house of her dreams, the perfect motel was
always the one we had just passed, glowing like a beached
ocean liner on the flat desert at dusk; as we went across the
country visiting old friends from Aruba and inspecting
their houses, their towns, their solutions to the terrible
problem of happiness, I began to feel it did not exist. To my
great surprise I came actually to hate my mother; and at no
time was the emotion fiercer than when we entered one
more superfluous motel, sat down at a crisp white table-
cloth overlooking Chesapeake Bay, as the waiter overturned the thick amber glasses and said, "Would you care
for anything from the bar?"

What did she want of me? How could I flee? Was America clothes, cars, motels, drinks from the bar? Could she be
merely a woman sitting in a Cadillac convertible in a nutria

stole and dark glasses? For the first time in my life I felt my
future was not with this prosperous couple, and my father
actually had to remind me to hold the chair for my mother
when she sat down.

Things got worse. My parents did not attend my sister's
wedding when she married a classmate shortly after their
graduation from a midwestern university. The wedding
was held in the small town in Pennsylvania where her
husband planned to attend law school; my parents were
still in Aruba. This was ostensibly the reason for their not
attending the wedding but my sister believed it was not the
real one. They disapproved of her marrying in the first
place—they wanted her to pursue a career, to live in New
York for a while free and unencumbered—and they did not
like the man she chose to marry. He visited us in Aruba the
summer before they married, and every evening while I
watered the plants in the bungalow of some neighbors on
vacation, my sister sat on the patio beside me weeping over
our parents' snobbery. "They're so cruel!" she said. "How
can they be so cruel?" she wailed as I stood there with the
hose trained on the gardenia hedge, not knowing what to
say. They felt he was unworthy of her. She loved him,
however, and my estrangement from my family began
when I assumed the role of mediator in their dispute.
"Can't you see?" my sister said. "Mother is cold! She's a
cold, cold woman!" And I had to examine Mother in the
light of this new perspective, this solidarity I felt with my
sister. It grew stronger each time I visited her during my
vacations from the boarding school my parents sent me to.

If my sister was far more rebellious than I as a child—
the day my mother discovered cigarettes in her dresser
drawer was but the culmination of a defiant spirit that
stretched back to her infancy—she was no longer. She went
to work while her husband attended law school, and when
I came to Carlisle during my vacations, tins of cookies and

fudge sat beside the cheesecake she knew I liked. She was
the most conventional of souls. In the evening we went to
the laundromat downtown to wash clothes. She cleaned the
house, washed dishes, and confirmed my parents' dark sus-
picions that she would become a chattel waiting on her
husband. He studied. The astonishment I felt at seeing my
sister in love, doing things her mother never did, subservi-
ent to another personality in a way she had not been till
now, was joined by a suspicion that I, her obedient, polite,
bookish, docile brother, was destined to become a rebel in
a way she would never be. I clung to the public virtue of
the dutiful student and pleased my parents that way. Evenings my mother telephoned me at the university to say,
"You're not involved in any of these demonstrations, are
you? Because if you are, your father and I would have to
reconsider our support of your education," or, alone in the
den in Jasper after cocktails and my father's retiring for the
night: "You're not taking drugs, are you?" I always said,
"No," wondering if I had disappointed her. But my apost-
asy was much worse: I was enthralled by the beauty of men.

These were the years when the family watches for romance, when my sister's "Are you dating anyone?" induced me to invent young women I made up out of thin air
to satisfy her persistent questions. I gave these girls names,
personalities, habits, a favorite ice cream, slight character
flaws to show I was not blinded by desire, and then liqui-
dated them before there was any need to produce them
physically for my sister's inspection. By the time I gradua-
ted I was a veteran of five or six failed romances, made
possible only by geographical distance and the magic of the
telephone. For a while the questions ceased—though not
my unhappiness at being unable to satisfy them in this way
—and then they were reintroduced through the mouths of
my sister's children, who would blurt in the middle of
Thanksgiving dinner the words that made me spill the

mashed potatoes: "When are you going to get married?"
My mother and sister sat innocently by, waiting for the
answer to this question they were too discreet themselves
to ask any longer.

After its retirement from Aruba the family became a
kind of government-in-exile. The train that stopped at a
small town near Jasper bore my parents northward, in
their fur and cashmere, while another bore me west along
the Susquehanna till we converged on a stone house beside
a golf course in the hills west of Pittsburgh where my sister
now lived with her husband and four children. We did not
know what to do together. We went to those vast shopping
malls which my father had no interest in, and collapsed
afterward in my sister's bedroom upstairs, where I lay on
the bed watching them discuss their purchases. It seemed
we had only one function now as a family: to shop. The
dark winter night just beyond the pane of glass I put my
face against to feel its chill, the snow advancing across those
lighted hills west of Pittsburgh, was what I wanted to be
out in, but when I did come back from a walk before dinner, I stopped to admire the glowing windows of the house
—a tableau I could no more be part of than those in the
windows of the department stores downtown. We took my
parents to the zoo, to the orchid show at the conservatory,
walked down the street to a cemetery planted with syca-
more trees, where Mother and I would read the gravestones
in the soft, wet snow. Standing there among the stone
angels, the crosses and mausoleums, as dusk thickened in
the valleys beneath us and the fine snow blew through the
mottled limbs of the naked sycamores, we looked at one
another. We did not need to speak. My sister was absorbed
in her own domestic life, whose perfume was the fragrance
of my nephew's pajamas, still warm from the dryer, as he
fell asleep beside me in the attic. At Christmas I went to
Jasper.

My mother knew no one in Jasper, Florida, when she first moved there except a woman and her husband who had grown up with my mother in Chicago. They had four married daughters living in northern cities and a son my age whose picture was on the fieldstone mantelpiece, but who was either in Europe during the summer or at Columbia the rest of the year. She was a tall woman with deep blue eyes around which the skin crinkled when she laughed —a silver sound spilled often on the air. She could be seen in her son, whose mention caused her to glance up at the photograph on the mantel and say: "Look at my baby!" as if it were a source of astonishment to her that she had produced a man of six feet two with broad shoulders, and eyes and a smile like hers. His room was just as he left it, I noticed during the tour she gave us of the house; peering in, I recognized the room kept while the son was away at school for that long, expensive education given children of the middle class. This particular room looked out into a garden of azaleas and palmettoes, and a patch of blue lake sparkling with the subdued brilliance that characterized the soft, profoundly peaceful weather of Christmas week in Florida—too cold for bare feet, too warm for overcoats. The room smelled of Christmas in that part of the country: the bland perfume of the forest that crept into that town whose gardens were carved out of the sandy pinewoods. In Jasper there was not much to keep young people—they left as soon as they could and joined the army or got work in a distant city. The whole town had about it the air of a place that is paradise for small children. Everyone else left—even though the room where we stood looked lived in; a bookcase was filled with an encyclopedia, textbooks, the Hardy Boys series, and a stack of *Horizon* magazines; and a perfectly made bed was even furnished with a blue blanket folded at its foot, as if someone were to sleep there that night.

"It's such a mess when he's here," she said, laughing as we stood there. "He was admitted to West Point, but got very sick last fall, and couldn't go. I don't know how he would have kept his room up there," she said as we went out into the cavernous living room to sit beside the fire. "He's living with a family in Mexico City this year to learn Spanish."

Winter was still in Jasper, and the overcast sky made it seem even drabber some days, but most of all the sensation that time had stopped, that there was nothing one had to do after this, characterized those visits I accompanied Mother on. She had a curious desire to own a hardware store, but as we drove down the brief main street even she was discouraged by the forlorn look of the tiny stucco buildings gleaming under the streetlights. Her friend— whose husband owned the local water works, and sat on the board of the local bank—told her that most people drove to Monroe for hardware. There was not much business in this town at all. It was so quiet I felt sorry for my mother. She knelt beside me in the dim, drab light of the small cinder-block church in clothes far more attractive than their surroundings, when I visited Jasper at Christmas while I was a student at college. We were different now: I had a secret, and she a new cashmere coat.

My father still went to bed at his customary early hour, even though the next morning he rose only to plant azaleas and oak trees and date palms. My mother—seated in her chair with cigarette and drink in hand, still beautiful— found herself in another theater altogether with an audience considerably altered, including me. Furnished with friends at school, a life of my own, even if bookish, at the university, I thought her life in this town as forlorn as Ruth's, following her family into exile. On the day I finished the physical examination required by the draft board housed in a rotting old hotel on the banks of the St.

Johns River, the black man from a town near Jasper dressing next to me burst into tears.

"What's wrong?" I said.

"They said I got asthma," he said. "They won't take me."

"But you could get killed in Viet Nam!" I said.

"I don't care," he said. "I just want to get out of here."

I too felt confined. Since I had no idea what I was supposed to do in life, the very privacy and freedom my parents afforded me to make up my mind only made my inability to do so more painful. That academic education in which I had been immured for nearly ten years since leaving Aruba was accompanied by no other kind, and when they drove me out of Jasper one morning before dawn I felt with deep dejection that it was right that I was going into the army. I could not even select a career, and as we drove to Green Cove Springs in the sickening humidity of an August morning which still lacked an hour till sunrise, I remarked casually that I was not sure I had taken the right valise. "Indecision!" my mother said, her face glowing in the light of the dashboard as she lighted a cigarette and turned to look at me. "I hope you haven't inherited that from me." I said I was afraid I had, and, in the darkness, continued to list the various qualities I had received from these two people I seemed unable to escape. When I finished, my mother said, "You must remember you are a separate person, you know."

As the bus drove off in the predawn darkness, the vegetative air both chill and warm as it lay stagnant in the groves of live oaks and potato fields around Hastings, I actually felt guilty for having an escape when she—returning in the other direction with my father to Jasper—did not, prematurely buried as she was in that tiny town. So we went our separate ways.

2

Two years later I awoke in an Army barracks in Heidelberg on Sunday and spent the morning in bed thinking, like my father, while everyone else slept. My mother would have wept to have me injured or dead in Viet Nam—it was mere chance that I was in Germany with the American Army stationed there since World War II—but she would have understood it. ("I'm an American and don't ever forget it!" she said.) Now I found myself free of the life the Seventh Army was in West Germany to defend. She was in Jasper and I was in a town that illustrated the century she said was her favorite, and part of an organization like the Church in many ways—hierarchical, ceremonious, traditional. When I awoke in Heidelberg on Sunday mornings, as my fellow clerks slept off their debauch in the bunks around me, I lay there in an odd kind of limbo, watching the icy rain slant past the window.

At the age of twenty-three I felt that the only rational use of life was not to go to Heaven, in which I no longer believed, or to avoid Hell, which was the motivation of so many of my actions as a child, but simply to achieve happiness—to give and receive pleasure; and here in the Army, with all the mechanical necessities of life (food, work, shelter) satisfied, I was left free to enjoy those things which in my virginal state did bring happiness: books, a hot meal at the end of the day, friends, the valley darkening at dusk, the beauty of faces.

The man who plucked me out of the stream of replacements landing in Frankfurt had detained another draftee from Jasper: the son of my mother's friend whom I had seen only once before, in church, his face covered by his hands, apparently deep in prayer till I saw his shoulders shaking and realized he was laughing at the comic, quavering voices of our little choir. He introduced himself to me as I waited for my orders my first morning in Heidelberg. "Hello," he said, "I'm Vittorio Donnelly. I know your mother. We live around the lake from you in Jasper." He was as tall as his mother said he was, and broad-shouldered, and wearing a neat moustache which was the only difference between his face and that in the photograph on the mantel. But the photograph did not convey his confidence, ease and friendliness. He shook my hand and smiled, a smile not unlike his mother's, whose blue eyes he also had, and her sweet expression. "How would you like to stay here in Heidelberg?" he said. "It's much better than the boondocks."

It was clear Vittorio had been here a few months already —knew and joked with everyone in the office; and when I was finally admitted to their number, it was understood that I was to get coffee, run errands, stay late, and do favors for everyone else until I was replaced by someone even newer. My nickname was simply "Newbie," and I belonged specifically not to Vittorio but to the man who had detained him in Heidelberg and had power in these matters, a personnel specialist whose nickname was the Clam because of a film of sweat which covered his hands no matter what the weather. As we walked home that evening from work at six o'clock the Clam lighted a cigarette with a trembling hand and asked Vittorio in a nervous voice what Jasper was like.

Vittorio said, "Oh, it's like a village on the steppes of Russia, one of those little Southern burgs where Carson McCullers said the soul rots with boredom."

"Well," said the Clam, "as long as the soul rots with something. Like the tea in Kirchheim tonight we must insist Newbie come to," he said, turning to me.

But I was sure I would not—and as I watched him dress for this event which he attended every Tuesday evening in a little suburb near our barracks (a tea he invited others to with no success) I made an excuse. "But they'll have butter cookies in the shape of windmills!" he said in that sharp, brittle Boston accent, turning his large, almond-shaped eyes on me. Watching him dress (as I watched my mother in Aruba prepare herself for the official parties she found so tedious) brought to mind accounts of the toilettes of the Sun King the public was allowed to watch. The others sprawled on their bunks after supper watching the Clam assemble what he called his nine-piece suit, while Vittorio sat, more simply attired, on a bunk leafing through *Stars and Stripes*, which gave its readers that summer the impression that the entire country was in flames, and war between the races was in full gear. The Clam sprinkled his crotch with cologne and turned to the room. "How do I look?" he said, as he tucked a pink handkerchief into his breast pocket, his face gleaming in the light of the fluorescent tubes suspended from the ceiling.

"Like a glazed doughnut," said one of his less admiring roommates.

"Then eat me," said the Clam with the smile of a madman as he paused at the door. "Coming, Newbie?" He arched one eyebrow. "No? Afraid of tea and crumpets? Afraid of being raped?"

"You got it!" yelled O'Neill.

"Afraid of the chance of a lifetime to mingle with the local yokels?" the Clam went on. "So be it, Newbie. I should only say I did not suspect you were as devoid of *Gemütlichkeit* as the other occupants of this room. One cannot spend one's *entire* life in dread of syphilis. Or Europe. Or both. Adieu! *Auf Wiedersehen!* It's been a business doing pleasure with you. Come, Vittorio!" He closed his wall locker, which had taped to its door two reproductions: one of "The Roses of Heliogabalus" by Alma-Tadema, the other of a mushroom cloud over the Nevada desert. Vittorio stood up. The Clam looked out the window and said, "The evening is such a *pale* green!" And off they went.

The rest of my roommates opened their paperback novels, or began yet another anecdote about the legendary exploits of their football coach in Longview, and I went to the library. The night was balmy and ripe with the decomposing spring. The white gloves of the MPs directing traffic at the entrance to Patton Barracks flashed in the gloom. I went to my desk at the library where my window allowed me to watch the Clam and Vittorio disappear into the field of corn that separated our barracks from the village of Kirchheim. Once they vanished I continued to stare at the corn. When I first arrived in Heidelberg, life seemed to be outside these tall windows, but I was not sure what form it took, and what it was I should be doing with these commodious evenings of internment. The librarian—a German woman who worked between an aquarium of tropical fish and a large radio tuned to a station that played Strauss waltzes quietly—smiled at me. I smiled back and opened my book. Most of the people in my barracks refused to leave their room because Longview, Texas, was not outside the door. But as I sat at one of the desks along a wall lined with tall windows that looked out on a row of chestnut trees and the spigots at which off-duty Americans washed their cars while talking about the number of days they had left in the army, I felt I was missing the point too. I knew just what the invitation to tea in Kirchheim meant but I had no desire to accept it. I did not want to belong to either camp: the soldiers discussing their cars, or the soldiers discussing each other. So I found myself as solitary as the librarian—who looked up at me suddenly and smiled with the instinctive bond of one spinster recognizing another. Eventually it turned dark. The voices of the car washers ceased, and I was staring at the reflection of the librarian going through a drawer of her card catalogue while her parakeet hopped in its cage.

At ten o'clock the library closed. I took a long shower. When I went to bed that evening the Clam was not back. The others straggled in drunk. They spun, they swayed, they fell into bed, and soon were snoring deeply. A thunderstorm was rumbling in the distance, and a sudden gust of cool wind blew the branches of the lilac bush that grew outside our building against the wall. I fell asleep—only to awaken hours later at an especially loud clap of thunder to find Vittorio, fully dressed, sitting on a bunk, weeping. I asked him what was wrong.

"I'm in love," he said.

"In love! With whom?"

He looked at me between his fingers. "Life!" he gasped. "I'm in love with life!" He rose onto his knees and said, "With the brevity and the beauty of life!" He knelt beside the windowsill, pushed the window open and put his head out. "Smell the air! The air actually smells like something! Dead leaves and lilacs, and roses and vomit. In love with a face that has the power to summon up the whole world, and all its beauty!"

The door opened. The Clam entered and came to a stop in the middle of the floor. He held up an unlighted cigarette. "Ah, Newbie. The Greeks said the four best things are these." He began to undress unsteadily as he recited, removing a piece of clothing with each item on the list. "Health. Beauty. Money honestly earned. And!" He raised a forefinger as he stepped out of his pants. "To be young with one's friends!"

Vittorio stepped down from the bunk with a dazed smile on his shining face. "To be young with one's friends," he said.

"The Greeks knew everything," the Clam said, sitting down on his bunk, trousers in hand, with a blank expression. "Except the location of my underwear. Where is my underwear?" he said. "My blue French briefs?" He put a hand to his mouth and bit it. His eyes grew wide and he said, "Oh no!"

"Where *is* your underwear?" said Vittorio.

"In a bush beside the Neckar River," the Clam said, with the radiant expression of the drunk. "Beneath the bridge Goethe called the most beautiful in the world." And he fell back onto his bunk and was snoring within a minute's time, his message undelivered, his trousers fallen across his lap with uncharacteristic modesty.

Vittorio picked his legs up and swung them around so that the Clam was lying on the bunk and then wrapped him in the blanket. He drew the sign of the cross in the air over his form and left the room. I rose to close the door and went back to sleep.

In the morning I went into the chilly latrine, filled with the sound of birds singing in the bush outside the window, and found Vittorio in a puddle of vomit on the floor. At work, the moment was not referred to. Like a man who babbles in his sleep, the Clam no doubt did not remember it. Vittorio stopped me in the hall and said, with the same embarrassment my mother exhibited the morning after, bedspread drawn across her mouth like a *chador*: "I'm awfully sorry about last night. I consider waking people up like that a capital offense. I always have, and always will." I said there was no reason to apologize, but the rest of the day he was silent and kept to himself.

The Clam glided up and down the hall at full steam, threatening newcomers with assignments in the boondocks, telling anyone who annoyed him, "How would you like to be in Baumholder tomorrow? Wielflicken or Grafenwöhr? How would you like to spend Christmas Eve on a

mountaintop with a hundred GIs from Newark shooting
smack?"

I found Vittorio in the stairwell at five o'clock, waiting
with everyone else till the flag was lowered so they would
not have to salute. I asked, "What happened at the tea you
went to? Who was there anyway?"

He said in a tired voice, "Oh, just some rather bored,
innocuous people, desperate for a new face. They were
crushed when you didn't arrive."

At that moment the MP detached the flag and folded it
in his white gloves, and the doorways of the office buildings
spewed forth hundreds of bureaucrats anxious to get home
and begin their real lives, which began, as do those of
clerk-typists everywhere, at five o'clock. Vittorio went
back to the apartment he had off-base to sleep, but the Clam
was indefatigable. He rushed back to the barracks to
change clothes and splash cologne on himself with the feverish hysteria of a man who hears Time's chariot hurrying
near, and disappeared. To my surprise he went no farther
than the EM Club across the road, where he installed himself at a large round table, began drinking beer, and pre-
sided over a little band of clerks who were inseparable and
spent the evening shrieking over their own jokes while a
woman on stage sang songs to a boa constrictor wrapped
around her limbs. Why the Clam preferred to remain on
base perplexed me. He knew Germans and Americans who
lived in town. Yet he changed his clothes every night and
marched over to the EM Club to spend the night there,
leading his entourage in single file behind him like so many
ducks across the lawn.

One of them, I discovered, was someone I had not seen
since leaving Aruba: Wheatworth. I did not recognize him.
He was shorter than I now, compact, his dark hair falling
across his forehead in a boyish haircut. He was as taciturn
as he was in Aruba when he drove home with us from

church. But now he had a cigarette in hand and was—even after telling me his parents now lived in Connecticut, and he himself was an alumnus of a monastery in Pawling, New York—just as great a mystery as before. It was the Clam I asked one day: "Why did Wheatworth leave the monastery?"

"Because he decided the clever Nazarene was just a clever Nazarene," the Clam said. "And because in the army one can have camaraderie, sex, *and* chocolate. Yes, once Wheatworth made his mind up, that was that. He has been far more sensible about these things than Vittorio, who will always twist in the wind, in the no-man's-land of the undecided." But this remark only left me more confused. "If only we could get you out of the clutches of Lily Trautwein!" said the Clam as I set out for the library with my books and he stood dressing at his wall locker.

But he couldn't. When Fraülein Trautwein closed the library, we took walks in the Odenwald. She told tales of Germany during the War, and then said good-bye on a terrace of the Filosofenweg, blinking her eyes, red-rimmed from the chlorine in the municipal pool she used daily, like some mermaid who cannot come down into the world of men because the auto exhausts irritate her.

And when the Clam and Vittorio took a night off from his bilious duties at the EM Club and consented to accompany me to the weekly concert at the castle—the rest of his little band never visited museums or listened to music on anything but a jukebox—one had the sense that it was but a prelude to their real evening, a kind of time killer, to occupy that vague, greenish hour between the afternoon and darkness. "Everyone here is an American. Where are the Germans?" I asked as we sat on our folded chairs in the courtyard, surrounded by tourists in printed cotton clothes, waiting for the chamber orchestra to come out onto the cobblestones.

"The Germans?" said Vittorio. "Home watching *Bonanza*," he said.

The Clam cackled beside him and said, "You don't think they want to listen to these clowns eviscerate Bach, do you? They want to be living in California around a swimming pool shaped like a penis, preferably with a Negro lover. Oh, Newbie, your dream of Europe is just that—a dream of Europe."

On the last words polite applause rose from the crowd as the sweaty flautists emerged from a doorway. "Do you see that man over there?" Vittorio said in a voice just audible to us. He nodded at a gaunt, bearded fellow staring mournfully at the concertgoers from his seat on the steps.

"He used to be a crafts instructor at Campbell Barracks —woodworking, I think," the Clam said. "I haven't seen him in months."

"He left his wife and kids when he fell in love with a bricklayer from Istanbul," said Vittorio in a low voice, "and now all he does is hang around public places hoping to pick up Turkish guest-workers."

"Let that be a lesson to us," said the Clam.

"He looks as if he's starving," I said.

"He is," said the Clam. "For what, I will not say."

"A dreadful taste to develop!" said Vittorio.

"No worse than Telemann," said the Clam, turning his attention to the program. He perused its engraving of the castle and then looked up. "You know what I'm going to do the day I get out?" said the Clam. "I'm putting on a WAC uniform and going around to all my sergeants to say good-bye."

"It wouldn't tell them anything they don't know already," said Vittorio calmly.

After the concert the Clam and he disappeared on the way back to the barracks—jumping off the streetcar at the Bahnhof to catch a train to a town in the industrial waste-

land across the river called Ludwigshafen—and I did not
see either one till the Clam caught up with me in the gardens I walked through on my way to work the next day.
The gardens were composed of small plots, tilled by Germans in their spare time, which formed a patchwork of
orchards and flowerbeds between the barracks in which we
lived and the barracks in which we worked. I walked out
of choice, to enjoy the flowers and avoid the daily traffic jam
that brought our bus to a halt under the shadow of the
Königstuhl and the blue Ford Motor Company flag, which
fluttered in the air where once ensigns of Roman legions
had caught the morning light. Vittorio usually drove to
Patton Barracks in a small red sports car purchased for him
by the same woman who paid the rent on his apartment on
Fahrtgasse: a beautiful German with faintly pitted skin
who worked as a prostitute at the brothel in the mud-
colored stucco building opposite the entrance to the PX,
and was reputedly in love with Vittorio. Clam walked because he missed the bus nearly every morning, and Vittorio
when he had to spend the night in the barracks in order to
be present for inspection.

"Life would be simple if you didn't have to sleep," Vittorio said the morning three young men carrying their
personnel records passed us on the path.

"Stop!" said the Clam. "Let me see your 201's." The
Clam examined and returned them without comment to
the two plain youths. To the third—a pale man with large
dark eyes—he said, "A cook. Can you do *bûche de Noël?*"

"Boosh what?" the man said.

"*Bûche de Noël.* No matter," the Clam replied. "A simple
hamburger will do. How would you like to remain in Heidelberg on the Neckar? Come to Room Nineteen after
lunch."

"I've seen that guy," said Vittorio as we resumed our
walk, "at Crescent Beach, this beach we go to from Jasper
in the summer."

"Building a sand castle?" said the Clam.

"Among other things," said Vittorio. "I wonder why he's here. Just about everyone in Jasper got married or joined the reserves. At least my senior class. Let's face it. The only people the army got were the poor, the black, and the undecided," he said, his last category reminding me of my mother's wish that I had not inherited that particular vice from her. But unfortunately I had. Some afternoons I spent in the library only because I could not choose between going to the *Schwimbad* and taking a walk to the Königstuhl. I ended up doing neither. A strange passivity pervaded my personality, and blended perfectly with my duties in the army, where action of only the most insignificant sort (typing memos, polishing boots) was required.

I was obsessed with a postal clerk whom I saw every day on the mail run. He wore his hat pushed back on his head, and stood waiting for the van with his hands in his pockets, chewing gum with a cold, arrogant, supercilious expression on his face. I never spoke to him but he was the most significant feature of my day, and one evening while I was brushing my teeth at the barracks, a hand reached into the basin next to mine to test the hot water and I recognized, without even looking up, my fellow mail clerk—like an archaeologist who could, from a few limbs and fragments of pottery, construct an entire ancient statue, or the villa that surrounded its pedestal in a garden. And the force of this instinct, which wished to transfer its allegiance from my mother, exiled, remote, in Jasper, to some new object, left me astonished.

That evening I arrived for supper with the Clam to see the cook standing behind the mess hall with his white blouse open in the late-summer heat, one hand grasping the chicken-wire fence that separated the barracks from the street, talking with a German girl who moved a stroller with a baby in it gently back and forth. His white paper hat was pushed back on his sweaty forehead, and his black hair clustered in curls. The cook was from a town on the other side of Lake Jasper so small it did not have its own post office—one of those southern boys with eyes the color of Coca-Cola: a color spilled over and smeared across the tops of his cheekbones as two gray shadows that in an older person would have indicated fatigue but in his case seemed due to the size and color of his eyes. The wind blew open his shirt as he stood there talking at the fence.

"Mother of God!" the Clam gasped. "The last time I saw a tummy like that was in London. On the Elgin Marbles."

The cook passed one last cigarette through the fence to his German friend as we entered the mess hall, and then came inside to serve his late customers. He stood behind the metal serving trays heaped with food and, holding the tongs, said to the Clam with a smile, "Broccoli, lima beans, or a piece of pussy?"

The Clam said, "Is the pussy hot?" The cook laughed. The Clam beamed. He sat down, after filling his tray, at a table in the corner with Wheatworth and two short, blond men with pitted skin whom the Clam called the Terrible Twins. I chose a table separated from theirs by a counter lined with snake's-tongues and geraniums in plastic pots— still refusing to belong to their company—and opened up an issue of *Stars and Stripes* to read about the horrors of life in the more remote Army posts: drownings, brawls, racial melees, arrests, and accidents.

As he sat down the Clam tilted his tray so that the lima beans fell off onto the tray of one of the Terrible Twins: a boy from Tampa named Stone. "What is this?" said Stone in a piercing voice that rang out through the room like a fire alarm. "You think I want your lima beans? I hate lima beans! And so do you. Who are you after now?"

"Whom!" whispered the Clam as he picked up a fork and pressed it onto Stone's hand. "Just because you're a scream-ing faggot is no reason to think you can ignore the rules of grammar. *Eat* the fucking lima beans and shut up!" And he returned to the line for more. The table turned to look.

"*Oh,*" said Stone. The Clam returned to his table with a bowl of vegetables, his face flushed and gleaming. "Cute," said Stone. "Cute and dumb. He's from Florida and his I.Q. is slightly lower than this lima bean's," he said.

"But a lima bean doesn't have a dick," said the Clam in an intense, trembling, and unusually low voice. He sat down and said, "Besides, how many lima beans can you outthink? It's not as if we discuss Proust every night in the EM Club, is it, ducky?" he said. "No, we tend to talk about less elevated topics. Like cock. And we do so in voices no one hears because there is so much noise from the jukebox. Here there is no jukebox," he said in the same compressed, trembling, furious tone. "So lower your stinking voice."

"Why should I lower my voice?" said Stone.

"Because anyone who hears it knows immediately that you should be sitting across from me in a brassiere, that's why," hissed the Clam. Stone exploded in laughter even louder than his speaking voice, and the Clam, his face visible between the snake's-tongues and the potted flowers, pursed his lips in fury. He then lowered the cigarette he was about to extinguish in the ashtray and pressed it onto the back of Stone's hand. Stone's eyes narrowed. He smiled as the lighted butt seared his flesh, competing in some strange way with the Clam to dominate a scene. "I didn't know you cared." He grinned.

"I don't," said the Clam. And then the scene was ended: Stone jumped up from his seat, overturned a tray, three glasses of iced tea, and a bowl of catsup, and screamed as the Clam hurriedly rose, took his tray to the window, and scurried out of the mess hall.

When I described this scene to Vittorio the next evening as we walked back from the office through the gardens, he just laughed. He was, I concluded, one of those amiable devotees of Eros who sees no distinction among the objects toward which lust leads us against our will, so helpless that I viewed the sexual objects of people as mere numbers they had drawn in some cosmic lottery. Some were luckier than others in the draw, at least in the chance they had of pleasing society. The chief advantage of loving women was that one could marry and then move on to other concerns (business, politics, science) more worthy of the mind and more likely to give men satisfaction than the endlessly neurotic negotiations people who live for love are condemned to. Or so I imagined. I was tired of my damp walks to the Königstuhl, the scowl on my face when I passed someone like the postal clerk whose beauty ravished me but whose face I could not look at. The lover of women married the face that inspired such joy in his heart, acquired a household in the bargain into which he could retreat from the forlorn public life forced on those without families. (My real goal in life was simply to shape amidst its barbarism a haven, a room in which someone else was reading and watching the hours pass with me: a lover with whom I could share the news as if it were occurring on a planet different from our own. The urge was simply to escape existence; if a saint would not appear to me and extend his hand, then marriage would serve.) I admired Vittorio. He was proof that men are divided not between the heterosexual and homosexual, but rather the puritan and the cavalier, the tolerant and intolerant. When I saw him arrive at Patton Barracks outside the gate in his little red sports car, driven sometimes on these cool, foggy mornings by the woman whose kept man he was, and she kissed him good-bye and he stepped out of the car, he was just the image of what I thought a man our age should be: in love and free of the monotonous surroundings of the post, which I found erotic only because men entranced me.

"Of course it all must seem crazy to you," I said after describing the scene in the mess hall.

He turned and looked at me and said, "No more than to you."

This remark confused me (unless it meant he thought I was heterosexual myself) and I fell silent as we walked between the garden plots, which were, individually, like a tiny orchard on the illuminated page of a medieval manuscript, where the letter *C* contains in its embrace a pear tree and a princess reading a book, on a bench exactly like the one on which a Ford auto mechanic still in his uniform sat now, eating a cheese sandwich with greasy hands. "But I think it must be especially perverse to you," I said.

"Why?" he said. "I'm as nuts about the cook as the Clam is."

"But not," I said, "in the same way."

"Of course," he said. "Only the Clam has absolutely no inhibitions and I have nothing but inhibitions."

"Nothing but inhibitions!" I said. "You're living with a woman in an apartment off base. She bought you a Triumph. You've been selected by a prostitute—a connoisseur of men!"

He stopped, dropped his cigarette and ground it out with his foot. "You've got me confused." He smiled. "I'm not kept by Maria. Is that what you think?"

"That's what the Clam told me."

"Maria and I are friends," he said. "We met in a bar in Ludwigshafen. She does keep someone, in fact—a woman. Who works as a waitress at the Feterstall. We're roommates." He looked at me and then resumed his walk, adding, as our shoes made the gravel crunch, "I'm the lover of a man you've not met, a doctoral candidate in botany at the university here. Only he's in Ecuador at the moment gathering mushrooms with his professor. Now I see I've destroyed all your illusions."

"No, no!" I said. He had simply replaced them with others. He had changed the nature of the glamour in which he was surrounded in my eyes because—whatever its object—he had a sexual life. He had what even my psychology textbooks in college assured me was the next goal in the life cycle: intimacy with another person. The textbooks added, "of the opposite sex," but one had to improvise.

"You won't say anything about this in Jasper, will you," he said, looking over at me with an expression of concern on his face. "I don't think *they* would understand. Even though I have no intention of ever going back there unless I can help it. Funny, isn't it? It was the army that freed me from a life in which I was trying to be the perfect son. The army, which I thought was depriving me of freedom. It was in Viet Nam that I melted, so to speak, in the wrong way."

"At least," I said, "the inconvenient sort of way."

"I'll say," he said. "That long, deep kiss Maria and I exchange when she drops me off at work is just to give the MPs a hard-on."

Our footsteps bit into the gravel and we fell silent. We came to the railroad tracks that bifurcated the gardens. The shining curve of the rails ended precisely on the horizon in a perfect brown Romanesque church with two black steeples, set against the wooded hills which here cascaded onto the plain like enormous breakers frozen in space by the fact that they were made of earth and not water. The sight of that church at the end of the curved tracks soothed me. Its pleasing proportions seemed to me only one aspect of the beauty of a world that included, too, the quartet of soccer players crossing the bridge now in the twilight. The air was green and so were the uniforms and high socks which left only their thighs exposed, pushing back the viridescent air like the legs of swimmers, flashing as they waded into the surf. "Did you see that face!" said Vittorio after they passed.

I said I had.

"Extraordinary!" he said. "I'm stuck on faces. And bodies. On *hands.*"

"Does it bother you that in the eyes of Jasper—your parents—all of this is wrong?"

"A little," he said. "But the only thing you have to do in life is deal ethically with people. The rest is unimportant as long as you don't hurt anyone."

"But you love your parents."

"Of course. Or rather, yes—since some people do not. Don't you?"

"I do," I said.

"But you want to be free of them."

"How do you know that?"

"I could tell the moment I met you."

I had no idea what he meant—I even wondered if he had really perceived anything of the sort—but this remark served to remind me that we may spend our whole lives ignorant of a quality in our characters which is instantly visible to a perfect stranger.

"What do *you* want to be free of?" I said.

"What is this," he laughed, "an interview?"

"I'm sorry," I said.

"I just want to be free," he said. "Period."

"But you're not," I said. "You're homosexual!"

He looked at me. "Well, not completely. And I don't plan to let it take over my life," he said.

"You don't?"

"No." He smiled. "You don't have to, you know. You have nothing in common with Stone, for instance. I'll never ever refer to a man as she," he went on, his face in profile as I watched him, walking briskly through the last stretch of gardens before Patton Barracks. "I'll never ask how sex was with someone, or how big someone's cock is. As bizarre as the Clam is, he does have *manners*. Which is more important. I'll never be like Stone. Who talks about, thinks of, nothing else. I have no intention of devoting my life to it."

I thought about this a moment as the red sun sank behind the stalks of green corn that separated our barracks from the village of Kirchheim, where the Terrible Twins kept their own apartment. The air was full of gnats glowing in the light between us and the pear trees. "Then what do you think you'll devote it to?" I said. "I mean, what do you want out of life?"

"To be happy," he said. "To do what I want. That's all." This was so startling to a youth of a Catholic cast of mind that I was grateful when he went on to explain. "To have Wilhelm back from Ecuador," he said, "to bicycle to Greece. To never go back to Jasper," he said. "But then, it's Jasper that produced the cook—and he's a masterpiece. He looks just like a painting of Saint Sebastian by Antonio Moro in the Alte Pinakothek in Munich. That same skin that seems never to have seen the sun."

"But so dumb!" I said. "Or at least so quiet."

"Everyone is intelligent in his own way," he said. "Even Sergeant Slager."

And with that we entered the gates of Patton Barracks —where the Clam was hurrying across the street to the mess hall. He saw us and stopped. "*Meine Freunde,* I am not going to the concert tonight," he said when we approached. "You'll have to go on without me."

"You're not going to hear that country-western singer at the EM Club!" said Vittorio.

"No," he said breathlessly, "but I am tempted."

"Well, what are you doing?"

"Taking a shower."

"Taking a shower!" said Vittorio.

"I can't explain," he said. "Come on, dinner is almost over. I always wait to the last minute so I don't have to listen to Stone *bray.*"

And we followed him to the mess hall. The Clam no longer sat with Wheatworth and the Terrible Twins at their table in the corner. All his habits had changed. He was no longer in the EM Club every night, caustically presiding over the little band and the less sympathetic clerks who liked to try their skill at bantering with him— in the same spirit they went out onto the basketball court after supper and bet quarters on the number of free throws they could make. The Clam stayed in. He waited for the cook, and took his shower when the cook—his hair, eyebrows, arms, dusted with flour from tomorrow's bread— walked in. They spent at least an hour in the shower room, smoking cigarettes on the low bench that ran along one wall. Even in summer the nights were damp and cool, and they turned on the hot water in all the spigots so that the room filled up with clouds of steam. The Clam came back to our room with wrinkled hands and feet. "What is this, Clam?" said O'Neill when he returned to our room wrapped in a purple towel, carefully removing his rubber shower shoes. "Are you trying to wipe off the ooze once and for all?"

"Never," snapped the Clam. "My subjects would not permit it. The Imperial Ooze has been handed down for generations. No, I have simply learned the lesson of the Orient. Gooks find the odor of Western flesh nauseating. We eat meat. We stink. We have a smell that is quite offensive. And since I wish to be worshipped by the masses I have to cleanse myself. No meat! Lots of showers!" he said, and slammed his locker shut.

The Clam grew almost calm. He remained there now when everyone else was still out drinking, gathering his soap and cigarettes and towel to go down to the shower room. He was circumspect. He did not touch the cook. He lent him his bar of soap, and watched it roam across the cook's flat white stomach in the grip of his beautiful hand. But he did not touch him. They stood side by side in separate streams of water while the Clam watched the bar of green soap revolve around the slightly concave bowl between the cook's rib cage and his navel. The cook had one of those bodies that has been the standard of beauty through historical epochs. When the Clam compared his stomach to one on the Elgin Marbles he was correct. His pale flat chest was not so much muscular as it was broken by a shallow groove, which divided it into two square panels. The Clam watched the bar of soap in the cook's hand touch the body he found more beautiful than anything else he knew; finally washed a portion of the cook's back he could not reach himself, nervously and without much pleasure; and returned to the room with the plastic soap dish cradled in his hands. He replaced it on the shelf of his wall locker wordlessly and began to oil himself to alleviate the dry skin so many showers inevitably caused, and sang a song popular that year: "Memories of Heidelberg mean memories of you."

"Clam," I said when O'Neill left, "are you really in love, or is this just more imperial madness?"

"Really in love," he said. "You have no idea, having just arrived, Newbie, in this desert we call Life, how long one has to trudge under the hot broiling sun before one finds water. I thought that Horst—last December on the *Schnellzug* to Berlin," he said, "—was my relief from these monotonous Turks who cannot even speak English, much less appreciate the niceties of foreplay, or rosy afterglow. But that lasted all of a week. Horst wants to design jewelry and live on Fire Island. Like all Germans. No, just when you are most depressed, just when you think you will have to tear your hair out root by root, just when you want to put your head in the toilet bowl and *shriek*—along comes someone you would never have expected, much less looked for. It's so odd," he said. "Love occurs, despite the thousand reasons it should not. And why? I'm afraid to ask. Love is not something you take apart like an M-14. You never know why you love or why you *are* loved," he said. "Not exactly, anyway." He lighted a Gauloise and stared out the window, and expelled a stream of smoke. "I only know his eyes are like rivers, like those black, black rivers at Fort Benning. I only know his feet are ex*tremely* aristocratic, not to mention his patrician shaft. His blue-veined charger. And he does not like to sleep alone," he said, standing up suddenly and gathering together his shaving kit and cigarettes. The Clam was going down the hall to the single room the cook was fortunate enough to be assigned because his hours were irregular, a room in which the little band smoked marijuana and listened to *Abbey Road*. "Ah," the Clam said to me as he turned at the door to see me gathering my books together, "it is only when you fall in love that you realize how dreary the world is when you are not. It is only when you fall in love that the words of all those stupid popular songs become mere statements of fact, and one understands at last that memories of Heidelberg really *do* mean memories of *you*."

In summer the long, gloomy hallways of the barracks were almost always deserted. The windows at each end of the hall were covered with vines, so that little light entered and what did was green, as if we were living in an aquarium. As we passed the brightly lighted washroom, the Clam stopped. The cook stood shirtless at one of the basins. His head was back, his neck white with lather, his hand poised beneath his neck, holding the razor with the careless grace of a god who has just doomed an army on the plains of Troy. I paused as long as I could beside the Clam, hearing the drip-drip-drip of a shower in the shower room, whose door stood open, watching the cook draw the razor slowly down his neck. Then he turned and saw us—like Susanna noticing the elders—and called: "What's up?" The Clam went into the latrine and I went to the library, wondering what beauty was (its power over me, its independence of life), made a list in my notebook of the various kinds there were in the world—weather, nature, art, character, face, body—and asked if there were any connection among them.

There seemed to be none as I went walking by myself in the hills above town after work. Fall arrived. The forest near the Königstuhl was absolutely silent, and half the time drenched in clouds. Down in the valley the little band sat in the cook's room smoking marijuana and listening to the Beatles and laughing over their own jokes. I stood in a sparkling cloud watching an elderly couple walk down the hill toward me, the canes on their arms rocking back and forth like metronomes. "*Guten Abend,*" they said. The consequences of my decision to remain aloof were not only moral but physical: There I stood in the fir forest looking down on the roofs and steeples and bridges of the town. I now knew all the back streets in Heidelberg, so that I could walk from Patton Barracks to the footpath that led up into the hills without seeing a soul. The world was something to avoid. When I descended to the castle and walked out onto its broad terrace above the valley, it was devoid of people. Along the balustrade overlooking the river, the stone gods and goddesses cradled the gold and umber leaves in their arms. The fountains were dry. Once I passed my German teacher, Fräulein Wolf, arm in arm with another young woman. "*Guten tag.*" We smiled and nodded. When I asked Vittorio that evening, he assured me the sight of two young women holding hands as they took a promenade had no sexual significance. It was a custom between friends. The Clam disagreed: "Of course she's a dyke!" he said with that joyous insistence that the whole world was in line with our tastes. "All intelligent women are! She wasn't walking with her *boy*friend, was she?" The next evening a tipsy American woman regarding the view of the valley at dusk invited me to dinner shortly after introducing herself. I shrank from the opportunity—from her lone-liness. She reminded me of my mother.

Snow came, and the dull pearl-gray skies, the tiny crys-tals fluttering down onto the parade field as I trudged across it with the canvas sack of mail, had a curious effect: They made life more, not less, erotic. In the dry silence of the falling snow, insulated by my hooded parka, I was conscious of the blood beating behind my ears. The huge stone buildings that enclosed the parade field looked like palaces. The cheeks of the postal clerk waiting in a cloud of fluttering snowflakes when the van picked him up were splotchy red. He blew on his hands to warm them up. The close-cut blond heads of the MPs directing traffic at the gates stood out vividly against the snowy parking lot be-hind them; their waxed black boots, beaded with drops of water, gleamed against the pale gray and white slush of the snow melted by the ceaseless passage of trucks and cars through the chilly, shadowed entrance tunnel. The sight of the cook, roseate and sweaty behind the closed windows of the mess hall on a cold night when we hurried up the steps, and the sound of a song by Loretta Lynn, and the warmth of the room when we opened the door and went inside, and the cook's "Well, look who's here!" made me determined to fall in love.

It was not possible for me, I suspected, but I was glad to be in the company of someone who seemed undeterred by the scruples that paralyzed me—and I went along with the Clam when he took the cook downtown to the apartment of an American woman married to a lieutenant who lived near the Markplatz. We sat in a high-ceilinged room filled with candles and vases of paper flowers, drank wine, and talked of art and beauty. She was grateful to see us. Her husband, a telecommunications specialist who admired her so much he seemed bewildered that they were married, apparently did not care about these topics (except as they interested her). We went weekly during the month of January. The cook never said a word during these visits. He just drank his beer as the Clam chattered on beside him about the Peruvian tapestries, the history of the Electors Palatine, Proust, the Austrian writer Robert Musil. We learned that the only two climates in the world in which textiles were preserved were those of Egypt and Peru, that Mozart performed in the theater at Schwetzingen, that Proust admired Emerson. Our hostess had a face as fine, as translucent, as delicate as a youth painted by Georges de la Tour; she sat forward listening, her gray eyes shining in the candlelight, her soft lips parted, as eager as a child hearing a story made up to soften the blow of being put to bed. But when I looked at her I knew my heart was mortgaged to my mother. She seemed infinitely more serious and deep. At the concert we attended afterward in one of the churches in the old town, as my eyes searched the interior of the church for some architectural detail on which to rest during the Agnus Dei, the cook dozed between me and the Clam, his head back, a bit of spittle on his red lips. The Clam stared at him with a smile. He was all the more in love. At work he wrote poems whose composition he camouflaged by inserting the requisite pink, green, and yellow carbons behind his sheet of paper so that it looked as if he were typing orders. He was composing sonnets to the cook's penis.

The long bureaucratic day ended only when the cleaning ladies lumbered upstairs with their mops and buckets, and we finished our last assignments and were allowed to go home. One evening as we sat behind two lieutenants on the late bus, one said to the other, "I'm getting married. The army can make you pretty cynical, you know, but I think it will put my head on straight."

"Absolutely," his companion said. "After a point, it's hard to live only for yourself."

Beside me the Clam removed the cigarette from his lips and murmured, "Exactly. Exactly."

"So he's saying you have to get married and have children," said Vittorio.

"Nonsense," said the Clam. "You fall in love with a cook."

"Well, I hope you're right," sighed Vittorio, grasping the seat in front of him, anxious to get to the barracks in time for dinner.

The lieutenants began to discuss women's breasts. Men and women—creatures as different as my parents—were joined by this magic physical appetite, which I felt no more than a deaf man heard a symphony. I merely wanted to take a long, hot, steamy shower; only in that decrepit room, at the end of the day, after the salutes and uniforms, the feuds and office politics, did one find the beauty that lay beneath it all in the form of a supply clerk from Ottumwa, Iowa, soaping himself slowly in a white cloud as he sang "He's Not Heavy, He's My Brother." Daily existence was exhausting, but there was a general's chauffeur lounging on the wet bench in nothing but his dog tags.

When we had to go to a party at Sergeant Slager's one Saturday afternoon after work—to celebrate the impending marriage of a shy clerk from Maine who had enrolled in Bible class in preparation for his wedding—I was furious. On our way to the little stucco house Sergeant Slager shared with his German wife on a street in Kirchheim, we stopped to pick up Vittorio. Our knock woke him. We entered a room filled with the milk-white light of a winter afternoon—the rumpled sheets of the bed were the same color as his skin, the air, the afternoon. He and the Clam spoke of office politics while Vittorio dressed, but I hardly listened. I sat while they talked in a daze of romantic longing. The dense light in the room, the limbs of this smooth young man in his underwear, this personnel specialist from a small town in Florida who lived with a prostitute, made me wonder what it would be like to spend the cold winter afternoon in this nacreous light on a bed whose rumpled sheets seemed composed of the same substance as the milk-white air, the forearms of Vittorio. Yet I was not sure what I coveted more: selection by a woman who was a connoisseur in such matters, or a gentle, handsome clerk hidden in one of the drab cement houses in the new part of Heidelberg, captive at the end of a long cold winter afternoon.

In summer Heidelberg was a rose-red city but in winter the stones of the churches and castle turned a pale nougat color in which the windows shimmered like pools of oil as we walked to Sergeant Slager's. In the gardens the pear trees were encased in ice, and their heavy branches scraped against one another in the wind. As we passed the barracks I saw four black soldiers shooting basketball in a clearing on the snowy court behind the mess hall, and reflected that in regard to the rest of society I was as isolated as they in their all-black barracks, sitting at their all-black tables in the mess hall. For the first time I found myself alone—a solitude that seemed both a crisis and an opportunity. So impatient was I suddenly with my fate that when we came to our sergeant's house I stopped on the sidewalk and voiced my dislike of these parties. "Come, come," said the Clam, "get it over with."

It was just as I predicted: The Clam and Vittorio kept up with everyone but myself and the blushing bridegroom in supplying the off-color jokes that were inevitably called for after an hour of drinking beer and discussing the absence of pubic hair on Vietnamese women. On the street outside, drunk and light-headed for the first time, I said to the Clam, "How can you bear those jokes? How can you put up with the phoniness?"

He replied, "Simple. I always keep in mind that the moment I am out the door, I can get into a taxi"—he pushed us into one of the little black Mercedes in which he went everywhere—"and tell the driver to take us to"—and here he leaned forward and spoke to the man at the wheel —"the Yellow Rose of Texas, *bitte. Mach schnell.*"

The Clam never got into a taxicab without saying *go fast, please*, partly I suppose because it gave him pleasure to speak German and those were the three words he knew in that language, and partly because he really was in a hurry. Like a man whose injuries demanded attention, he leaned forward in his seat until the car was under way, anxious to get to the hospital; and then, convinced the driver was obeying his orders, he sat back and smiled a serene, demented smile, lighted a cigarette, held it before his lips, and sighed: "As Doctor Johnson said, there is nothing quite so delightful as flying through the countryside in a four-in-hand!" And he settled back, as the tires bounced crazily across the cobblestones, to watch the corners and doorways, the *Platzes* and chestnut trees, flash by. I felt I was floating on the night wind which blew through our cab. The Clam's eyes glittered in the amber glow of the passing streetlights.

We got out of the taxi at the Yellow Rose of Texas—a plain wooden door I had passed often in a facade of buildings beneath the castle, which loomed above us in the fog, tinged amber by the spotlights embedded in the hillside beneath it, like a fantastic set for an opera of Berlioz or Gounod's *Faust*. We followed the Clam inside. Everyone looked at us as we came in. The waiter came to our table, bent down, and kissed the Clam on the lips. This kiss lasted so long Vittorio and I began to wonder if we should say something while we waited. I was too drunk to formulate words however. "His name is Erhard," the Clam said when it ended, his eyes sparkling, and the waiter withdrew. The Clam put his cigarettes on the table and said, "He's a mad dolly who refuses to give me his complete devotion because he is interested primarily in blacks. The curse of the krauts!"

The Clam looked around the room with the steady swing of a radar scanning the heavens. Then he turned to us and sighed. "Look at that boy," he said in a calm voice as he stared at someone across the room. The Clam glanced in that direction: A laughing, stocky German who had removed his shirt sat on someone's lap, wearing a conical straw hat. His chest was deep.

"He's pretty, I admit," said Gallimard, "but if you could hear the dialect he's speaking, you wouldn't find him so appealing. It's as if sewage was streaming from his mouth." Neither Vittorio nor I could hear the dialect he was speaking, however, and he continued to rivet me the drunker I got. Our table was joined by others; introductions, laughter; people came and went. At one point the Clam crawled under the table to retrieve his cigarette lighter and remained there even after I shouted that his lighter was right on the table.

"Your lighter is here!" I bellowed.

"He knows that," said Wheatworth. "Stop shouting."

"He knows that?" I said incredulously. "Then what is he doing down there?"

"Having sex," Wheatworth said.

The Clam rose up between us. He reached for his beer while on his knees, drank, wiped his lips, hoisted himself up, and leaned forward to pick up his cigarettes. "Ah, Newbie," he sighed, as he held one up for a light. "Youth. Beauty. Life."

Then in the drunken haze I heard Vittorio say in a loud voice to the Clam as he sat down beside him: "What do *you* see in the cook? What is it?"

"He's sweet," said the Clam.

"But what do you talk about?" yelled Vittorio.

"His car in Florida, his best friend Timmy, and Creedence Clearwater Revival albums."

"You see?" said Vittorio. "He doesn't even know the best part of you!"

"The best part of me?" said the Clam, smiling in wonderment.

"Your intelligence, your wit," said Vittorio, "your mind!"

"Oh, darling," said the Clam as he lifted a cigarette to his lips, "I don't think the mind is the best past of me, or anyone else, for that matter."

"He doesn't even value what makes you loved by your friends!" said Vittorio, grabbing the Clam by his wrist.

"But none of my friends," said the Clam in his most sinuous tone, "have that snow-white stomach, that gorgeous ass, that pendulous dick!" Vittorio dropped the Clam's wrist, covered his own eyes with a hand, and moaned. The Clam called to me: "Oh, isn't life crude? Isn't it just too dreadful? In Mexico they pay by the inch!" He now leaned close to me and said in a murmurous voice against my ear, "Wolfgang wants to know all about you. He is too shy to speak, however. So *I told him* about your patrician shaft. He plays the violin for pleasure and designs computers at work. He visits his mother in Bonn every Sunday and would like to ask you how you find Germany."

There was no need to reply. Soon we were floating in a windy automobile between the modern swan-throated streetlights of Heidelberg, through the new cement portion, and there were several people besides Wolfgang in the car with me. The Clam smiled and patted my hand and sang in a low voice "Memories of Heidelberg mean memories of you." I was then in bed with the computer programmer who played the violin. His flesh was like paper: dry, tasteless, smooth. Bodies lay in sheets all over the floor. I awoke my host just after he dozed off and demanded to be driven home. We returned without a word to the barracks and I went in to do what my own mother had done to me as a child when I said naughty words: In the empty, gleaming shower room I washed my mouth out with soap. As I put my towel away I concluded that the Catholic Church was right: The body was the temple of the Holy Ghost— nothing more, nothing less. Then I lay down and felt myself plummeting through the mattress, the floor, the earth.

The following weekend, while the Clam and the cook were in Berlin on a pass, Sergeant Slager picked a document out of the Clam's desk and started reading: "Your cock is yet to me . . ." in a loud voice until his laughter ceased, his face flushed, and he turned and left the room as pink as the carbon copy. On his return the Clam was called into the major's office and told he was being transferred to one of the towns with which he frightened so many newcomers. As we stood beneath the window of his train one evening, he reminded Vittorio that the cook did not like to sleep alone, and could not be handed over to the likes of Stone. But Vittorio could not bring himself to accept—the very ease of the invitation guaranteed that. For a while that winter the cook belonged to Wheatworth, and then to the wife of the lieutenant downtown. Admiring beauty, she esteemed the cook as much as the Clam did. By March they all had gonorhhea. Shortly after Easter her husband got drunk at a party at the Officers' Club and fell, or threw himself, down a flight of stairs. The rest of us returned to America.

3

When they returned to the United States to be discharged by the army, the little band was like those families from Aruba who brought their maids back with them. Lives could not be transplanted exactly. The maid, considered part of the family after their life together in Aruba, found herself imprisoned in a big white air-conditioned house in a suburb of Orlando with no trees. Within the house their world was intact. Outside, the tropical gentility of an Aruban afternoon was replaced by a river of automobiles flashing past their blazing lawn. The maids were trapped indoors. I knew the moment I returned my book to the handsome librarian at Fort Dix—with a curious sense of regret—on the morning of my departure, that the world in which our amorous escapades had loomed so large was completely artificial.

The Clam did not. He tried to re-create his reign over the homosexual clerks of the personnel office in Heidelberg when he settled in New York City. He even sent for the cook. But housed in a tiny penthouse on the roof of a building on Eighty-fifth Street—whose broken windows that winter let in the cold winds that made it necessary for all his dinner guests to keep their coats and gloves on—the imperial insouciance was hard to sustain. The cook hated cold weather and left the Clam for a wealthy record-company executive with a capacious apartment in the East

Fifties whose rooms were so warm one had to open the windows for relief. The Clam taught school that year in Spanish Harlem. Shortly after Christmas he slapped a Haitian girl who was insolent to him and was relieved of his position when her parents sued. He borrowed money from Stone, to be repaid in a year by cleaning Stone's apartment once a week. Then he got a job selling ties at Brooks Brothers until an uncle in Queens found him a position on the maintenance staff of the public school system there. "I would much rather sweep up after the shits than have to talk to them," he said, and began taking the subway out to Jackson Heights at three o'clock every afternoon to clean the classrooms of P.S. 69.

On the edge of southern Harlem he found a paneled room in the turret of an old apartment building whose splendor had deteriorated with the evacuation of the Jewish middle classes to the suburbs. After assembling his souvenirs of the Rhine, he became a reclusive janitor, and when he was not sweeping out the schoolrooms, whose emptiness thrilled him, he began a feud with a Puerto Rican postman on the same floor of his apartment building over the importance of Puerto Rican literature, and the rank of Caribbean culture generally—as its people began to fill the streets around him. The details of his days we heard about on the telephone. Like some erstwhile agent of the C.I.A., the Clam retained a nostalgia for his years in the service, and would from time to time telephone members of the little band in the city and reminisce about Sergeant Slager. Otherwise we had little in common now, for if half of a friendship is its circumstances, nothing could have been less like the cloistered life of the barracks, the rose-red somnolence of Heidelberg, than New York City, where everyone, suddenly on his own, began pursuing interests that necessarily got more dissimilar as time went on.

The cook remained in New York, invisible when he had

a lover, omnipresent when he did not. He was one of those people who depend on lovers to order their lives, and collapse without them. When attached to someone, he worked, stayed home in the evening, was sober. Then we would see him waiting tables at a hotel on Fire Island, or in every bar we visited on Christopher Street, drunk, morose, looking significantly at people across the room—embarrassing Vittorio (who had, I saw now, a more romantic conception of him than the others who treated him in Heidelberg as a descendent of Cupid) by his availability and lack of will. Vittorio didn't like to see him standing in a bar, part of the waiting crowd, either because the cook was associated sentimentally with his own youth and freedom as a soldier in Heidelberg, or because he thought the cook objectively valuable. He saw him still as the youth tied to a post on that canvas in Munich, bristling with arrows—or so I imagined when he excused himself and went across the crowded room to talk to him on those summer evenings our first year in the city.

For a month they lived together in an apartment on West End Avenue lent Vittorio by a classmate, and Vittorio listened to the cook's escapades with the cool appraising air of the manager of an actor or singer giving advice on a career; only the cook's career was apparently nothing more —or less—than that of a lover. Vittorio was the product of an educated family and could hardly permit himself to live life on those terms. He listened to the cook's tale about his little adventure of the night before—when one first arrives in New York, every pick-up is an adventure (if nothing else, a new apartment)—and gave him advice: He told him not to go to a gymnasium because his body was perfect as it was, and that beauty consisted of proportion and proportions could not be altered by lifting weights. The cook went anyway, because Americans must labor to make themselves feel they are accomplishing something.

These denouements did not discourage those of us who came to New York in search of love and happiness; even the sight of the cook (in a bar between lovers) in no way disproved our belief that permanent happiness could be found in union with another person. In the case of Vittorio it did not even preclude the ultimate happiness of a conventional union blessed by his family.

"What do you want?" I said to him one evening as we stood on the esplanade in Brooklyn Heights looking at the city lights.

"I want to be successful," he said, "and have a family." That his dream was standard startled me. He was at the time a temporary typist addicted to the Everard baths.

He spent his first winter in New York typing up a report assembled by an advertising agency on the shift in American drinking habits from hard liquor to wine. Then he worked for a professor of linguistics investigating the development of the word *anymore* in the argot of street gangs in the Bronx. The Clam compiled a copy-writing portfolio and took it to agencies. "The quintessential ice cream?" said the woman at McCann-Erikson as she viewed the sample advertisements he composed. "What does that mean?"

"Quintessential," said the Clam in a faint voice, his hands rising in the air to portray the connotation of this word. "The ice cream of ice creams, the extreme essence of ice cream, the *echt* ice cream," he said.

"Nobody will know what you mean," she said, closing his portfolio and handing it back to him. "*I* don't know what you mean. Work on these some more and see me in a couple of months."

But the Clam was too embarrassed to go back in a couple of months. He felt as chastised as he did while wandering through the mists of perfume and face powder on the ground floor of Bloomingdale's the previous week, when out of the scented cloud surrounding the display of a cosmetics line he wanted to investigate, a woman with a sharp Bronx accent intoned, "You have an irritated area."

"I do have an irritated area," he said the evening of his visit to McCann-Erikson. "My soul. You see, what's wrong with us is that the Army accustomed us to a life in which everything was taken care of. Now we stand in one very large department store. We've got to learn what makes this country go," he said. "We've got to learn to sell."

"What?"

"Anything," he said. "The principles are the same." He picked up the Pimm's No. 1 Cup he always ordered in the Oak Room of the Plaza Hotel—where he led the little band after work—and said, "My maternal grandfather, actually, was the premiere salesman of hats and gloves in Boston." Seeing we did not know how to react to this piece of information, he leaned forward and said, "I've found an advertisement in the newspaper that promises travel, vacation in Europe, high income, and a chance to become your own boss."

When we went to the introductory meeting in the Flatiron Building we found Wheatworth sitting there. "It's selling encyclopedias," he said. A man in a dark pinstripe suit, with theatrically large black eyes, was seated next to Wheatworth. He smiled, wiped his forehead with a handkerchief, and introduced himself as Mister Friel. He looked as if he were on his way to or from a dinner party.

"Don't tell *me* it's because of the color of your skin you can't get in a single house in Syosset!" yelled the Greek in charge of the meeting, as he entered the room with a black youth in red pants, vest, and tennis sneakers. "You are not using the approach we taught you. It's foolproof. It will open any door, and once you're through that door, you use the rest of the speech!" he shouted, while Mister Friel flushed.

"Perhaps we are too sensitive for this job," he whispered as we left to go to lunch. "I know it was actually kinder, more honest of Mister Couletas to accuse the *shvartzer* of using his skin color as an excuse—even though a housewife in Syosset is hardly likely to unlock her door when she sees a black man on her steps, if she even answers the door at all, or manages not to faint. But did he have to *yell* at him in front of all the others?" He sighed as we took seats in the coffee shop down the block. "I suppose it's absurd in the nuclear age to dislike a man for raising his voice—and yet, as my mother said, it's a pity manners and compassion were not written into the Constitution."

Wheatworth said nothing, but a week later, after our training was completed, when he was finally dropped off at a street corner in Port Jefferson, he whispered to us through the window as he got out, "I feel like a frogman ordered to blow up a ship in the harbor. I think we should have stayed in and reenlisted." And as the car sped off to drop the rest of us salespeople off in various neighborhoods, it seemed very much like a military operation.

Sometimes I simply knocked on the door of a house to ask for a glass of water. I sat in the kitchen as the woman watched me drink, and the voices of children playing in the backyard, the flutter of a water sprinkler, mingled with the suburban silence. I liked clean kitchens, boxes of cake mix lined up on the Formica counter, paper cutouts taped to the refrigerator. Such a kitchen was as cool and clean as the kitchen of my dreams. But I saw no way to enter this domestic life. When I sat face to face with a husband and wife on their sofa, I felt a profound guilt stealing through me: How I could ask this pair of lovers to plunge themselves further into debt was beyond me.

"Exactly!" said Mister Friel when we sat together on a bench at the end of the green, humid twilight waiting to be picked up by our supervisor. "Hospitality is a sacred trust.

To plunder it requires a conscience less finely wrought than ours."

"But people are bored!" said Vittorio. "They want a visitor! They beg to buy encyclopedias from me. They want advice on their furniture, too! Can you understand the scale, the monumentality of the boredom of most people's lives?"

Mister Friel nodded and said, "It only confirms Schopenhauer's dictum that once a man is free of his material needs, he is only confronted with the consciousness of life's essential emptiness." He wiped his forehead with his square of handkerchief and sighed. "And where is the mother ship when we need it?"

Wheatworth took his duties more stoically—he simply sat there smoking cigarettes and watching the suburban boys playing basketball in a driveway. There was no trace of that religious mania which characterized his childhood —unless it was telling me one evening he now followed the Sufi doctrine that God is in the arms of a beautiful youth —until he sold a set of books himself. Then he returned to our pickup point so pale, so agitated, we thought he had been bitten by a dog, until he gasped, "I sold a set."

"Placed," said Mister Friel with a smile, using the verb preferred by the supervisors. "Placed a set."

"With a family whose children are too young to even read! They were like my parents. They would have bought anything, they were so nice. Do anything for their kids! I shall burn in hell for this one day. I shall burn in hell!" Wheatworth said.

"Now, now," said Mister Friel in a soothing voice. "It's not as if we were selling something harmful. We are selling encyclopedias, and encyclopedias can only do people good." But his single success made it impossible for Wheatworth even to knock on another door.

Toward the end of August no one felt like working—it

was too hot. Corn and peaches were being sold along the highways of Long Island and northern New Jersey. The wild grass was waist-high along secondary roads. Even Mister Friel—who was always impeccable in a dark suit and fragrant with cologne, his silver-flecked dark hair combed neatly, his tie secured by a sterling tie pin—lost his composure. "No, please, don't bother to get up," I heard him saying to a screen door as I stopped in the road. "Sink back into your swamp of Tupperware! Watch your Jell-O mould acquire a fungus! Sit there and wait for your cellulite to harden! Plato was quite right about the soul—I see that now!" As he turned away, two Doberman pinschers hurled themselves against the door. Mister Friel ran down the steps and across the lawn and followed hot on my heels.

"Really," he said when we finally came to a stop on the gravel apron of the highway. "How about a Dairy Queen? How about a summer on Fire Island?" he said as we walked down the road. "I know several people who need houseboys. Including my ex-lover. I wonder who's pulling *his* wagon from the liquor store," he said, wiping his forehead with a handkerchief. "What do I know of heat?" he panted. We sat down on a smooth stone beside the road in a patch of oakshade to catch our breath. "We were always in the Pines at this time. We went in May and did not come home until September. Ah, the academic year! I used to pull the wagon back and forth to the grocery and liquor store, and meet arriving guests. I had few other duties, except to amuse at dinner. And I did amuse." He looked at me and smiled sardonically. "I was not always as you see me. I once was a professor of American history at Brooklyn College. Until I was assassinated by four colleagues in a men's room. Until I was refused tenure," he said. "And life began to fall apart."

The silence and the sunlight were so intense that when a kitten appeared in a nearby hedge and looked at us, I started.

"You see, I am a teacher," said Mister Friel, "the way that is a cat. And since I could not be what I am, nothing that has happened to me has been a surprise. Including the coarseness of my former lover."

"Who was that?" I said.

"John?" said Mister Friel. "A professor *with* tenure at Rutgers. The author of several books on the Bourbons, and the son of a doctor who owned some three blocks of downtown Wheeling, West Virginia. A man insulated, so to speak, from life." Mister Friel unbuttoned the top three buttons of his vest and sighed. He was a black Irishman whose large dark eyes were always slightly moist. He noticed my looking at him and said, "Of course I was a different person altogether when I met him twenty years ago on the corner of Third Avenue and Stuyvesant Street. Fresh out of Holy Cross. I glowed. Mothers introduced their daughters to me. My looks all came from perishable things —hair, complexion, eyes—like so many colleens. The eyes are the first to go, of course. And here I am, as if those twenty years had never happened, looking for my first job," he said. "Well, not my first. A year after losing tenure, after being thrown out of the Casa di Mille Tormenti, I went to work at an answering service. But I could not bear to soil my mind with the disgusting trivia of other people's lives. Their pompous little careers, their nasty ambition. I got tired of being yelled at because someone *else* chose not to leave his name. So I quit that. I became a chauffeur. I drove Mick Jagger to Montauk, Diane Keaton and Warren Beatty to a premiere; I drove a Latin American representative to the United Nations on what I'm sure was a drug run. Then I worked in a travel agency but that was depressing. So I took a position in the shoe department at Saks. Then I worked for a skinflint at a print gallery on Fifth Avenue, and then I came here." He sighed again.

"You mean we have to do all that?"

"Skip Saks," said Mister Friel. He lighted a cigarette.

"No, no," he said, "you are young. You must avoid my mistakes. Just don't give twenty years of your life to a man whose town house and beach place and farm in Rhinebeck are all in his name."

"But what happened? Why did you break up?"

"I . . . lost my head over a youth from Moline, Illinois, who had just moved to New York," said Mister Friel. "If the truth be known. I met him on the same block, in fact, where John met *me* in 1954. We were in love. Then he met a grand master of bridge who promised to take him to a tournament in Monte Carlo on the *Queen Elizabeth*. We all lost out, I'm afraid. But here I am, in touch once more with the only decent portion of my life—education." He patted the sample volume (*Fish* through *Gerontology*) he carried in his presentation kit. "The road not taken, unfortunately, but the road I must track my steps back to. So! Let us press on!" he said, getting up with a smile and a little grimace as his knees stiffened. "Let us attempt to civilize this suburb. I have done little myself the last twenty years, God knows, but mix martinis and make sure there was toilet paper in the guest bathroom." And the two of us began walking down the highway, our eyes narrowed against the sun blazing on the asphalt and the pale gravel alongside.

As the summer wore on, we found ourselves in more remote and rural towns, for the suburbs were like a farmer's land which has been plowed and farmed to death. We arrived sometimes in neighborhoods ten minutes behind young Mormons and Jehovah's Witnesses, only to be picked up five minutes later by the mother ship, with our supervisor's terse explanation: "George Kovacs's group was just here." The most likely suburbs had been combed so thoroughly that the women said in bored voices without getting up from the table in the kitchen where they were paring apples: "We have an encyclopedia, thank you." The supervisor instructed his troops to look for "mooches": the couple on the block who were either so nice, or so bored, they would buy anything. But these were precisely the people who reminded me of my parents and I refused to take advantage of their kindness. As I sat on a park bench in Sayville watching boys toss a football on a green meadow between walls of copper beeches, I wondered how I was going to justify my parents' investment in me. I hadn't a clue as I listened to Wheatworth and Mister Friel discussing the lives of the saints, Schopenhauer, Saint Augustine, and Plato, while trudging through the hot little towns in which I felt I was with each block discarding elements of a genteel education.

The Twins and I lived that summer in a Brooklyn neighborhood populated primarily by Hassidic Jews, who stood in clumps of black hats watching us rush back and forth to the subway. From the roof of the building one could see Manhattan wrapped in a gauze of hot silver moisture. The fact that the geographical limitations of an island caused this city to rise as a fantastic group of spires and towers in no way explains its effect when viewed from a distance. We had one desire: to live there. In August an entire company of performance artists who lived in Mister Friel's building in the East Village left to reestablish their base in Columbia, South Carolina. Five apartments fell vacant at one stroke. Wheatworth took the first one and we followed him a week later: like ducks, like immigrants.

Some people come to the city for love, and some come to make money, and some come simply to disappear. My motives comprised all three. The building on St. Mark's Place in which I had found three rooms bore across its lintel, in German, the words GERMAN HIGH SCHOOL, but since those days it had given way to Ukrainians and then to middleclass bohemians seeking flats with cheap rent. Across the hall lived a lesbian who every year acquired a thin lover whom she took in and fed foods she would not allow herself to eat—cakes, pies, cookies, pasta, homemade bread, ice cream, rice pudding—until the woman became obese, and then she kicked her out. In a few months another waif appeared, a scared street kid with short black hair and large dark eyes, skinny, angular. Within the year she was a blimp. Down the hall lived a male prostitute who kept fish, dahlias, Confederate jasmine, climbing roses and sunflowers, and who never went out into the sun. In summer he refused all invitations to the beach and he would not even go shopping until eight o'clock, when we would meet him coming through the gray dusk in the middle of August, glimmering-white as cold cream, or some prehistoric fish that lives in the lightless depths of a mid-Atlantic trench. He guarded his skin for the same reason my mother covered the sofa on her porch in Jasper with a sheet: so it would last forever. Transvestites lived in the apartment beneath, and across from them a drug dealer, and down the hall a young man and woman—he blond, she black—who once ran out of their flat as he screamed, "You're fucking with another man! You can't sleep with two men at the same time!" in a furious voice. It was a building filled with oddities, and one evening while standing near the police who patrolled our block I learned they referred to it as "Love American Style" because it was occupied by people like ourselves.

But that was why I lived there part of the year. Where else could one pursue these personal tastes? Down the hall from me, Mister Friel dressed to go out each night into a city whose parties seemed innumerable. I would pass his room, hear *Lucia di Lammermoor* playing, knock on the door, and find him fixing himself up. He used both a martini and the mad scene from that opera to help him choose clothes. His apartment was a mess: His bedstead was composed completely of stacks of old newspapers, on which he'd scrawled "Read Kerr on Albee" or "Review of Gielgud" on the margins, articles he had never got around to reading but refused to throw out, and which supported him as he slept. One room was impossible to enter because when you opened the door a crack, you saw that it was a pile of newspapers and magazines that reached to the ceiling. Bookcases covered every other wall; and, on a cork wallboard over the bathtub in the kitchen, were pinned invitations to openings, dance clubs, and parties. Mister Friel spoke of everything—fashion shows, murder trials, the baths—with indefatigable joy and excitement. "The thing is to remain interested," he said as he tried on ties before the broken shard of a mirror. "And in your case, to fall in love."

"Not yours?" I said.

"At my age," he said, "it becomes less and less probable. For the not-so-wealthy widow, it's nothing but cocktails and dinner parties," he sighed, "and salads with five kinds of lettuce. But for you! Love is everywhere! In the laundromat, for God's sake!" And he waved his hand in the general direction of one on Second Avenue that always lost his shirts, but which was run by a Puerto Rican family he felt sorry for.

What he said was true. In Jasper I would hardly have been able to search for lovers on the street. In Jasper our life was so quiet my father urged me to take a drive, stay overnight somewhere, at least explore the state. As far as they could see I had no interests except those of the people who lived around us: gardening, feeding birds, taking walks. During a visit there one rainy afternoon, while searching for a vacuum cleaner I discovered a box of my letters from Heidelberg. The false tone adopted by the son censoring his life, the real adventures of his heart, as if they were secrets which could not fall into the hands of the enemy, made me unable to read more than a few lines. They were earnest, affected, fraudulent, and polite. So

shrouded in mystery was my life now that when we went
to a coffee shop during my parents' visit to New York one
day, my mother gave me a quarter to put in the jukebox and
said, "I want to hear what *you* like." There was nothing I
particularly did admire on the jukebox. The music I danced
to was black music played in homosexual clubs Vittorio
took me to which seldom surfaced on the radio, much less
the jukebox of hotel coffee shops—so we sat there listening
to Carole King sing "It's Too Late, Baby" as we ate our
pancakes, and I hoped she would not read anything into the
lyrics. She received no other clues from my conduct during
their weekend in Manhattan. Each morning I picked them
up in the lobby of the hotel at which we'd always stayed
going to and from Aruba—a melancholy memory now—
and took them around all the beads of the tourist's Rosary:
the Empire State Building, the Metropolitan Museum, the
Circle Line. They no doubt wanted to sit in a bar in comfort and have a drink. I took them places I was sure I'd see
no one I knew. Even on the water I was nervous, however,
as we floated slowly around Manhattan, counting every
hour till their departure. Yet when I met them for the last
time to say good-bye, when I saw them leaving New York
bemused (and uncomplaining of my terrible treatment), I
realized their Manhattan no longer existed; I was replacing
their city with my own, just as people in a crowded restaurant waited for us to give up our table. And my cruelty—
my inhospitality—struck me with such horror that when
their plane took off, I was not sure which I felt more intensely: relief at their departure or hatred of myself. "But
what could I do?" I asked myself aloud on the subway going
home. "Introduce them to the Clam? Mister Friel?"

"How did it go?" Mister Friel said when I came back and
he saw me on the stairs ripping off my coat and tie like a
man choking to death.

"I drove them through the streets with everything but a
whip," I moaned. "Like *dogs,* like *cattle.*"

"Poor you," murmured Mister Friel as he looked down at me, and frowned. "Poor them." And he continued down the stairs.

His own parents were very old, he told me, and lived in Brooklyn. The rest of us were separated from our families by great distances stitched together by the Bell System, a fact that created odd juxtapositions. Wheatworth answered the telephone one evening in his apartment, picking it up with his free hand while the other remained in the rectum of the bartender who lay on the bed beside him, head back, gasping, and heard his mother say, "Hi! Your father just said I should give you a ring. He's sitting across from me now. He watches TV from the small sofa instead of the big one now."

But several of the little band (including Wheatworth), finding themselves launched finally on a new life in New York, went home to get the things they needed to furnish their new apartments, and in the first flush of excitement at finally living alone, decided to set things in order with their past. Stone spent a weekend at his family's house in Tampa and told his mother, as they were cleaning out his closet, that he was attracted to men. "Well," she said, "it's not so bad. Look at that bitch your brother married."

Gallimard flew home to Ohio to tell his mother after a session with a psychiatrist. But she held up her hand and said, "There are some things a mother has a right not to know."

Wheatworth went home to his parents' house, now in Connecticut, and told them he had an important announcement to make. They gathered in the library at twilight. The woods were bare already; a fire burned in the grate; an autumnal wind rattled the windows. His parents sat in their separate chairs, his mother poised on the edge of the cushion, his father knocking tobacco out of his pipe. Wheatworth stood up and announced that he was enthralled by men. His mother let out a sigh of relief, and said, "Oh, good. We were afraid you didn't know."

Who knew was precisely the issue in the Clam's eyes. He told his sister, and she agreed the news should stop there. He did not want to give his father a heart attack. He did not care who knew in Manhattan.

That fall we walked all over the city together, tireless and excited, in search of adventures. One night not long after Halloween we were walking down West Street when we saw a transvestite prostitute who worked a corner there free her arm from the grip of a handsome black man who had been twisting it. He turned and saw us following him up the block. "Faggot boys!" he called in a singsong, and grinned as he returned to his garbage truck.

The Clam took out a cigarette, went up to the man as if asking for a light, and said, "Excuse me. My friend and I were having an argument. Are you a nigger, pimp, or garbageman?" We walked away to a stream of curses. "I haven't heard that many *motherfuckers* since the army," said the Clam, who sat beside me the next week at the tennis courts in Central Park on a warm fall afternoon watching the players. The man on the bench behind us was telling his friends about "this little fag who plays great piano in the Village." The Clam got up and went over to the man and said, "Excuse me. When I go to this piano bar, should I tell the pianist the little kike in Central Park recommended him?"

It was only his own family he kept the truth from, and when I asked him why as we walked out of the park, he said, "Because no one is quite like our mummies. Now that I'm back at school, I get to watch these bruisers terrorizing their classmates. Goons seven feet tall holding knives to kids and stealing their lunch money. Only last week one was in the office of my friend who's the assistant principal. He had just stabbed a girl from Ecuador—and when my friend told him he was going to notify his mother, the goon burst into tears and said, 'Don't tell my mom—she's got a bad heart!' No one's quite like our mummies," said the Clam with a cackle as we left the park and began walking down Eighty-first Street.

We took the train the next weekend to Philadelphia to visit Vittorio, enrolled in business school there to please his father, who wanted him to return to Jasper and take a position in the local bank. But in the small room in the cement high-rise in which I found him, he was unable to concentrate on the books piled on his desk. He lived between a Japanese studying international tariff agreements and a boy from Kansas studying ophthalmology. At night the lights on the plaza between the high-rise he lived in and its twin came on, and he sat at his desk with the United States Tax Code open before him, eating Swedish Kreme cookies and staring at the windows of the building opposite glinting blankly in the violet dusk. He watched the dusk deepen and then he got up and went into the bathroom he shared with the two other students and prepared himself for a night in the bars he had discovered accidentally one night while walking to the Academy of Music to hear Ormandy conduct the Great Symphony of Schubert. "I could stand in them forever," he said. "And do. When I come home at three and take off my shirt, I can smell the hours I've wasted, all that stale cigarette smoke in the fabric."

He stood up, tucking in his maroon polo shirt, and said: "I've got to stop all this nonsense and buckle down."

"What about the examination you took for the Foreign Service?"

"I passed," he said. "But I didn't go for the interview. I couldn't bear the idea of some bureaucrat behind a desk wondering if I was homosexual. I'm too proud. I've got to start studying."

But he didn't. Instead, he stopped attending class and

finally withdrew from the school in which he had no interest. "It's so boring I'd rather dig ditches," he said. He sent his parents a carefully written letter. They called him while he was in New York at my apartment; it was a long call, and he put the receiver against my ear at one point and I heard his mother say, "We only want you to be happy." When he finally hung up he was flushed and teary. "Is that all they want?" he said. He turned with his hand on the doorknob, still wild-eyed from the shock that his parents only wished him to be happy, and said in a low voice, "We've been given everything. Health, intelligence, a good home, *every*thing!" His eyes narrowed and he said grimly, "We have no excuse. None!"

And he disappeared out the door into that city which contained so much freedom and so much on which to squander it: like the people one saw in Union Square selling drugs in even the most inclement weather, their umbrellas clustered together in the middle of the park in a dense snowfall like lily pads in the center of our fishpond in Aruba. They were there at all hours of the day and night. In summer they lay on benches as if in the municipal park of a Caribbean port, asleep or teasing one another. A man sprang forward who said, "I have a variety of drugs," in broad Jamaican accents, followed by a white man with mad eyes who wore a black raincoat with the collar turned up and who lowered his cigarette to snap, "Meth!" Around the monument the drugged and sleeping lay on the rotting benches, while a slender cocoa-colored youth in red polyester pants standing at the water fountain gave himself an impromptu bath, splashing the water under his arms with his free hand, Vittorio watched him, transfixed, as he murmured "No thank you, no thank you, no thank you, not today" to the sellers, with the distracted air of a man beating off a cloud of gnats in the woods.

"How beautiful he is," Vittorio said as he watched the

youth bathing, "and even more beautiful, he doesn't know it." He turned to me and said, "This is just what I live for. You see why I never want to go back to Jasper? You can't reconcile the two worlds. Don't even try. You can have boys like that, or you can have all the pleasures of family life. But you can't have both. Adoration of the penis has nothing to do with what produced us."

And he walked away through the crowd of drug sellers, drug buyers, and women watching their babies as they argued with their friends in words Vittorio did not even hear. He disappeared. I left the park certain he was wrong. I was determined to unite the two: my past family and the one I was hoping to establish here. But how? I was now a citizen of a world nothing had prepared me for. I was a man whose past and present were divided by an abrupt schism, raised with dreams inappropriate now. For one thing, the impulse to establish a domestic life of my own was so powerful that I made no distinction among the creatures whose physical shells attracted me. We were mere sights in that little society: as detached, arranged, and connected to our roots as cut flowers. We fell in love not with a man's mind but with his moustache—and lost interest the moment he shaved it off.

My program was simple: find a lover in the city and get out. What was more of a rebuke than those golden, soft October afternoons in Manhattan? I had a farm in mind, and one of those men in the plaid shirts stylish then, whom one saw on the boat to Fire Island in the late fall and who came into the Sandpiper on cold nights bundled up in baseball jackets and woolen caps. What did it matter if one saw them only once or twice, or was too awed to speak to them? It was their beauty, which made the depredations of the city irrelevant, that I wanted to transport to the country. Yet I could not go up and speak to them; the manners instilled in me prevented that. One didn't go up to a perfect stranger and talk about the weather when in fact you wanted to say, "Marry me." One didn't say what was in one's heart.

But one tried despite all: When Stone told me a man in the bar—so handsome that people refused to look at him— was actually "a nice guy who likes to talk more than anything else about this house he's building by himself in New Jersey," I was overjoyed to hear the news. I thought, I'll be glad to listen; I'll happily lie there and let him pour his soul out. I was touched by people whose grammar was not flawless but who could repair refrigerators and install a pump. But love is above all a subjective pleasure, an egoistic appetite, and I found that, once I had possessed his beauty, the outpouring of his soul became more and more intolerable. This handsome, strapping, kind man from New Jersey was fascinated by railroad switches, hated the Postal Department, and spent Saturday nights before he discovered the Eagle's Nest driving in his van through shopping malls in Paramus, dressed in a suit and tie, with Moody Blues tapes on the cassette. The memory of his loneliness made him weep—he was alone for so long he had distracted himself by memorizing odd things. We drove one day to West Point, and as we sat regarding the majestic bluffs, the silver river, he recited by heart "The Masque of the Red Death" by Edgar Allan Poe.

It was at moments such as this that I learned love was more difficult than I had been prepared to think, that I was quite selfish, and certainly very different from this person reciting, in the low, breathless hum of a man trying to walk a tightrope, a description of the ball at Prince Prospero's. And I viewed him with the same coldness my parents brought to bear the summer my sister invited her fiancé home. It was as if I longed to be rescued from my banal life by Love, and then, once having obtained the object, found a new form of banality stretching before us: that of lovers.

When he took me to the brick ranch house he had constructed in a clearing in the pine barrens of New Jersey, the glutinous gray light gathering in the woods, the sandy soil, the silence and the loneliness reminded me immediately of Jasper, and a little voice within said clearly: Get me out of here. And so—after tears and threats—I fell in love with a mysterious dancer who lived in my neighborhood in a building with no security system, so that he had to throw the keys down to me when I went to see him on Avenue B.

None of these people could I describe in Jasper, so that any parental wisdom on the subject which might have mitigated the errors born of my romantic vanity was lost. I did not even tell my parents about the roommate I acquired when it became apparent my long absences were an invitation to thieves. He was an intelligent young man, obsessed with building up his body, who relaxed when he came home after a hard day at the bank he worked for by putting on a pair of white sling-back pumps and walking up and down the room until his tension unraveled. The personality that inhabited his muscular body (whose breasts were now larger than his mother's) was in control when he answered the telephone in these shoes, in a sinuous, silken, unctuous voice that said: "Walter Reed Memorial Hospital. Department of Surgery." Or: "Bergdorf Goodman's, Lingerie, may I help you, please?" My mother assumed she had a wrong number until he shouted, "No, no! Is this Helen?" (He took pleasure in using the Christian name I never could use.) "Just a moment, he's right here!" And with a broad smile he extended the telephone to me: "*Helen* wants to talk to you!"

"Your roommate seems very e*mot*ional," Mother said after I explained his presence as a merely temporary, useful deterrent to thieves, somewhere between mothballs and window gates.

"He is," I said, "but very bright," for intelligence was admired equally with good character in our family.

But we never mentioned him again. He and the rest of my life were a dim mystery. This was by no means a source of pleasure to me. Surely my secret gave me a power over my mother that was the reverse of that she had over me as a child when, reading at her feet, I would be asked to leave the porch because some item of information that was adult and confidential was to be exchanged with my father. This did not so much annoy as thrill me then: that my parents had secrets and lived in a world where life was far graver, more tragic, more sordid than anything a boy in fifth grade could imagine. My protests over my banishment to the kitchen—the recommendation that I "ask Inez how dinner's coming" so transparent a pretext that I snorted—were theatrical. Now that I had a secret they did not share, I was by no means thrilled. Secrets, it seemed to me, gave their possessor an inflated sense of himself—like the person who indicates he knows something about someone but says, "I've been sworn not to tell." Secrets lent mystery to things that were in fact quite ordinary without their borrowed grandeur. Had I not kept it secret, my homosexual life would have appeared banal, no doubt. Yet when I ran downstairs at night I felt guilty not only because I was alive in a city far more exciting than Jasper, and free to pursue erotic pleasures my mother was denied, but also because it was a happiness I could not share with her. I had no desire to keep this adventure to myself, unknown to those who had, after all, made it possible. Even when I finally shared it with my sister—who merely asked, "Is it a hard life?"— she agreed it was perhaps best not to tell our mother. And so I watched Mother thrash about in ignorance of my life, trying to decipher an existence she had very few clues to. This sense of helplessness on her part—this feeling that she was irrelevant to our lives—produced, if nothing else, dull dinners when we gathered together at my sister's for Thanksgiving.

The only ones who enjoyed these feasts were the children, whose worst worry was that they would have to eat all their peas. The grown-ups did not know what the dinner would bring. My sister hoped her children would not display the lack of manners my mother accused them of, my brother-in-law was conscious of the historical coolness of his reception into the family, and I waited for my niece to say, "When are you getting married?"

And if we survived the Thanksgiving dinner, the danger was not past: I was nervous when Mother sat quietly in the den watching a television show she spoke highly of in Jasper, with her arms folded across her chest and a set mouth which made me suspect she was not watching the show at all, even if her eyes were on the screen. The snow fell outside the windows as we went about our business—reading, washing clothes, making snacks in other rooms: that domestic life I missed so—and her anger grew. Convinced she was being ignored—a reasonable conclusion in a busy house (the kids went out to play, their father watched football, their mother played paddle tennis, shopped, baked, conferred with a decorator, and fell asleep every evening exhausted in front of the television)—she sat there mentally cataloguing our sins. Finally she came upstairs to the bedroom where my sister and I were lazily discussing the rearrangement of her living room and folding laundry. She stopped in front of us, crossed her arms on her chest, swayed momentarily in her stockinged feet and said, "I finally had to ask myself: Why am I sitting downstairs all by myself in front of the TV? I can do that in Florida. I don't have to come here to be ignored."

My sister sat up and said, "Mother, we're not ignoring you. There was nothing on I wanted to watch. But you're welcome to sit up here with us and talk."

"I just want to know why." She frowned. "Just tell me why."

"Mother, no one is ignoring you," I said.

"No? Then why am I sitting down there watching *The Brady Bunch* by myself?"

"*The Brady Bunch* bores me."

"That's not the issue. You could at least keep me company. Your father and I did not come thousands of miles to be ignored. We can be ignored at home. Your father has told me," she said—and here my ears pricked up, for it was my mother's role to convey my father's thoughts to us— "that this is our last visit. We're not doing this again. He didn't want to come this time," she said, "and neither did you!" She unfolded her arms and pointed dramatically at me.

"Well," my sister said, folding a last towel calmly and then picking up the stack to take to the linen closet.

The moment she left I jumped off the bed and hissed, "Mother, you may consider yourself a Christian because you go to Mass, but that was the cruelest thing I've seen in a long time! You had no right to say that. Whether it was true or not, you had no right to say it!"

"The truth hurts," she said.

"*Who* does it hurt?" I said. "Betty! How cruel! I will never forget this!" I said, my fury so great even she rocked back on her stockinged feet and blinked, unprepared for this reaction.

She turned and left the bedroom. She sat down on the steps to the attic. Fury turned my heart to ice. The knowledge that my position was morally sound hardened my heart further when I heard her begin to sob. "Nobody loves me," she said, huddled on the stairs, her shoulders shaking. The children began to leave the rooms in which till now they had been listening to records, reading books, playing with toys, talking on the telephone, and walked across the landing to comfort her.

"Granma, *we* love you," one said.

"Don't cry, Granma," said another.

And as I heard their words—the same I'd used on similar occasions in Aruba—I reflected that family life was eternal and changeless, and only the actors were replaced. "Nobody loves me," she gasped.

When we left Pennsylvania this and all the other scenes were forgotten; we embraced, kissed, held one another, and parted with the certainty that no matter what happened, no matter where each of us went, we were a family. In fact, I returned to New York wondering how I could please my mother, justify all her hopes, her love for me, what accomplishment would allow me to bring her finally not merely to Manhattan but to the Manhattan of her (or my) dreams: some penthouse on Fifth Avenue from which she could watch the snow falling, surrounded by boxes from Bergdorf's, a limousine purring thirty-four floors beneath her, her cheeks rosy, like Deanna Durbin in a film I had seen in Aruba years ago singing on a satin bedspread "Spring Will Be a Little Late This Year."

These dreams evaporated more quickly than snow the moment I hit the grimy pavements of Manhattan, however. The Lower East Side was a neighborhood former generations struggled to get out of as quickly as they could. If my mother imagined New York in terms of Fifth Avenue, shopping, restaurants, nightclubs, passenger ships docking and departing, the city that thrilled me consisted of empty streets late at night in the poorer neighborhoods where a handsome youth stood warming his hands over the fire in an oil drum beside a fruit stand on First Avenue. The tenements that former generations had put behind them had for me all the romance, glamour, and allure that a mansion in the suburbs had for them. But that was because dreams are all equipped with revolving doors: Someone is always walking into the one you are leaving, and vice-versa.

4

I saw little of the group from Heidelberg during the next decade. Sometimes on Fifth Avenue I would run into the Terrible Twins, but they hadn't time to talk because they were following a shopper who had just gone into Saks Fifth Avenue. "Stunning corporate, cracked lips!" Or "Organic mountain man! Hot daddy!" Gallimard would say, and disappear into the revolving door with Stone so close at his heels they shared the same compartment.

Or out of the blue one afternoon Vittorio would call from a pay phone and say in a more level voice, "Listen, you must go up to Kaufman's Army-Navy Surplus Store on Eighth Avenue and Forty-second Street. There is the *most* incredible security guard. He could be Lebanese, Syrian, I'm not sure what—even Iranian—but one of the great faces of this or any other century. Just go up and pretend to be looking for knapsacks. How's everything going? I've got to run!" And there was a click. Sometimes I went. Sometimes I didn't. More than once Vittorio alerted me. He was frequently appalled to see some person (whose beauty enrolled him in the only aristocracy Vittorio cared about) trapped in a milieu Vittorio thought unworthy. But physical perfection was scattered through the population with no connection to any other quality. It was a random gene. And if Vittorio found it unjust that some physical paragon was incarcerated in the dim depths of a dingy surplus-clothing store off Times Square, there was nothing he could do about it except invite him to a party.

There was always a party in the seventies. Sometimes I saw the Terrible Twins shopping for clothes at the costume shops in the East Village, or the stores on lower Broadway where the fashions that defined our generation first appeared. Or I would see Vittorio on the boat going over to Fire Island for one of the fetes that were given at the dawn of the decade for nothing and ultimately moved to the city, cost fifteen dollars, and required a plastic membership card. But he, and the rest of the little band, were not the people I saw most frequently.

In New York one had friends for everything: to dance with every weekend, to see the autumn foliage up the Hudson once a year, to seek out for advice about work or matters of the heart, or to visit sometimes late at night when you happened to be walking past their door. There was an artist on Twenty-third Street I saw in this manner and each time he taught me something: that Wittgenstein felt we shouldn't torture ourselves about questions like "What is the purpose of life?" for instance. Seeing the artist once a year was like the annual physical examination I never took: It measured in an offhand way the progress of our lives.

The city was full of people you saw every two years on the street, for that matter, because it was the kind of town in which—because some people sleep late and others rise early, because its citizens are able to pursue their tastes at their most idiosyncratic—one could live two blocks away from someone but never see him. When you did, you stopped for twenty minutes and told each other about your lives since last meeting. Did he still live in the same apartment? What was the rent now? Was he still seeing the doctor on the Upper West Side, the one who played the piano every night for two hours to relax after surgery? Was he painting again or still writing a novel? What happened to Gallimard—driving a limousine for the producer of *Saturday Night Live*? Working for Halston? Going to Bogota for three months to live with Sam Turpin? How marvelous! I wish I could leave the city—he has the right idea! Still going to the Loft? No, I went to Flamingo; the music wasn't so great.

Shortly after parting you realized you had done nothing but extract a dull set of facts. What you really wanted to know was if there was any progress, any evolution, any goal toward which you were all moving. In fact you were simply growing older. And meanwhile the airplane fare to San Francisco went up and down, depending on the competition.

That was the only other city in which I saw them. I went back and forth several times over the deep, brilliant snow of mountains and plains I planned to visit but never got around to seeing. The country beneath the tip of the airplane wing looked cold and pure and rugged; I imagined trudging up one of those rumpled ravines to a better, healthier life. But the West (which every American holds unconsciously in reserve, including my mother, who longed for Colorado often) was practically off limits for me: I couldn't live on one of those gold-and-white prairies alone. The West in the end meant only one thing: San Francisco. Everyone in the little band went to San Francisco. In Jasper our priest referred in almost every sermon to his student days in Rome. The fact that he did so, the things he recalled, the look in his eyes when he did, made anyone who sat in his tiny audience at the five-thirty Mass realize this was the happiest time of his life, when he was young, and in Europe. Priests went to Rome. Wheatworth went to San Francisco. When I asked him how he could leave New York for periods of six months, he replied, "Oh, they'll all be here when I get back—standing in the same places."

And they were. They were simply living the routines of bohemian New Yorkers, who when I first arrived seemed the most self-possessed and glamorous creatures on earth. Then, I walked down Ninth Street, depressed by the sight of a young man rushing to dinner with a spray of irises in hand, wishing I knew him, and his friends. Eventually I did, and rather than go to the dinner party, made excuses, and found myself walking home by choice through the summer dusk to a solitary supper wishing that I could arrive in Manhattan all over again for the first time, absolutely ignorant on a summer night like this one, knowing no one.

But the constant roaming was not the reason I seldom saw the little band together, if at all. It was rather that elements in their characters hardly noticeable in Heidelberg had been given a chance, in this inexhaustible city, to assert themselves. At its most concrete they simply lived in different parts of town: Wheatworth had no material ambitions whatsoever, kept a cheap room on Avenue A, and seldom went north of Fourteenth Street unless it was to visit the Everard or Continental baths. If Wheatworth went to the Metropolitan it was the movie house on Fourteenth Street which showed heterosexual pornographic movies to homosexual men looking for sex in the balconies and aisles. The Clam went to the Metropolitan Museum; its objects pleased him more than the real city, and in a few years he knew the collections so well that when he took me there one weekend, he said, "The Buddha of Infinite Illumination has been moved." Or, "That scroll depicting the burning of the palace is gone. It must be in the basement being cleaned."

Wheatworth equated museums with morgues. I would visit the baths and see through his open door a man kneeling on the floor licking Wheatworth's rectum with a passion so sudden and startling that Wheatworth was still stubbing out the cigarette he had been smoking.

The Clam on the other hand took a job teaching English in Saudi Arabia because he found the puritanical society of that country a welcome relief and because, he said, the students were polite. "In this country," he said, "everything's a *tchotchke*. Including us." He had reverted to the proper Bostonian he had been as a youth at the Boston Latin School. He hardly had sex at all and seldom left his apartment unless it was to go to Jidda for six months. When he returned, the city made him angry. We went to the Metropolitan Museum to see the portrait by Velazquez of Juan de Pareja: a face reproduced all over Manhattan in the kitchens of restaurants, the backs of trucks being unloaded outside warehouses, the men's room of the IRT when we took the subway home afterward. Inside, a group of men, clouds of vapor at their lips, were masturbating in a circle while two elderly gentlemen sat on the toilets, waiting for a bowel movement or love, one could not tell which. The Clam came to a halt in the center of the room and stared at them. "Can't you people go on a date?" he said sharply. "Stay home and take a correspondence course in computer programming?"

"Come on, man," said the hippie who had zipped up his pants when we entered, unsure what our sexual tastes or official position would be. But the Clam was unembarrassed. Stone stopped inviting him to parties because guests asked "Who *is* this person?"

Wheatworth declined to come to parties because he had no desire to meet anyone. He did not even slightly believe in love. "It may happen once or twice in your twenties," he said to me once, "but that's it. I feel sorry for people who think it exists—something you can get, like a car." This left him curiously calm, in a way that those laboring under the belief that life was worthless without a lover were not. His own sexual objects evolved as the decade wore on; when he came back from his long sojourn in San Francisco, for example, homosexuals bored him. He knew them too well. He now went to decrepit gymnasiums in the boroughs surrounding Manhattan where adolescents with greased hair dropped the weights simply to make noise, had bad skin, and were compelled to express themselves by making jokes about farts, while Wheatworth stood quietly by, curling a barbell, bathing himself in their crude insecurity. It was their company he desired two hours of every day in Brooklyn—not the throng whose parties he had attended so assiduously when he first moved to Manhattan. And, like Vittorio alerting me to some security guard in a dingy clothes store off Times Square, Wheatworth would tell me breathlessly about some roller-disco in the Bronx or a bar in Bensonhurst "where no one has even *heard* of Fire Island!"

That everyone had a type was assumed. I was not sure I did, unless it was anyone who was not middle-class, intelligent, and burdened with those critical faculties that I longed to burst free of whenever I fell in love. If ever I wondered just what I thought of the milieu in which I had been raised, I need only reflect that I could in no way associate an erotic significance to it. Love was an escape from the pressure to be successful, a requirement so human (or American or middle-class—I didn't know which) it made me one of those people who, like the Frenchmen I knew who refused to return to Paris because their intellectual gifts had made their families expect great things of them, ran off to New York or Montreal. That is what we all were in a way: the dutiful son who goes to the colonies. I sought lovers who were not critical, did not complain, but I seemed to find them most often in the mechanical class—which always seemed more virtuous, more romantic, to me than any other.

As for Vittorio, he did not care what class the person belonged to. Faces were all that mattered. And he found most of them in that society whose importance he had vowed in Heidelberg would never take over his life. I saw Vittorio most often at the parties he sent me invitations to —and Gallimard, who drove a limousine and often was leaning against its fender while he waited for his customers dancing inside. There were three party-givers in New York during the seventies whose parties managed to attract dancers even after the celebrations began to cost fifteen dollars and required membership cards or mailed invitations if you were not a celebrity. One was the son of a Cuban general in Batista's army who reputedly sold a train car full of ammunition to Castro during the troubles there and then decamped to the mainland. The second was a Haitian woman by way of Brooklyn who was originally a manicurist and inserted an aristocratic *de* in her name. The third was Vittorio. By 1982 no one on Fire Island was even giving parties anymore—they were discussing over small dinners who had cancer (or they were not discussing it, depending on the wishes of the host)—much less the extravagant fetes given for their own sake in the early seventies. As the parties moved to clubs, and the clubs got bigger and the crowds more faceless, we went dancing less and less. The next time we met we weren't even dancing at all; we were at Bond's in a room the size of an airplane hanger watching the Dancing Fountains spurt in time to the music.

But because I had once gone out dancing, when I went downstairs in the morning my mailbox held invitations to new discotheques and New Wave clubs opening up every week in Manhattan. One re-created Berlin in the thirties, another Rio in the forties, a third a high-school cafeteria in the fifties. Occasionally I put one in my pocket in case I should be near that particular club while on one of the walks I began taking late at night. Sometimes on a dark street in the west twenties I would see a light in a facade of factory buildings, the ones from which Jamaican women issued every afternoon at five o'clock talking to one another in accents that reminded me so of Inez (whose granddaughters lived in Queens and were secretaries at a Park Avenue law firm, and who wrote me letters asking if I was married and to please send a photograph) that I followed them down Fifth Avenue in the falling snow to hear them talk with those broad, graceful vowels. In my pocket was the invitation I thought I might use that night. When I went inside I always saw Mister Friel, who lived only at night.

And as we stood talking, Vittorio came in and walked over to us. "What is this?" he said. "An homage to Cher? Straight or gay? Chic or bridge-and-tunnel?" We didn't know. And when I asked Mister Friel how he came to be there, he replied, "Once your name is on the Rolodex, dear, it's on forever." And he was off through the crowd greeting the people he knew, whose faces were to me so dramatic. They were people who did nothing but go out at night, and yet in the red glow of that universal bar-light, the dimness of the stairwells, they all assumed a drama, a romantic significance they did not have when you saw them on Second Avenue the next day, waiting for the bus under an overcast November sky. The three of us danced till it was six o'clock and then went home through the streets which at dawn were as empty as those in a village in Vermont.

On my way home I stopped at the baths, an unfashionable baths populated mostly by people I did not touch for fear of contracting disease, and I walked down the dark halls in my bare feet and towel, as proprietary as a doctor on the rounds of his beloved hospital, recognizing occasional patients lying in the rooms whose bright open doors broke the dark facade with pleasing infrequency. I didn't want crowds anymore (though my first year in New York we went to the baths only when a friend telephoned to assure us they were packed). I was searching, as the magazines said, for intimacy, and crowds made that more difficult to attain. I was searching not for the person of my own social class with whom I could expect to find compatible qualities. I was searching for the improbable person one never expected to find in this place at two in the morning, showering on the sixth floor in perfect solitude. I lay in wait for people in the same way muggers waited for old women returning from the grocery all alone. The young patrons lay mute on their pallets with dark questioning eyes—I had forgotten how serious the search was when I first went to the baths—as I went by. Once a blond held out his arm desperately. He told me about his friend Bob, the one who used to tie him up in Roanoke. He babbled as his body tossed like a branch buffeted in a wind, a person possessed by a demon, and I listened to his fantasy, silent as a priest hearing a confession. Then I continued on my way—past the room where every night, on peering in, I saw an ass that writhed, rotated, rose and fell above the pillow placed beneath it, with feverish energy. The rest of the room was dim. It was not that The Ass writhed only when its owner heard footsteps approaching in the hall. Once I tiptoed to the door and glanced inside. It was bucking as furiously as one of the mechanical bulls in the Lone Star Cafe. It shook for hours every night on that deserted floor, reverberated in the night like the motor of a water fountain always there for someone who might need it. One night, while sitting at the end of the hall, I was surprised to see a person leave the room and lock the door behind him. It was Mister Friel. He walked with eyes downcast to the bathroom and then returned to the room to become simply, once more, The Ass In The Night, an integral part of the peace and quiet of the baths. Nothing unpleasant happened there. Once a cherry bomb went off in a stairwell and I lost my hearing for a day. But by and large, unhappy things were banished—including Time. Hence I was astonished to come home one day and find my cat dead. Time was passing; people were mean; but at the baths one did not notice either.

In the baths there was no history, weather, time, or any of the other elements that compose life—and so addicted was I to visiting them that I was shocked one day when I rushed past a handsome man smiling at me on the sidewalk a block from the entrance. I did not stop. And I said to myself as I checked into the baths that I was now like my roommate, who refused dates because they would interrupt his workout; both of us had forgotten the original reason for our habits.

Mister Friel knew the reason for all his, however, and by this time it was no longer sexual; he was beyond the time of life when, as he put it, one is ruled by the penis. Nor did he go out to dance anymore, as far as I could tell. When I asked him one day, "Where do you dance?" he said, "In my living room." He just went out. Having taught at a university, having written art criticism, having lived in New York longer than ourselves, he belonged to several demimondes that I knew nothing of; but often I would see Mister Friel whizz past me on a summer evening in a crosstown bus, standing in dinner clothes beside a woman whose long formal dress peeked out beyond the hem of her raincoat. He belonged to that cultural colony which had something to feed on every night in New York. And it was not only the opera, the one-man show, the book promotion, he went to. He liked parties: the bigger the better.

I dropped by to watch him dress. He was going to a Brazilian costume ball one evening and needed assistance in placing the elaborate headdress, composed of fruits and flowers, on his head at the right angle. Mister Friel wanted to go to Brazil the way my mother wanted to take lessons on the guitar: things they would never do. He had corresponded for years with a young man from Pôrto Alegre whom he met on a visit to New York. He was a medical student when they began writing and was now an established eye surgeon in São Paulo. "His voice was like a waterfall," said Mister Friel. "He was so quiet and grave and beautiful. With green eyes." His family—two aged parents in Brooklyn and four married brothers, three in Queens and one in Albany—had no idea what his life was like. "That's one of the advantages of a hideous apartment," he said, looking around the room as he stood before the mirror buttoning his cuffs. "They don't visit. They hate Manhattan anyway. Let them. It's not wise to let them think you're having too much fun, either," he said. "Especially *brothers.* I learned that the year I shared my plans to visit Brazil. Brazil! You'd think I'd announced plans to leave the church! Why are you going to Brazil?" he said, fixing the necklace of shells. "Where did you get the money? What's in Brazil but jungle bunnies? If you've got so much money, loan me some for an air conditioner! Oh, my, the roof blew off several houses in Queens," he said. "I told them if they stopped buying guns for the I.R.A., *they* could go to Brazil, too. Although what they would do there, I can't imagine," he snorted.

"How many brothers do you have?" I said.

"Four," he said. "Three of them could be used very nicely to find truffles in the woods."

"You mean—?"

"They're pigs," he said, "who don't want to see *me* going to Brazil. So I've learned to keep my mouth shut. And take care of Mother and Father, which they don't have to do, of course, since they have families of their own." He adjusted the necklace and said: "Why do the wrong people reproduce? I ask myself that question every day—along with Why do the wrong people have money? And Why do the wrong people have big cocks? There is never an answer to life's most pressing questions." He held out a hand toward the crowded table. "Would you pass me that bronzer?" he said. "I'm afraid at my age one needs a little color in the face, and since I am no longer asked to Fire Island—my generation now lives on farms up the Hudson—and since I am not allowed to leave the country, I have to get it where I can. Thank you. Yes," he said, regarding himself in the mirror, "I believe in that maxim of the New Hampshire Friels: *Make do.* I see so many boys your age throwing away their youth in self-recrimination, unable to accept their sexual situation, shall we say. Stricken with guilt and self-loathing. Or lost, like the little mermaid who fell in love with an inappropriate object. A human being!" he said. "Ha!" He held out his ruffled sleeves. "And who no longer felt at home in the sea. We, too, are creatures caught between two kingdoms. That of sea and land. But we mustn't weep, like the little mermaid. We must *make do.* Whatever you do," he said, turning to look back at me, "*don't wallow.* If Vienna is fogged in, and the plane lands in Rome, then get out. Do as the Romans do. *Capische?* Oh, God, how I long to travel! My hat, please," he said, and held up his hands for the headdress, which I lifted off the bed and settled on his head.

He looked at himself in the mirror.

"I don't think I look like Carmen Miranda at all," he said. "I think I look like a priest. Put a pound of bananas on my head and I still resemble a bishop." He frowned. "Have I left any shells in that drawer?" He held his hand out and fluttered the fingers at a night table. I found some earrings and handed them to him. "Thank you. When I do go to Brazil," he said, "and I shall, I will do so quietly, on the QT. I will *tip*toe to Rio and *tip*toe back. And tell no one I went. Mario has the most wonderful ranch in the interior. We will ride horses all day in the Mato Grosso and be met on our return by servants bearing trays of champagne. Vulgar? I suppose so. It is the flaw in my soul, the cross I must bear. My dreams are so ordinary!"

He covered himself with a cape and went to the door

with his invitation—a paper pineapple—in hand. "And what is your cross?" he said as I followed him out. "Every Catholic must have one—it's just a matter of selecting the right model."

"Why?" I said. "Why must there be a cross?"

"Why must there be a penis?" he said, turning at the top of the stairs. Seeing I could not answer the question, he smiled and descended the stairs like a barge, a float in a New Year's parade, even more bizarre in the spasmodic fluorescent light that fluttered in the tubes the landlord seldom replaced and which gave to our building a nervous aspect.

The next day I saw Mister Friel, pale and sober, in the dark three-piece suit he called his May-we-view-the-body-now? suit, hurrying off to Brooklyn because his mother had misplaced her glasses and he had to look for them. "She's becoming a bit dotty," he said, "although I now suspect she hides things on purpose just to get the attention." And he rushed off to the BMT.

At a club later that week, while we waited for our jackets at the coat-check, a young man came up to Mister Friel (who that evening wore faded jeans and a black T-shirt) and said, "Take me home with you."

Mister Friel replied, "I can't, darling. I have to go out to Brooklyn and look for the remote control on my parents' television set. Some other time."

The shuttling back and forth had no regular pattern; sometimes he was gone for a week, and I learned his mother had been ill with the flu. He would telephone me and say, "My dear boy, how are you, would you do me an enormous favor? Go to my apartment—the key is above the door—and see if the invitation to the Magic, Fantasy and Dreams Party is tonight or tomorrow night?" He sighed. "I'm afraid I won't be able to go, whichever it is. My father has a painful case of gout and can't move from his chair. Thank your stars, my dear, you are not seventy-nine. If you'd like to use the invitation yourself, please do. It will only go to waste and it is, I believe, free. I never leave my house unless it's free, of course—"

Mister Friel talked in so low, so silken, so continuous a murmur that the only way to bring him to a halt was to yell "Wait! Wait!" into the phone. "Where are you?" I said. "In Brooklyn?"

"And *how*," he said. "Everyone is shuffling around me in tennis sneakers. I'm in a little grocery on the corner." If Mister Friel's brothers did not want to see him go to Brazil, his father did not like to see him on the telephone. "My father thinks the telephone should be used only to announce the end of the world," he sighed. "So I come down to the *bodega* to make my calls. Dad wants me to stay over of course. But the only way I would do that is if kept penises in the icebox, like Popsicles. Oh, and when you check that invitation—I hate to miss that party; Benson Paul was kind enough to send me a complimentary admission—when you check the invitation, my dear boy," he said in that breathless murmur, "would you also see if I didn't leave a pot of rice boiling on the stove? It must have evaporated by now. And there *may* be a chicken in the oven, my three-thousand-and-eight-hundred-and-fourth chicken of the year. Maurice, if I'm not mistaken. Would you then, oh, you are such a dear boy, I shall remember this, you are, believe me, one of the few people left on earth with manners. And manners, despite what our culture tells us, are *every*thing. Moreover, you have that quality which is so rare but which I value more than any other in people."

"What?"

"Goodness," he said. "I'm a Catholic, you know, and it's important to me."

He was still speaking when I put the phone down and went to his apartment and came back to tell him the party was tomorrow night, the rice was on the stove in a pot of tepid water, and the chicken was nowhere to be found. "Odd," he said. "Well, back to Nightmare Abbey, then. Don't call me, I'll call you."

I never called Mister Friel in Brooklyn. I knew his father did not want to see him on the phone, and I did not want to speak to his father. It was part of that general embarrassment I felt about parents, at least the parents of all my friends: I couldn't really believe they had any. Not long after his return to New York on the subway—which connected the past and present, the two worlds of Mister Friel, in a way I could not imagine ("I used to read Proust on the subway," he said, "but now I always look up to see who's coming in the car.")—we were leaning against a van parked on West Street on a Sunday afternoon. There were so many people there that the crowds spilled out of the bars onto the sidewalk, and we saw a man go by with his parents behind him. He wore leather pants, cap, and jacket. Chains composed his belt. He wore dark glasses and looked neither right nor left. Behind him walked a woman in white pants and a flowered blue-and-pink nylon blouse. Her white vinyl purse grazed the sidewalk. Behind her, at the same interval that separated her and her son, came a man in pale gray slacks, a short-sleeved Dectolene shirt, and beige desert boots. His silver hair was combed neatly back from his forehead. He wore glasses with silver frames. Their eyes were lowered and they did not look up from the sidewalk, like children being taken home to be punished. Only their son, protected by the mirrored sunglasses and the visor of his leather cap, strode ahead into the bar with his head up. His parents followed. "Now *that*," said Mister Friel, "is really sadomasochistic! To take one's parents on a tour of your favorite bars! Just trying to show them what he does on a Sunday afternoon. Can you imagine? They might as well be dragging a cross behind them!"

"He's telling them the truth," said Vittorio.

Mister Friel shuddered: "Well, I know I couldn't do it."

"Don't your parents know?" said Vittorio.

"No," said Mister Friel. "I can imagine Martians landing on the roof of that bar, but I cannot imagine my mother or father the moment they learn their son loves a surgeon in Brazil. You younger boys have an advantage. Your parents weren't born in the shadow of Queen Victoria. My father has yet to accept the telephone. Only last week, watching *Donahue* in Brooklyn, Mother asked me what a lesbian was."

"And did you tell her?"

"How could I? It would have involved discussing sex," he said. "Do you think your parents know?" he said to Vittorio.

"Of course they know," he said. "They've been watching me since I was a baby shitting in its diapers. They know me better than I know myself. It's just not what they wanted for me. It's not what they had in mind. They worry, because I'm not married."

"They wonder who will take care of you when you're sick," said Mister Friel. "They wonder where you will die. Everyone does. In whose arms? In what house? That is what the family is all about, dear. But not everything must be stated. Don't tell them because someone says it's the thing to do. Do what *you* feel is right. Are your parents intelligent? Do you trust them?" he said.

"I don't know," said Vittorio, frowning. "I know it must be a crushing disappointment to them. But—"

"I'm sure they've had other crushing disappointments," said Mister Friel. "They've weathered those." Then: "Perhaps the problem is you. *You* don't want to tell them, because *you* are ashamed of it."

"Look," Vittorio said, suddenly standing up, throwing his cigarette down, and grinding it against the pavement with his shoe, "it's pointless to be ashamed or not ashamed. It's pointless to hate homosexuality for not providing the things a family does. The joys of this life are joys the family can't provide—of course it can't give you kids, Christmas, relatives, and all that, but it can give you something else."

"What?" I said.

"That man," said Vittorio, looking at a handsome cowboy entering the bar.

"Oh, *her*," whispered Mister Friel.

And Vittorio walked off and followed the man into the bar. "Isn't it odd," said Mister Friel, "that to enter the mansion of love, you must slip in through a side door? A mask over one's face, a mystery." He fell silent as we watched the parade of handsome men stream by between those of us leaning against the cars and those leaning against the buildings in poses they hoped were inspiring. "Something happens after a while," Mister Friel said. "You just can't sleep with strangers anymore. In the same way."

"What do you mean?" I said.

He was squinting at the throng. "I mean that when you are young, you have the luxury of time. You can explore, investigate, experiment. But when you get to be my age, you start to feel a certain chill. You start to realize your supply of time is limited. Like the oxygen of a man trapped in a coal mine."

"But you're still young!" I said.

"Oh, my dear, not at all, how good of you to say so," he said. He looked at me and said, "My face happens to be *rotting*! I no longer dare sleep over! Each morning when I awake I have a different face altogether, till twelve o'clock. My skin is like the bodies of those Romans in the time of Petronius who had to visit the baths, had to be slapped into life by a masseur, by hot plunges and cold showers before the blood would circulate. I hardly ever look in the mirror anymore. But when I do, I see the blueprints of the eventual collapse. Blueprints I would rather not see, furnished by an architect I did not hire! I am about to grow old, my friend. The sin for which there is no forgiveness."

"And that's why you won't sleep with strangers?"

"Not really," he said. "Because even as you get older, you become more attractive to some people. Looking for a Daddy," he said. He glanced away even as a young man walked past staring at Mister Friel. "No, I can't sleep with these people for another reason. The spirit deserts the body, my dear. It's not always the other way around, although that is the chief complaint of poets and beauticians. The problem is I can no longer believe," he said.

"In what?"

"In this," he said, waving his hand. "In the importance of copulation."

Vittorio came out of the bar, walked over to us, and said, "He's not interested."

"And neither would you be, if you went home with him," said Mister Friel. "Like so many of these people, he is not what you suppose. Good taste prevents me from saying more. Why don't you come out to Brooklyn and have dinner with my family instead?" he said. "Roast beef and the Irish Folk Hour." We both made excuses. "Well, I must be going then," he said. He stood up and turned to us. "And may I say how nice it has been to be able to talk about my family with you? Most people don't want to hear about Mother and Father. You'd think most people in New York were hatched from an *egg*," he said.

In fact our contacts with our own families were confined to telephone calls after five o'clock, or postcards giving our new address, and even these made us impatient. "By the way," Vittorio said to me, "if you go to Jasper for Christmas, would you go to my house and look for my typewriter? It's in one of those boxes I stored there after school, and I can't ask Mother to look for it because one of them contains a love letter I wrote someone."

"Ah, my dear, in my case it was a dildo," said Mister

Friel. "Won't the two of you come out some Sunday for dinner? You're welcome anytime," he said, and walked off toward the subway.

It was an invitation we ignored that autumn when I encountered Mister Friel on Sunday mornings going off to Brooklyn for this weekly feast—walking down the same street I was coming home on at ten o'clock after a night of dancing—I said good-bye to him as if he were going to the guillotine. His parents lived next to the Verrazano Narrows Bridge. Whenever I surveyed the harbor on one of my walks to Battery Park, I looked out over the water and imagined Mister Friel—just where the dark span touched Brooklyn—cooking dinner for his parents. He visited them chiefly to prepare meals. That fall Mister Friel and I were proofreaders at the same law firm on Park Avenue. We worked the night shift, read to one another, and shared a taxi home. The taxi was one of the perquisites of the night shift, arranged chiefly because women could not be expected to travel on the subway at that hour. Mister Friel told me the subway was enchanting then, however: You never knew what would be seated in the car when you got on, slumped over, half asleep on his way home to Brooklyn. So we took the IRT home instead. I got off at Astor Place, and Mister Friel often stayed on. He got to his parents' place around five in the morning and prepared their breakfast. Or he went directly from the baths. His father liked to walk, but in recent years the esplanade along the Narrows had become dangerous for an elderly man because of teen-age thieves; so Mister Friel escorted him on a promenade after breakfast, while his mother (who went in and out of lucidity like a country radio station) watched *Donahue.* After they returned home Mister Friel prepared lunch and dinner, put them in Tupperware containers in the refrigerator, and came back to Manhattan.

It was the sort of double life I never had to think about

while I was in New York, a city which, if it held for me all
the possibilities of a tale from *A Thousand and One Nights*,
was nevertheless anchored in a sea of brick houses whose
walls contained families just like the one I was separated
from. My New York held no families. My New York was
a late-night city, its streets occupied by prostitutes, taxi-
cabs, roaming homosexuals, its parks trysting places, its
ruined neighborhoods mere stage sets on which isolated
figures appeared to fulfill my romantic dreams. That these
figures all came from families enclosed by the walls of the
numberless houses that stretched in all directions around
Manhattan was not a fact I dwelled on. When Wheatworth
went to Connecticut to visit his parents, or the Clam went
to Boston because his mother was sick, these exits from the
scene seemed like mere interruptions soon forgotten when
they returned. When the Clam invited me to lunch at his
aunt's in Queens, I declined; I had no desire even to see the
house, much less participate in the charade of politeness
such a lunch must entail. I loved, nevertheless, to lie beside
some youth I had met only a few hours before and hear him
talk about the family that had kicked him out, or with
whom he still lived, who knew or did not know about his
sexual tastes, who were or were not happy. Every tale was
unique. Every lover had a family. And when I met one on
the street late at night who told me he had spent the day
in Floral Park celebrating his niece's christening, I was
both attracted to his avuncular piety and thrilled that now
—with all that behind him—we stood together on Second
Avenue on a late summer night, all alone, reduced finally
(at the end of our clamorous, sociable days) to sharing kisses
made possible by people we had never met.

   One never met the family—that was the moment which
didn't occur in these relationships. One heard tales of families whose members you would never lay eyes on. When I
met some stranger we eventually spoke about our origins

—like the warriors in the *Iliad* who describe their family trees to one another in the midst of battle—in the aftermath of erotic love, his white limbs glowing in the pale radiance reflected on the brick wall outside my window, or when, nearly hidden in the gloom of a rainy night whose drops zigzagged down the windowpane as he talked, he spoke of his family, it was like hearing the description of a puzzle that possessed endless variations. Each word only endowed his body with more interest. Like the young men I saw at Mass in Pennsylvania, flanked by their families, the stranger's beauty was enhanced.

From the lips of these somnolent refugees I heard about families very different from my own: a cold mother so sarcastic to her son that he still twitched twenty years later; of a four-hundred-pound woman who sat on her children when they misbehaved, who locked them in closets and threw them down the laundry chute. I heard of the mother who—in a provincial city in Brazil—convinced her perfectly healthy, handsome son that he was dying of cancer and so should not leave home. I heard of a woman so unhappy on learning her son desired men that—after inviting beautiful young women to her house, one of whom ran off with her husband—she slept with him herself. I also heard of a mother who took her son to house parties in Capri and fell asleep beside him discussing which men at dinner were the most attractive. I met young men who were to their mothers as curators to a museum collection—who served as hair stylist, confidant, dresser, hailer of taxis, escort in restaurants; and others who were grateful when theirs went to Florida at Christmas because it meant they would not have to see her for their annual dinner. A visitor from San Francisco remarked to me that his mother lived in a town across the bay beside which we lay taking the sun on Fire Island one afternoon; he could see the roof of her house amongst the trees on the Long Island shore. She did not know he was in the East, however, much less a boat-ride away across Great South Bay. He called her that evening and pretended he was still in San Francisco, "because," he said, "if I tell her I'm here, she'll be hurt if I only have dinner with her and don't stay the week." So he went back west without even seeing her. One man told me he fought bitterly with his mother until he told her he was homosexual; now they were friends, and she came with his father to the party he threw every New Year's Eve and bantered with the weight lifters and the boys from Yale. I loved stories of families—at a distance.

One weekend Mister Friel and I had to work overtime because a loan agreement between Citibank and the Republic of Nigeria was being prepared on New Year's Day. I went home with him because the documents we had to compare were so long we decided Mister Friel could not take time out to attend his parents. He would have to do both at once.

We did not leave the office until four in the morning—the lawyer finally went home himself—and we emerged from the subway in Brooklyn behind two young men on their way home from a party in Manhattan. The streets were lined with red-brick row houses in every direction. There was an air of quiet and repose which one felt whenever one left Manhattan. We went up the stairs of a house like all the others, four blocks from the subway. "Welcome," Mister Friel said as he turned the key and opened the door, "to Nightmare Abbey." We went in to the kitchen and unpacked the food Mister Friel had purchased earlier that evening. "Come," he said. We walked through a small living room and went upstairs. Mister Friel paused in a doorway—beyond him I saw his parents sleeping still in their beds—took me by the arm and whispered, "One day I tell myself I will find them not breathing. I will have to act. Go to the telephone, phone whom? The ambulance, a funeral home? I dread it more than my own death. I will have to invite people to the funeral, choose the dress in which Mother is to be laid out. Doesn't life stink?" he whispered, and led me downstairs. "Even if everything goes *well*, it stinks." We set our documents out on the dining room table and then Mister Friel began to prepare breakfast. He unpacked the bag from Balducci's: the kippers, sour cream, croissants. "My mother loves starch. She's in ecstasy eating rolls that cost a dollar nineteen a dozen at Daitch, but I bring her these extremely expensive croissants anyway." He set these on a plain white plate with fluted edges and a blue border, and put them on a tray. He waved his hand toward a cabinet in the hall and said, "They have all this Rosenthal china she refused to use all her life. But what am *I* going to do with it? Serve hustlers tea? Look what I got," he said, producing a cluster of irises which he put in a glass vase and placed on the tray. He turned to me and said, "Remind me to ask Mother about her soap opera. I watch it with her from time to time—so we have a topic in common." He put a jar of Fortnum & Mason's apricot preserves on the tray, a silk scarf he had bought his mother at a discount-designer store, and then prepared his father's tray with a neatly folded copy of the *Irish Echo*. We took them upstairs. I waited in the hall. Mister Friel took both trays into the bedroom. I heard his father say, "Well, good morning, son, and Happy New Year. Your mother and I were in bed last night at ten o'clock."

"You and the Lindsays!" said Mister Friel.

"And the what?" said his father.

"The Lindsays—the former mayor and his wife," said Mister Friel. "The *Times* did a piece on how people spend New Year's Eve. Most of them said they liked to stay home. Mayor Lindsay said he and his wife are always in bed sleeping when the New Year comes in." Then he said:

"Good morning, Mother. What happened to Ned yesterday?"

"Oh, Ned," she said. "He's still being poisoned by Vanessa and doesn't know it."

"And is Sheila going to tell him then?" said Mister Friel.

"She's tried, but everyone knows how she hates Vanessa, so no one will believe her when she's telling the truth," she said. "But Elaine was told off, at least, and I'm glad for that."

"Was she the one dealing dope?" said Mister Friel politely as he stood, his back to me, between their beds, while a white curtain at the window bathed the room in a pearl-gray light.

"Yes. You've never tried any of those things, have you? Dope?" she said.

"Of course not," said Mister Friel, turning now to leave the room. "As James said, 'Consciousness is everything.' I'll be up in a few minutes with your omelettes."

We went downstairs, into the kitchen, and he began chopping up a large mushroom and a small onion on a cutting board. "I can't bear to watch soap operas," he said. "I would much rather sleep with the actors, half of whom I see at the baths. I don't see how I can tell Mother that the man who plays the chief surgeon in *Gull City* is a man who always has his boyfriend stand in the street beneath the window of his apartment before he comes inside, so he can massage his crotch and then hold up a piece of paper with his apartment number written on it. As if the boyfriend were a perfect stranger being picked up on the street! Much more interesting than the scenes he has to play as Doctor Ramsey," said Mister Friel. He broke two eggs in a bowl and stirred them with a whisk. "On the other hand I'm quite shocked by what does go on in these shows. *We* may live for sex, but I don't like to think the rest of the country does! I would *never* allow children of mine to watch television," he said. "I would raise them abroad. In rural Japan." He poured the eggs into the warm skillet and shook it back and forth to prevent the eggs' sticking. "I do so long to travel," he said to me, looking over his shoulder. "But how can I go to São Paulo when my parents can hardly make it to the icebox?" And he went upstairs with two plates of eggs.

At ten o'clock we went to church—his parents in black coats, his mother with a small black hat, arm in arm with Mister Friel. His father, a few paces ahead of us, looked up at the sky, remarking what a fine day it was. The church was only two blocks away: one of those immense, grimy edifices whose interiors are far more magnificent than anything a modern church possesses. If New York was a city full of fountains that were never turned on, it was also a town full of churches that were empty. In the afternoon on Fifth Avenue I went into them to rest and get away from the crowds. Here the church held far fewer people than it might have and those were chiefly families from Central and Latin America. The paint on the wall just beneath the gilded ceiling was peeling off in patches, but the service was modern. The priest began the service by turning to us as he reached the altar and saying, "Good morning." The congregation shouted, "Good morning, Father!" Mister Friel leaned toward me and hissed in my ear: "And now what, calisthenics?"

The priest began to talk about the fine weather and his hope that everyone had celebrated the New Year in moderation—while Mister Friel continued to whisper to me: "Look who's around us—latinos! White people have no more religion. They're too busy examining their biorhythms!" He fell silent when the Mass began, following it in his old, faded missal, whose pages were clogged with tiny prayer cards which he would turn over from time to time, revealing on the back the name of some deceased person beneath a small black cross. His mother said the Rosary and his father stared straight ahead with an alert expression, trying to follow a Mass he could not hear. The words, amplified by a microphone whose effect was considerably diminished by the echoing spaces of this once-rich and once-crowded church, came to us in fits and snatches during the sermon. At one point the priest warned against "fictitional beliefs that lure us to the desert of self-satisfaction."

"Fictional!" Mister Friel hissed beside me. "It is either fictional or fictitious. There is no such word as *fictitional.*" He sat beside me, swept with thundering sermons only he himself heard, jolted out of his daydreams by occasional crimes against syntax on the part of the priest. "When will people understand," he said, leaning toward me and speaking in a whisper, "that there is no such thing as 'most perfect.' Something is either perfect or it is not. There are no degrees of perfection." Mister Friel sat back and frowned as the sermon continued: rambling, discursive, and metallic in sound.

At the Communion his parents went up to the altar, slowly, his mother already hunched over with the pinched posture that comes to women in old age. Mister Friel turned to me in the freedom their departure allowed and said, "*Every*one goes these days. There are no standards anymore, whatsoever. It's impossible to find a good cotton lisle polo shirt, or a Catholic who does not go to Communion. A Jesuit I know who lives on Eighty-first Street told me not to worry about going to Confession. He told me that if I wanted to go, I should walk into Central Park and confess to a *tree*! Can you imagine?" he said. "This encouraging advice only confirmed my belief that the Church is on its way toward oblivion. I wouldn't *dare* go to Communion without having confessed," he said.

"Why don't you confess then?" I whispered.

"Because the Church considers *it* a sin, and I don't," he said. "Or rather, they consider homosexual acts a sin, and homosexual acts saved my life! Whoops, it looks like Dad has lost his way," he said, and stood up. Mister Friel left the pew and walked up the long aisle to his father, who stood on the tiled floor with hands joined, looking around at the sea of strange faces and empty pews, unable to remember where we were sitting. Mister Friel led him back down the aisle and went up again to retrieve his mother.

Within a few moments the priest turned to us and gave the final blessing, which Mister Friel took with the eagerness of one who was glad to receive anything—from invitations to costume parties to the blessing of God—free. By the time we left the church he was much calmer, almost reluctant to leave, and he lingered in the foyer, dipping his hand in the font of holy water, turning to look back at the altar and kneel once more.

"Can't hear a word the man says," his father remarked as we walked home.

"You didn't miss much," said Mister Friel. "There should be a school for men who must deliver sermons. Surely these poor people deserve to have the full splendor of the Catholic Church break upon them! One does not take as one's text *Raiders of the Lost Ark* even if you want to suggest that Christianity is also a treasure hunt. That concedes too much to the enemy. It makes you think of the scene in which she kisses Harrison Ford on his wounds."

"Oh, what a lovely day. The New Year! So much to look forward to! The Masseys are already in Florida," his mother said, looking at a house across the street, and then we went inside.

The remainder of the day passed quietly. Mister Friel and I worked on a big round table in the kitchen. Across the hall from us we could see his father in the den constructing on a card table a model of Rockefeller Center made entirely out of toothpicks. His mother read the newspaper until *Gull City* began on television, and then she closed the door and watched this show for an hour. At five o'clock Mister Friel's father rose and put his toothpicks away and came into the kitchen to mix cocktails for himself and his wife, while we searched the minutes of a United Nations conference on rubber for data the lawyer we were working for needed. By the time we went into the den with the dinner Mister Friel had prepared, his parents were voluble and excited by their cocktails. His father played with his false teeth as he watched the evening news, lifting them up with his tongue and pushing them forward and backward.

"Well, who threw her baby onto the subway tracks today!" said Mister Friel as he set up the television tables and made sure they were secure.

"Some Rastafarian! There are no Americans left in this country," his mother said as the tenants of a building in the Bronx were interviewed about the murder that had just occurred in a hall on the fifth floor. "None!" She said grace and we began to eat our dinners.

Just before the local news ended, I saw Mister Friel begin to stare at his father; he frowned as he watched his father bring his plate close to his face, mashing the remaining bits of food together with a frantic thoroughness. At one point it seemed he would begin to lick the plate it was so near his lips. His chin jutted forward so that in profile he resembled Popeye. I saw Mister Friel, still frowning, glance over at his mother as if to see if she was not horrified by the sight of his father nearly kissing his plate, as the mad fork went on pressing, scraping, mashing, rubbing the surface to get every last morsel. We were both astonished when his father sat up suddenly, put the plate down, turned to my friend and said in a normal voice, "That was very good, son. Thank you." Until that moment we were staring at a drawing by Goya of Saturn devouring his children; suddenly we faced his father, composing himself and turning his attention to the CBS Evening News.

"Mark my words," his mother said, turning to us with a roll in one hand and a knife smeared with butter in the other, "when I am dead and gone, you'll see—Walter Cronkite is a Communist."

"Oh, Mother," said Mister Friel. "He lives in Westchester."

"And where else do the Communists live?" she said. She held up the knife, and then turned to watch the television. News of the French takeover of a contract, which an American company withdrew when the President imposed sanctions against Russia, elicited from her an impassioned denunciation of the French. Coverage of an AFL-CIO convention increased her ire. "The unions have destroyed this country and no one has the guts to stop them!" she said.

Mister Friel said, "Now calm down, Mother," and served the chocolate mousse.

After the news a game show began which his mother asked us to watch because she liked to hear Mister Friel answer the questions. When the master of ceremonies of *Tic Tac Dough* said, "On what play was the famous opera *La Traviata* by Verdi based?" Mister Friel called out: "*The Lady of the Camellias* by Dumas!" and his mother turned to him with an ecstatic expression. "Why don't *you* get on these shows?" she said.

Mister Friel smiled, and began clearing the tables during the commercial. "Because a bachelor of forty-six is not what America is comfortable with on its game shows," he said in the kitchen. "The unmarried have always occupied a place in human society similar to that of the undead," he said.

Suddenly the sound of the television stopped. A voice came to us from the den: "*Aren't* you going to watch this with us?" his mother called in a tone so plaintive it froze

Mister Friel in the act of putting the leftover broccoli into a Tupperware bowl. "We have so few moments together as a family," she said.

Mister Friel resumed his work and called, "I'll be right in." The television burst out afresh as she released the Mute button on the remote control, and Mister Friel turned to me with moist eyes and said, "Of all the words in the New Testament, the saddest ones I've always thought were those Christ addresses to his slumbering apostles. And now my own mother has asked the same question. 'Could you not watch an hour with me?' " He took down the cups and said in a sharper tone, "Only in this case it is not to make sure the priests of the Sanhedrin do not arrest the Messiah; it is merely to watch a housewife from Yuba City win a week in Acapulco."

We returned to the den with coffee just as the organ began the wild, hysterical theme of *Tic Tac Dough* while a new contestant came out onstage: a sales promoter from Redondo Beach so handsome that Mister Friel glanced at me with an alarmed expression. Mister Friel and I remained for the rest of the show. He missed only one question, about the Sargasso Sea, an exotic name that made Mister Friel think it was located off the coast of Indonesia, when it was in fact in the Atlantic.

After the show we left to work; and the sound of the television went on and off as his mother muted the commercials with the button on her remote control. During one of these silences, I heard her say in a quiet voice, "Where are we going to be buried, John? Here or in Rhode Island? We've got to decide. It's not fair to the kids."

"Mother!" Mister Friel said, raising his head from the document on the table. He frowned, stood up and went across the hall to the den.

"It's nothing to be afraid of," I heard his mother say. "We're going to die someday."

"Mother!" he said, louder and more frightened this time.

"Well, don't be silly," she said. "I *am* going to die. And you'll have to choose the dress they lay me out in. I think the navy-blue dotted Swiss."

"Is this what you think of during the commercials?" he said. "Perhaps it would be better if you didn't mute them, then."

"Or should we be cremated?" she said.

"If I had my way," said Mister Friel, his voice rising and turning colder, "I'd bury you in the backyard on a moonless night. Between the garbage cans and the clothesline. I *loathe* funerals! Cremation is simplest. Mother, the show is back on. Press the button!" he said. She did, and the television erupted into laughter. "Would you like some ice cream?" he said. Mister Friel passed me on the way to the refrigerator. "Thank God for television," he said as he scooped the ice cream into a bowl. "It is what Allen Tate said about civilization—the agreement to ignore the abyss." He sighed and returned to the den with a bowl of Sealtest Heavenly Hash.

At eight o'clock his father bid us good night and went upstairs. At eleven o'clock his mother rose and Mister Friel helped her up. As she passed the kitchen door, leaning on Mister Friel's arm, she said in a gentle voice, "I love you, you know, not for what you're doing to help us, but because you're you." And Mister Friel—who had turned so cold when his mother referred to her own death—looked stricken and bit his lip.

At midnight—after Mister Friel had opened all the Tupperware bowls and made sure that what he thought was in them was in fact there, like a man making sure his children are safely in bed—we left the house ourselves. The moment we stepped outside, the lights of the bridge, the cold, brisk wind, the distant figures of young men walking toward us in jeans, tennis sneakers, and blue bomber jackets, made Mister Friel put his hands over his mouth and shriek. "I'm

going directly to the baths! The fact that we are young—
well, *you* are young," he said, "and they are not, is so
radical, I sometimes feel when I finally shut this door
behind me that I have been born again. A born-again
flâneur!" he said with a laugh as we went down the stairs.
"And yet is it not totally unfair, as unfair as life itself, that
they should be lying there facing Death when *I* am on my
way to the Everard? I tell you, life stinks, it stinks, it
stinks!" He turned to me as we went down into the subway.
"You will come again, I hope, to Nightmare Abbey, when
we do not have to spend the entire time working, when I
can show you some of my scrapbooks, my first editions of
all Donald Wyndham's novels, and my back issues of *Horizon* magazine."

But I had no intention of ever returning to that house—
because I had no intention of leaving Manhattan at all. I
always inquired after Mister Friel's parents, a courtesy he
appreciated, even if it only allowed him to pass a hand over
his forehead, sigh, and say: "Oh, they're fine. As well as can
be expected of a family which reminds me more and more
of 'The Fall of the House of Usher!' " That every one of
those brick houses facing the Verrazano Narrows had behind its neat facade a tale by Poe I had no doubt. And while
I loved to hear them told by some lover in the still of night,
it was as a refugee that he lay there beside me—tied by
these elastic teguments that stretched indefinitely over
time and space, but momentarily free.

Vittorio refused to go to Mister Friel's for lunch on Sunday; he refused to go home himself that year except at
Christmas and then only to recuperate from hepatitis. One
evening not long after New Year's Day, Mister Friel met
a young man who drove him home to a town in northwest-
ern New Jersey. In the morning he awoke beside his host.
There was a knock on the door. His host called, "Come in!"
as he lifted his head from the pillow, and a middle-aged

woman in a white apron carrying a tray with two bowls of corn flakes and peaches, two glasses of orange juice, *The New York Times*, and a daisy in a vase walked in.

"Good morning," she said, and put the tray across their laps.

"Good morning, Mother," said his host. "Mother, I'd like you to meet William Friel."

"How do you do, William," she said, extending her hand.

Mister Friel—who was at his best making new friends, who always had something charming to say to a stranger —found himself unable to speak. After a brief conversation about the family car, she left the room. "You know how mothers are," his host said. "She always likes to meet the people I bring home. Sugar?" he said, turning to his guest.

But there was no answer. Mister Friel had fainted.

5

One day in 1976 a sister of my father's who lived in Missouri sent every one of her nieces and nephews a check for five hundred dollars. She was a doctor who lived alone and wanted to distribute her fortune among her nieces and nephews before she died in order to avoid inheritance taxes. Each one of us received a carbon copy of the covering letter with his or her name checked on the list, and an explanation: "Some bonds came due. Love, Edna." Beneath this she wrote in her own hand the suggestion that I spend it on something fun. I never did. Fun was beside the point, I thought. I put it in the bank, rather than go to Paris as someone else might have; in the bank it would contribute toward the rent and food I needed in order to maintain my existence in New York. My parents told us one evening they did not intend to leave much of an inheritance; money, in their eyes, was to be used while one was alive. (This was one more example of a philosophy that I—far more Catholic than they—found baffling.) In fact I did not want money from them; I was sure it would only induce a larger dose of the melancholy I felt when I wore an overcoat my father bequeathed me. But if I did not receive any monetary assistance, I was lucky in another way: I was always welcome at home.

To me this was a double-edged knowledge: On the one hand, I so resented having to go home once a year because my parents wanted me to that I spent the night before my return to Jasper racing around Manhattan on a sexual binge that would have made sense only if the next day I was to face a firing squad. I would then return to my apartment, lie in bed unable to sleep, in a fury, raise my head to look around at the scrofulous room heaped with pornographic magazines, books, clothes, a telephone out of which roaches sprang whenever it rang, and say, "This *is* after all my home!" If on the other hand I was going to Jasper of my own free will—because I was exhausted, sick, lonely, discouraged, battered by one more abortive love affair—I would leave New York deeply thankful that parents were still there to visit, as dependable as the clot of blood that formed when I pricked my finger, one of Nature's beneficent facts.

One winter I stayed nine months—grateful that no one asked any questions, because I hadn't any answers. I came home, as children do, because they are momentarily walloped. One night the rooms on St. Mark's Place which were so romantic in my eyes looked suddenly decrepit and very cold. And the prospect of another round of parties in New York seemed pointless. I was not sure if my life was drab because of my obsession with sexual encounters, or if I was obsessed with sexual encounters because my life was drab. But I went home for Christmas and just remained. The humiliating fact was there was no reason to go back. I could not pretend there was. The most curious thing of all—I had to admit the winter I remained in Jasper as a Christmas visitor still there on Labor Day—was my realization that having finally admitted my sexual tastes, and come to live among other men who presumably shared them, I had by no means solved the problem. As a young man in Heidelberg or New York those first few years, it was not unrealistic to think that—having left the society in which I could not find love because of my nature (the way a man changes rooms in a hotel because a clanking radiator will not let him sleep, and thinks as he lies down in his new bed, *Now* I can drift off—love was only a few weeks, a few months, away; that all I need do was search for it diligently in a place where men slept with one another. But now that I had thrown myself into the fray, I had to conclude, in looking around me, that a new set of obstacles to domestic peace existed which I had not dreamt of when I first arrived in New York: obstacles so obdurate that it was a relief to merely wash windows, clean gutters, and plant palm trees. Those one could accomplish. The other was impossible. As Vittorio said one evening, "Men are pigs."

But when I left for Jasper, I was certain that if only I could stay in the city I would solve all my problems. I left New York in the same mood my mother was in, leaving the casino in Aruba when we told her she had to come home: reluctant, furious, convinced she was about to hit the jackpot. I went to Jasper because I couldn't desert my parents. There was certainly no other reason to go to a place that any traveler driving through the countryside could justifiably call godforsaken. In fact, Jasper was one of those forgotten towns in north central Florida which all look pretty much alike until you have lived there a few years and begin to see they are quite distinct, even if the difference consists in nothing more than a row of camphor trees or a frame post office rather than one made of cement.

When one approached Jasper from the east—a journey I could imagine all too well as I lay in bed the night before going there—one drove across sandy hills covered with oaks so stunted and gray they looked as if they had all been struck by lightning. Only a few open fields interrupted the dullness, and these were merely bleached acres of faded grass in which white hunchbacked cows—Brahmas imported from India for their ability to endure this hostile climate—stood motionless in the dazzling sun, attended by two or three snow-white egrets a few feet away. Sometimes a solitary squat live oak collected a pool of ink-black shade beneath its limbs in the center of the field, and the cows all lay within it for relief. The salmon-pink gashes of abandoned phosphate mines gored the earth fifty miles into the interior of the state: craters glittering in the sun. Frame houses advertising houseplants nestled under live oaks on the roadside; signs were tacked onto the pine trees beside dirt roads disappearing into the woods' gray tremulous shadows, dappled like sunlight on a shallow river's sandy bottom. They announced live bait, boiled peanuts, revival services. The road dipped and rose and dipped again, past a filling station at which an old man sat in a rocker waving to every car that passed by; past a crossroads where a black man sat on the fender of a car outside a grocery store also waving; past another phosphate mine, a Bible youth camp, an immense golden prairie dotted with pine-islands which, when we first got to Jasper, shimmered in the sunlight with water and later dried up completely; and then a water tower on which high school seniors had painted their graduation year rose from the monotonous landscape: train tracks, a filling station, Jasper.

The road led to a tiny main street of shops which all were built of white stucco and looked like the stores children pretend to own, through a tunnel of camphor trees to a blue lake whose clear water was unusual in that region where cypress trees stained most lakes brown with tannic acid. The lake was seen through a grove of live oaks, and the deep, dark gardens of retired admirals and generals and colonels. Young girls walked down the dappled dirt roads with bottles of shampoo to wash their hair in the lake, while boys attempted to master the ski jump, and retired commanders wrote letters to the Jacksonville *Times-Union* warning of the country's collapse. Their wives came to church with the same perfect posture, the regal bearing they maintained in military chapels when they sat among cadets and the wives of lesser officers. The Catholic church was a plain rectangle built of unpainted cinder blocks; it had but one stained glass window. In hot weather the blackbirds roosting in the camphor trees outside filled the room with their chattering. There was a tiny library beside the cracked cement tennis court in the town park but its shelves were filled almost entirely by mystery novels and romances set in seventeenth-century Cornwall. An old hotel, abandoned during the freeze that killed the citrus orchards and offended tourists in 1933, sat beside the public beach on a sloping lawn: a tax write-off for a man who lived in Utica. The magnolia trees were dark-leafed and coated with the fine white dust that hung in the air long after a car passed on its way to collect the white-haired ladies in blue dresses waiting at the end of their drives to be picked up for lunch and bridge. The best gardens in town were kept by an old man named Clay. After funerals people brought hams and bean casseroles and lemon meringue pie to the relatives of the bereaved. The drug store in Jasper had two water fountains, one for Colored and one for White.

Summers were humid and hot, and every afternoon around three o'clock the sky—which provided more spectacle than any other feature of the landscape—was filled with massive, towering, purple thunderclouds. The rain fell hard and fast, amidst violent thunder and flashes of white light. The storms upset Mother so, she pulled the curtains and went to bed. After the storm she sat down to answer the voluminous mail she received from charitable organizations who, once her name was on the list of donors, deluged her with sometimes threatening, more often dolorous requests. She gave to Boys Town, Indians, Eurasians, Maryknoll, paraplegic veterans, men who painted greeting cards in an iron lung, and deserving congressmen. In September the storms ceased. The heat waned, and by December the days were cool, dry, and sunny. The first freeze turned all the lawns a pale gold, and liquefied the innards of the oranges on the trees so that the sun shone through them, and the lake was a flat, pale blue enameled surface. The town for a moment became enchanted, Byzantine. In March great winds swept across the lake and uprooted trees left untouched by lightning; then the azaleas, dogwood, and jasmine bloomed, and the town resembled a gigantic coral reef, lacy, delicate, pink and white. By May it was hot, the dust floated in the air, and, as if at a prearranged signal one afternoon, all the air-conditioners shuddered into life and the widows got into the chill green-tinted depths of their Cadillac de Villes and drove to steak restaurants near Ocala.

My mother disliked the place. Every morning she awoke with one question: Shouldn't they sell and move elsewhere? But when my father asked where, she could not decide. The Catholic Church considered the town a mission rather than a parish. One county in Ireland supplied the priests who succeeded each other there. Their duties lay not only in Jasper, but in Boone, Nimrod, and the state prison in Monroe. Our first winter there, the priest was a former actor from County Cork who entered the Church so his mother would still have a son in the priesthood after his brother, a missionary in Africa, died of cancer. He enjoyed the liqueurs my father liked to serve guests in our house, and recited passages from *Henry IV* as he sat beside the fireplace sipping Drambuie. The fireplace we attempted to use only once, and, since none of us knew anything about flues, the house filled with smoke; my father never tried again and forbade anyone to use it. So the decorative birch logs sat there for twenty years, like the plan to move to another state. The priest was witty and would raise his glass and say, "Well, at least we can amuse each other!" His wit had little effect on his parishioners on Sunday, however. My mother laughed loudly at his jokes each time he offered one, because she wished to show him he was not totally unappreciated in Jasper. He was always making jokes except when asked about the prisoners he visited on Death Row; then he cast his eyes down at his curaçao, and his voice sank to a murmur as he said, "I feel so close to God with them." My suspicion that he was in love with a prisoner or two could not be pursued; but it was an irony not lost on me that my mother, a woman to whom the thought was anathema (she once dropped a friend of the family's for coming to visit in a severe black bikini), was entertained by homosexuals. One was a mere senior in high school at the time, a youth who carried gossip from house to house with a cheerfulness that endeared him to everyone. Marooned in that living room with the forbidden fireplace, the priest, and the valedictorian, my mother attempted to sustain a social life in a town that doomed her efforts.

The only escape lay in drives through the backwoods to other places: shopping malls in Gainesville, the old precinct of Saint Augustine, seafood restaurants, motels on the beach, a steak restaurant inland, a revolving restaurant atop a skyscraper in Jacksonville. But when she returned home, Jasper was just as she left it. Life in this small town unsuited her for the hubbub of large cities. Even Gainesville, a city of about 100,000 people, seemed like Los Angeles when we arrived there from Jasper. Fast-food franchises gazed on acres of parking lots, and each corner resembled the next—the kind of endlessly repeated town in which sidewalks were purely symbolic, a holdover from a more pedestrian era. The old city in which women walked under parasols down streets lined with live oaks was gone. The cars weaving in and out of traffic as their drivers changed lanes frightened her. She sank down in her seat and put a hand over her eyes. Thunderstorms alarmed her so, she insisted we return home immediately. When we got there, on even the most peaceful evenings, Jasper itself left her uncomfortable. In the evening as we sat watching television she would sit up and say, "There's someone on the porch. Don't tell me I'm hearing things. Go out and see."

And I went out and turned on the lights and saw no one. But she would have none of it. "Turn on all the lights," she said, and I illuminated every room in the house with the indirect overhead lighting we seldom used, and the two of us walked through looking at the carpets, shelves of figurines, inlaid tables, and paintings in the ghoulish fluorescent glow.

"You really are mad," I said when we finally returned to the den, having investigated every room in the house and turned on the floodlights which made the lawn, cumquat and palm trees blaze against the dark night behind, so quiet that as we stood looking out we could hear the frogs croaking in the crescent of marsh weeds. "I can't help it," she said, wrapping the blanket around her. "I heard someone on the porch." She looked at me with raised eyebrows and the cool expression of someone sensible who knows that what she is saying is absurd: "I hope you realize I can never live here alone."

"But, Mother," I said, hearing in these words some registration of a claim to be made at a future date, "the house is locked; you're surrounded by neighbors, who all have dogs. No one ever comes down this road at night!"

"I don't care," she said, lighting a cigarette. "There is no way I will live in this house alone."

"But you're much safer here than anywhere else!" I said, thinking even as I said it of the owner of the beauty parlor she went to on Highway 100, her customer, and two assistant hairdressers murdered by someone they still had not caught, one of those itinerant criminals who sooner or later came south (Florida seemed to draw lunatics); and the shooting of a high-school student who broke into the pharmacy in Jasper the previous month to get drugs. Homes around the lake were frequently looted when their owners were visiting out of town. Residents no longer even wanted their coming journeys mentioned in the little gossip column, "Jasper Jottings," which came out once a week in the county newspaper. My mother had no qualms about going to the beauty parlor on Highway 100 after the murders there, but she heard noises every night as we sat quietly watching television and I knew she was simply stating a fact when she announced she would never live by herself.

She was both brave and timid, in ways I could never predict, and when the evening news came on, and the announcement of a plane crash caused her to put a hand over her mouth and moan with pity for the victims, I recognized the sound made by the woman at Student Health years ago when I went to the psychiatric clinic to ask for an appointment because I thought I was homosexual.

The evening news often carried some item about New York City and when it did she called me in, if I was in another room, and yelled, "New York!" I always entered to see it. But much of the television we watched was so uninteresting I often excused myself to read or take a walk. This hurt her feelings. I assured her the show was simply one I didn't like, but she took it personally, as if she had failed to entertain me. If my life in New York was a mystery to them—if they did not know who wrote me the letters I received in Jasper (which my mother envied; she received nothing but duns)—my absence from the room in which we watched television seemed but one more instance of that power I had to withdraw.

Our thoughts wandered during the shows I watched simply to keep her company, and during the intermissions provided by a button she pressed to mute the sound of the commercials, she often turned to me to converse. Once she said in the stillness of that room at the end of that dirt road in that little town on a summer evening: "Are you homosexual?"

I jumped up from the sofa, said, "No! Of course not!" in a voice as sharp as my father's when he was angry, and left the room. My heart hammered as I stood in the kitchen, however, thinking of the scene in the Gospels in which Peter denies knowing Christ when the woman asks him if she has not seen him with the Galilean. The comparison was disproportionate but in a sense exact: for if the Gospels told us one would have to leave one's family to follow Christ, the curious thing was that loving men had the same effect. Had I not converted my hopes from celestial to earthly ones, exchanged Christ for the boy at the baths? In that still kitchen I stood trying to slow my breathing as I stared into the refrigerator, and then out at the dark drive and the single lamp which marked its intersection with the road and picked out in the darkness the branches of a tree above it. I had only one passion: to leave, a son who had no desire to rebel, an exile who could tell them nothing about his life in New York but who was afraid even to change apartments for fear it would indicate some flightiness, inability to take root, mature. I slept with countless people during those years but always kept the same apartment and telephone number in order to appear reliable and fixed. In fact what I was doing with my youth was so ephemeral that when I considered moving to another flat I realized that all the lovers who had passed through the place had accumulated like the black on hurricane lamps on the walls, and that if I left the place I would surely have nothing to show for the years.

There was an unmarried woman my age in Jasper who during the late seventies left Los Angeles to come home and live with her mother. Her mother, a jolly, energetic, forceful woman who had buried a husband and another daughter, was undimmed by these tragedies or the exhausting night shift she worked at a large hospital in order to pay off her deceased husband's medical bills. I used to drive back to Jasper with her from Gainesville the summer I took a night course at the university there. Once a vulture slammed into the windshield. It would have shaken anyone else, but she burst into laughter. Her laughter was full and merry, and listening to her you always began to laugh yourself. But this dynamo was the mother of a daughter whose response to reverses was just the opposite: She came home and began to construct a rock garden in the backyard of her mother's house. Driving by, you would see her in the worst heat, under the noon sun, dragging boulders back and forth as she searched for the best arrangement, changed her mind, and replaced everything. Mother suggested one evening that I visit her. I demurred. There was no point. I knew her story without even visiting her: the acid trips, the Mexican boyfriends, the parties, the opportunities, the city in which one supposes it is enough to be beautiful. About women I was completely objective. There was nothing mysterious in them. How could I tell Mother that she alone was an enigma, and every other woman a character I could appraise instantly without the least occlusion of judgment?

One evening in Jasper I met her in the public park and we began to talk. She was a dull, conventional soul whose conversation gave me no pleasure. When I went home afterward I reflected: About women, in whom I have no erotic interest, I can think clearly, observe dispassionately, estimate, place. But about men I was completely foolish; if a young man in whom I was erotically interested seemed stupid, I said, "He's simply intelligent in other ways. Perhaps he hasn't read books, but he certainly knows people." Hypnotized by faint black hair on a graceful forearm, pronounced veins on a hand, I was so ensnared I made not the slightest effort to be objective.

And so I found myself on many nights in New York

standing in the street east of Tompkins Park, waiting for a dance instructor of Sicilian parentage to throw down the keys to his building, in rain and good weather, as if waiting for Love to toss me the golden apple. The keys would flash in the raindrops as they hurtled from a fifth-floor window and bounce on the sidewalk in front of me, and I would go wearily up the stairs to see this person whose beauty had me utterly enthralled—even as he spun up and down the room just out of my reach, performing dance steps with a vanity and frenzy that left even me embarrassed. There was no guarantee that we would sleep together that night, or that he would not sit up in the middle of sex and announce, "I have to see *Star Trek.*" One evening when he stopped his tarantella he panted to me as I lay on the bed watching him: "You're a patient and a tolerable man. Most people would have left an hour ago." I was a patient and a tolerant man. But I was also a slave. Even when he did consent to make love, and I went over and found him calm and amorous, another odd thing happened: I had, when I was finally in the arms of someone I had longed for desperately, the sensation of being in a vacuum—the eye of a hurricane. The noise, heroic energy, anxiety, haste, compulsion of Desire enclosed a void. Suddenly, all at once, the howling wind died. Everything was still. As I lay in bed making love to the dancer on Ninth Street whose beauty staggered me, I could hear the clank of the radiator in the corner; I thought of the laundry I had to do the next day, and actually began to listen to the conversation of two women talking on the sidewalk below about the best store in which to find a used refrigerator.

One night there was a knock on the door of the dancer's apartment on Ninth Street. He opened it and I saw the younger sister of a childhood friend in Aruba. She wanted to borrow some butter and had been living on this street for five years. We went back to her rooms to catch up and

I met the Puerto Rican student with whom she was living. The neighborhood in which she lived was so Hispanic, so poor, so decayed, that the only reason white middle-class people went there in cars from New Jersey and Long Island was to purchase drugs from the men standing on the corners. Each time she walked home someone inquired, "Looking for something?" (She might have said, "Yes. And I've found it, thank you. Just as my parents fled farms in Kansas for life with a big oil company in the tropics, cocktails, patios, Eastern schools, stocks, and suburban homes, so I have fled these for this decrepit slum, fragrant on summer afternoons with damp brick dust, the sound of gushing fire hydrants, and that monotonous salsa music coming out of your social club." She did not.) She simply said, "No, thank you." Why she did not marry, why she lived with Hispanic lovers in the slums puzzled me as much it did the drug pusher who wondered why she was there if not to buy heroin.

I thought I was there because I was homosexual. This put me in the bohemian world, among certain aspects of behavior which perhaps might have been unthinkable had I been heterosexual. Sleeping with men was so radical a departure from the life I was brought up with that nothing it led me to surprised me in any way. I stopped for the most part thinking it was odd for me to be sitting in the rain at three in the morning in a park on Second Avenue. This was my fate; this was the adventure it had led me to. Yet it did not mean my conception of society was not traditional. For I found myself wondering, with the same regret her father might have had, what drove her to lead so unconventional a life, so little likely to bring happiness to her parents, who were left with the fact that—despite the piano lessons, schools, manners—she had no intention of ever marrying. When she mentioned to me one afternoon that her lover wanted to have a child, and I asked her if she did not want one too, I was astonished to hear her reply coolly, "Sure, if he stays home and takes care of it."

The chill that spread through me on hearing these words made me realize that, while homosexual, I was a completely conventional person at the same time, like the man who, after a night of sexual debauch, joins his family at Thanksgiving and is horrified to learn that his niece is chewing her nails. If she was living on Avenue D with a Puerto Rican student perhaps *I* was not here because I was homosexual but for other reasons besides. After all, there were many ways of living a homosexual life; and there were homosexual circles that offended me because they were bourgeois. I was attracted to the romance of the Lower East Side. She and I were citizens of the middle class quite literally slumming. And so the children of Aruba ignored each other as we ransacked the city in search of love.

And their search was invisible to their families who waited in vain to send out wedding announcements. The signs for which they watched never came. One evening I went into the yard at home in Jasper to practice handstands. For a year now I had been trying to learn gymnastics because suddenly the body was more important to me than the mind. I threw myself into the handstand repeatedly for over an hour, and when I returned to the house my mother was standing at the door smoking a cigarette and watching me through the screen. "Your father is furious," she said. "He wants to know what a man your age is doing practicing handstands." I said nothing. They could not be expected to construct my life in New York from such clues, to deduce an invisible existence from activities as slight as this one. But no one asked any questions. My family respected its members' privacy so much that when my mother went into the hospital one winter for an operation, she told neither of her children anything about it because she did not want us to worry—and I suspected that if she could have arranged her death in such a way that it would not upset us, she would have.

The decision to explain nothing about my life—not even the handstand—left an odd void, however, where a life should have been. I was relieved when my mother turned to the anesthesia that numbed so many of our nights in Pennsylvania and Florida: She began to watch television. In Jasper there was nothing else to do anyway. When I came home from New York now and my father turned into the driveway after our drive from the airport, I was both hurt and relieved to see she was not waiting on the porch for me. She called through the window, "My show's almost over, just ten more minutes!" Eventually she came out onto the porch, kissed me and said, "Rachel is such a liar, I had to see how she would get out of that one!"

"Oh, what is she doing now?" I said, relieved to have someone else's lies the object of our attention. For the truth was I had nothing to tell her about myself except the fact that the plane was crowded from Atlanta to Jacksonville. I was grateful for the soap opera. I had nothing to report. And I continued to question her about the relationships in a purely fictitious community whose only taboo was that anyone should have a sense of humor.

And quite conveniently *Another World* took the place of the one I lived in but did not want to talk about. Jasper itself provided very little news. Within five minutes I heard it all: Ruth lost her wig while getting out of her car at the Whites' party; the priest from Detroit brought in to replace our Irish friend (assigned now to an even more remote section of west Florida where there were few towns even the size of Jasper) upset the women of the Ladies' Altar Society by breaking down during a sermon about a small girl kidnapped at a shopping center in Gainesville. He also wore his right shoe on his left foot, and his left shoe on his right foot, because he believed this saved the soles.

The county mobile health van now offered free blood-pressure tests once a month, parked outside city hall. The town nursery was up for sale and the lake was a foot lower because of the drought. The bishop was coming on Sunday to confirm the youth of the parish.

All this I heard while handing my mother the wet clothes she liked to hang on the clothesline between two pine trees because they always smelled fresher after drying outdoors. She had a strange passion for doing laundry now. She demanded my clothes the moment I arrived and, assuming they were filthy, put them in buckets of bleach as if to exorcise my residence in New York. Had I consented she would have put me in Clorox. She had a detailed and specific system of hanging clothes, how they were placed, the number of clothespins used. "There's got to be air between them," she said, "and put the towels at that end. Otherwise the line sags." This work exhilarated her—she brought order to the wash, and then sat down on the porch in triumph, as if her own soul, and not her bed sheet, were hanging on the line, wet and white and blazing in the sun. How pleased my German aunts would have been to see her now—lighting a cigarette with the odor of Clorox on her fingertips. Then the big maroon Thunderbird the valedictorian (now real estate salesman) owned roared up the drive in a cloud of dust. He got out with more gossip, gathered on the porch of a wealthy widow who lived across the lake from us.

My mother sensed, every time the feminist revolution was discussed on television, that she had missed, for purely historical reasons, an opportunity to have done something else with her life—what, she was not sure. "I've wasted it!" she said. So we wanted to tell the valedictorian that homosexuals no longer had to be alcoholic companions of wealthy women. But Vittorio would not even risk imparting that bit of information. He led a strictly celibate life there. He was so conservative, in fact, that the first time we flew down there together, he suggested on the plane that once in Jasper we see very little of each other. "I think it looks odd," he said as the plane descended to the flat farmland punctured with nameless, numberless lakes, "two grown men, both bachelors, spending their time together, don't you think? They have a phrase for it in the South when a man's sexual identity begins to appear. They come back from visiting Uncle Tommy and the women say, 'It's beginning to show.' Imagine that," he said with a smile composed of equal parts amusement and distaste. " 'It's beginning to show.' "

He looked out the window as we landed and said, "I don't know why I resent this so much—but I always feel I'm being pulled back into a past I'd rather leave behind. Pulled back kicking, in fact, into a charade of genteel hypocrisy, pretending to be something I'm not!" He gritted his teeth so hard the muscles in his jaw stood out with the dread his return induced.

Vittorio was not himself in Jasper—he came down and spent most of his time in his room at home. He did not even take walks, except at night, or go to the grocery store if he could help it. He was, when I saw him there, not more relaxed than he was in New York but less. When he arrived, his mother asked that he visit certain friends of the family whose feelings would be hurt if they learned he was home and had not come to see them. So he began a round of calls on people in homes around the lake who were growing older now and had to walk a mile a day on the order of their doctors, after heart operations, or who never budged from their chair on the porch, air-conditioned in summer, heated in winter, turning over cards and watching the color television. He went to see widows of coaches, teachers, men who had given him his first surveying job in summer, piano teachers, and local historians who had written privately printed histories of Jasper from 1889 to the present. As soon as this duty was done he became a recluse. When I asked him one winter why he was so antsy in a town I found so relaxing that I never had insomnia there, he said, "It's different for you. You're a newcomer. But, well, I was an Eagle Scout. Valedictorian! Basketball captain! Altar boy! I was on my way to West Point!" he said. "And that has nothing—absolutely nothing—to do with my life anymore. Nothing."

And so those first years we saw very little of each other. I would see him at a distance on the golf course, going around with his parents in the pale gold light of those crisp winter afternoons when the woods were so still one could hear a distant woodpecker knocking his head against the trunk of a live oak, and nothing else. Occasionally some low-flying jets, the bolts on their silver fuselages visible to the golfers, streaked past overhead on their way to the naval air station in Jacksonville with the effect of reminding the golfers that their lives were simultaneously protected and hanging by a thread. I would watch my mother straighten up from her putt and say, "Damn those things!" while behind her, beyond the woods separating our fairway from the next, I could see Vittorio and his parents walking down the slope; he disliked the game.

I saw Vittorio as infrequently in Jasper as I did in New York—where he moved in circles I did not. Sometimes a member of his set decided to visit him on his way back from Miami. Once he met me after church in the parking lot and said, "The most horrible thing has happened. This British guy I've met only twice in New York—a man I hardly know, a kind of professional houseguest—is on his way north at this moment from Brazil. He's with some guy who was in a Fassbinder film, and they're driving up—like killer bees!" But the next time I saw him after Mass, he was relatively calm. "They got sick in Miami—some fever—and

one of them died. So the other one canceled. Thank *God*,"
he said, and walked off to his mother's car.

Later that winter the same threat ruined my peace of
mind: A person I hardly knew, returning to New York
from Key West, called to ask if he could stop by. I found
myself the rest of that week viewing each party through the
other one's eyes: I looked at my parents as my guest would
see them; I looked at my guest as my parents would view
him. It was one of those moments when the lie—like some
corpse buried in the garden—was disturbed again, and I
had to find a new grave. The tension of this approaching
collision of two selves angered me so, I found myself talking out loud to the flowers I cut to put in the spare bedroom. "Why should I submit myself to this? Why can't I say
no? Why does he *insist* on coming by? Why do the wrong
people ask? I *never* ask!" And I clipped two branches clean
and walked back into the house.

"Your father and I are very happy that at last you are
having friends to this house," my mother said as we sat on
the porch the afternoon of the day the guest was supposed
to arrive. "You must admit this is the first one ever. Why
is that?"

"I don't know," I said. "I suppose because I'm selfish,
because one of the reasons I come down here is to get away
from them."

"Will I like him?" she said, looking up over the newspaper she took all day to read, she combed it so thoroughly.

"I don't know," I said, putting down my own paper.
"You might find him charming, and you might find him
. . . affected and pompous. I don't know him that well
myself."

"Why *have* you had no one here all these years?" she said,
as if this question was still not settled. We sat on the porch
we used in winter, looking out on the trees and the lake and
the marsh weeds: a landscape so fixed it was like a Chinese

scroll painting. It was so warm, so peaceful, so reassuring a moment—as we sat comfortably together reading our separate newspapers—I thought of giving the simplest explanation: the truth. As she sat there waiting for my reply a single leaf detached itself from the water oak nearest the lake and spiraled slowly down to the earth—but even that seemed part of the Chinese scroll, as if its artifice included from time to time a moving part. "Mother," I said, looking out at the blue and silver lake, the garden in which we sat sequestered in each other's calm company.

"Yes?" she said.

"I think that crepe myrtle by the flagpole needs fertilizer," I said. "And look at the weeds that have grown up around it."

"I wish I could get your father interested in yard work," she said, lowering her eyes to the newspaper which assured us the world was not nearly so calm as this golden garden, "but he seems to have quit for good. I blame the cards. I wish he had never learned to play that game."

And the moment was gone, and dusk found me going through the house removing objects I feared my guest would find objectionable. I took down the hanging baskets with the plastic ferns on the back porch, the wall calendar in the den sent my father by a ball-bearings company which featured a pretty girl smiling beneath a flowering apple tree. I took up the shag throw rugs and the plastic globe, the air fresheners and the cheap clock. I went into the garden and cut boughs of the late-blooming azaleas while I swore beneath my breath: "I am *not* explaining him to my mother!" I arranged the flowers several times before I got the effect I wanted. I put away the portrait of the Sacred Heart of Jesus in the closet.

"What are you doing?" my mother said when she came into the bedroom.

"Look," I said angrily, "it *glows!*"

It grew dark, the dinner hour came and went, and I stood in the driveway waiting anxiously for the headlights of the car my guest was driving to appear at the head of the road. He did not come. His car broke down in Orlando and he took a plane north. His rudeness in forgetting to tell me did not bother me in the least: I was glad to have been spared the confrontation. And when I went to church on Saturday afternoon I was able to tell Vittorio about an experience just like his own, with the relief of a man delivered from an execution.

Church in Jasper was—besides the annual free barbecue given by the Union Electrical Cooperative—its only social event. The organist was always there when we came in, her hands roaming over the keys, producing vague songs she did not take beyond the first few measures before replacing one with another. Her repertoire was eclectic. In the middle of the Communion hymn the parishioners were sometimes aware, and sometimes not, of a few bars of "Siboney" or the theme from *Spellbound*.

In New York I went to church rarely if at all, but in Jasper I did not want to offend my mother by saying I did not. It was part of that general desire I had to minimize the differences between our present and our past; it was easier to go. So I went off to Mass with her every Sunday morning or, more frequently, by myself to the Mass which was performed on Saturday afternoon at five-thirty. There was something I liked in the gathering of people on a winter's dusk in the clearing in the woods on the edge of town. Dusk was a beautiful hour in Jasper, and recalled that the disciples were gathered for supper when Christ instituted Communion. And so I mingled with the people converging on the new energy-efficient church constructed in 1972 across a sandy parking lot from the old one. I found myself, as we waited for Mass to begin, staring at the awkward adolescents who sat beside girls with blow-dried hair that seemed composed of spun sugar, in sweaters and bracelets, their backs so erect as they watched the empty altar, so motionless, so groomed, I imagined they were waiting for someone to ask them to dance. I found myself staring at the baby gurgling at me over his mother's shoulder and wondering what it would be like—as in some eighteenth-century English novel—to kidnap some beautiful infant from a country church and raise it to speak several languages. I stared at people's shoes. I stared not so much at the altar as at the altar boys.

Our priest now was a handsome, affable young man who drove a Porsche and liked to attend the practice sessions of the University of Florida football team. The Mass was said in English, the epistles read aloud by a member of the congregation, and the congregation frequently asked by an ex-nun at the organ to turn to a particular page in the hymnal and sing. We were not only asked to sing now but to shake hands: once at the beginning of the Mass with the people around us to greet them, and again during what was called the Kiss of Peace, when the priest said to us, "Peace be with you," and we were asked to murmur this to each other. The sentiment Vittorio admired—he was always searching for peace—but he had no desire to shake hands. He usually sat in a far corner of the church at a distance from the cluster of people near the altar, hoping that no one would go so far as to leave his pew and seek him out; but often they did, walking up the aisle to shake hands with Vittorio and declare, "Peace be with you."

Often when I got to church, Vittorio was already there, almost hidden in the shadows of his usual corner. The new church had a floor that sloped down to the altar and formed a kind of amphitheater; thus Vittorio hovered above the rest of the congregation, where (voyeur that he was) he could examine the parishioners during Mass. When I turned in my own pew and glanced up at Vittorio, he was merely a dark presence in the corner. My mother preferred to sit farther down, to hear the sermon better. Though I too would have been happier in the shadows, I was occasionally compensated by the fact that when I turned to shake hands with other people during the Kiss of Peace, I sometimes found a handsome young man beside me, murmuring "Peace be with you" with a grave sweetness.

Like moles who find their earthy camouflage falling away from them at the poke of a gardener's trowel, Vittorio and I were conspicuous only when the rest of the motley congregation descended the aisles to receive Communion. We remained in our pews. It was a moment used to scrutinize the figures of those people whose faces were all we had been able to admire. Sometimes a handsome face proved to be attached to a shapeless body. Sometimes it was the opposite. Vittorio used the sermon—which the priest delivered with his new detachable microphone at the foot of the altar —to inspect the various young men listening to the Gospel, as Vittorio had years before, a senior in high school. He was barely able to endure the sermon, and sighed with relief when the priest turned and said, "The Mass is ended, go in peace."

No one left less peacefully than Vittorio—he hurried out of church before anyone else, so he would not have to shake hands with the priest as he lingered in the foyer greeting his parishioners afterward. His mother liked to stop and chat on the walk outside church, and when she looked around for him, she laughed: "He runs off like a rabbit!"

He was already sitting in their car in the parking lot. "I feel like something at a bake sale that no one bought," he said, as I came up to the car. "And my mother is still sitting there after everything else has been sold. I am the only member of my class still not married! It's not fair to her!"

"Vittorio," I said, "you're being ridiculous. She's thrilled to have you in the pew beside her. It's you who think that, not your mother."

"Well," he said, "whoever is correct, I feel like a vampire

kneeling next to her. And during Communion, everyone in
the church goes but us. What's she doing now? Oh, come
on, Mother, stop talking!" he said, turning to look back at
the cluster of people lingering in front of the church in the
dusk to exchange news, their disregard of time making him
all the more anxious. "This drives me *nuts*!" he said, turning back to stare out the windshield, impatient. There was
no reason to be—the evening that waited for him included
little more than six hours of television.

When I said good night and walked off to our car, I felt
a great peace which always descended on me on leaving
church. The reason for it eluded me. I did not know if this
was because an unpleasant duty was behind me now (like
the dentist), or because the admonition to go in peace really
had affected me, or because the sky at that time of day, with
its soft gray clouds, its flocks of blackbirds flying from the
tops of the pine trees, was beautiful. I always felt my heart
lift on emerging from church, to see plum-gray and silver
clouds massed upon each other as they are in summer
storms filling the sky. Sometimes a light rain had fallen
while we were in church, and beneath the clouds at the
base of the horizon a washed red glow remained in the
western sky. The air was fresh, soft, moist. The wind scattered brown leaves across the edge of the woods, and the
bare trees were crosshatched in silhouette against a band of
pale green air. Even the drab, stunted turkey oaks, their
black skeletons between us and the dying light, were graceful. The woods took on a beauty they did not have by
daylight, when they seemed colorless and plain. As the
people streamed out of church in a widening delta to their
individual cars, the air was filled with the chatter of children anxious to eat supper or return to their homes, and the
gentler, slower voices of their parents calling to one another. And above us was the sky.

Vittorio was always gone by the time I got in our car,

disappeared down one of the dirt roads that led past quiet rows of houses through a tunnel of camphor trees. At home my mother was having a cocktail. My father went to bed at eight o'clock, for he still got up—a creature of thirty years of habit—before dawn. There was nothing to do at night. The valedictorian come by to gossip but I always excused myself and went into the bedroom to read. I did not even drive to the town thirty miles away which contained a homosexual bar. The reason was I preferred not to leave my mother alone. Most nights the valedictorian was somewhere else. My mother wanted me to watch television with her—she hated being alone—and I could not refuse. I did not want to lie (to say, "I'm going to see a movie," when I was going to a bar) and I did not want to leave her there, worrying I might have an accident. So Jasper was as devoid of sex for me as it was for the alcoholic valedictorian I would not help unravel his identity.

That winter a friend mailed Vittorio an advertisement that two lovers living on a farm near Jasper had put in a large national homosexual newspaper; they were seeking a third partner. We drove out to the tiny town in which the postmistress said Box 569 could be found—past abandoned phosphate mines, Bible campgrounds, boys sitting by the road with rifles on their knees, signs whose peeling paint proclaimed housing developments that never happened, bleached fields with scrawny cattle—and came to a halt beside a cemetery enclosed in a cyclone fence fifty feet from the pink crater of a phosphate mine. Across a dirt road a blue mobile home sat regarding the tombstones. The dirt road led us deeper into the backwoods as dogs chased our cloud of dust.

Finally we came to a dead end. On a tall pine tree were two signs. One said PIGS FOR SALE; the other, BETTY'S CUT 'N CURL. "Maybe they're both," Vittorio said. "Maybe you buy a pig and get your hair done." At the base of the tree were nine mailboxes. We peered at the numbers. One was painted black and had no name, only the number 569. "A bad sign," he said. "Like someone in New York with an unlisted phone number. The person is either fleeing a credit card company or has delusions of grandeur. The two almost always go together, in fact," he said, putting the car in reverse and turning around in a billowing cloud of dust. "Now this just shows how impossible it is to be homosexual in the country. So much for my dream of love under the live oaks."

And we drove back to town. For the next month Jasper was enchanted; whenever a handsome man with a moustache passed me in an automobile, I wondered if this were one of the lovers. The whole town became mysterious, romantic, vivid in a way it never was before. Every attractive man seen in the grocery store, the post office, Ace Hardware, was a candidate. The only place considered unlikely was St. Joseph's church. Then one Saturday while shopping for potting soil at Ace Hardware, I became aware of two men glowering at me. I watched them get in a truck, stare, and drive off, looking as if they had indigestion. "So grim and dull! Why don't we slip the advertisement under Alec's door?" I said to Vittorio, thinking of the valedictorian.

"Because they want someone super-hot," he said, referring to the advertisement, "super-hung, and willing to be both top and bottom. What else do homosexuals want? Alec's fat and has circles under his eyes. Maybe he knows about them already."

If he did it hardly improved his life. He spent his afternoons with widows drinking too much and transmitting rumors. My mother no longer even liked to see his car pull up in the drive. She despised malicious conversation and no longer took a drink before five o'clock. She began to drive frail old women whose husbands were sick to the hospital to visit them. She began attending, each Tuesday morning, the only other Mass said in Jasper besides those on the weekend. She attended Stations of the Cross during Lent, and one day while shopping in Gainesville she had me stop on a busy street at a plain cement rectory attached to the student chapel downtown. "I'll be right back," she said. It was two o'clock in the afternoon. The car was filled with bags of the moisturizers, night-lights, cheese graters, room deodorizers, and Chinese lanterns she purchased despite my protests.

When she came out ten minutes later I said, "What did you do?"

"I went to Confession," she said as she got in and lighted a cigarette. She might just as well have told me she'd held up the Savings and Loan.

"You went to Confession?" I said.

"Yes," she said. "He was very nice." And I stared for a moment at this renegade reconciled to the Church, a communicant thirty years after those mornings in Aruba when she'd poked me in the ribs and whispered, "What are you waiting for? Get up there!" She seemed to be making connections with the past: her own past, at any rate.

Occasionally we sat in the den in the evening in Jasper, the only sound during the muted television commercial the forlorn whistle of a train passing through town across the lake. My mother would turn to me and say, "What ever happened to that nice boy we met at your graduation, the one from Oregon?" And I would tell her he was now working his family's farm in the winter-wheat belt there, married, the father of two daughters. I did not tell her about the friends who sometimes broke the silence of that house by telephoning from New York to say they had taken a share on Fire Island next summer, or wanted to know when I was coming back. How astute my mother was, knowing nothing about them. After the few words she

exchanged with them before handing the receiver to me,
she would say, "He seems like a good fellow." (Each one
treated her in a different way: One spoke brusquely, in a
businesslike fashion, embarrassed by having to go through
her; another spoke to her at length in a bravura attempt to
charm her with his good manners; a third considered her
a witch keeping me in Jasper against my will, and hung up
if she happened to answer the telephone.) Or when I tried
to explain the tone of several friends who all called on the
same night to pour their troubles out to someone far from
the madness of New York: "Life in that city is very drain-
ing," I said, and she asked, "Why are your friends so easily
drained?"

At times I bristled under such remarks. These were my
friends and that was that. Even so, I knew her remarks
were merely those of someone starved for personalities to
observe. My mother was nothing if not social. Each time
she left the house to take a turn around the oval park that
formed the center of our neighborhood, she came home
two hours later like a bad puppy, having met so-and-so on
her walk and gone to their house to chat. When a group of
carolers came by, my father and I froze in our chairs hoping they would think no one was home. Mother said, "Go
out and ask them in!" But like some princess imprisoned in
a cheerless castle, she remained at the window peering
through the curtains while we made no move. We had no
desire to invite them in. "What's wrong with you!" she
said. She had an inexhaustible appetite for people. We did
not. And so these telephone calls from my friends in New
York—with news I could not share with her—tantalized
her unfairly. She never met a single member of that *de facto*
family which seemed so numerous to her; and when I re-
sponded to her question about the identity of a caller by
saying only "A friend from New York," she shot back,
"That's what you always say!"

Oddly enough, when I returned to New York I spoke to these callers who shattered the stillness in Jasper far less than I did while I was away—my chief point of interest to them (when was I coming back), my chief value (someone outside the fray to listen to their woes) negated by my return. Months went by sometimes before I saw an old friend. Yet when it came time to leave Jasper—a moment I dreaded as much as desired, for the unhappiness it would cause my mother—I could not think of anything else as I lay in bed my last night, too excited to fall asleep, but these friends whom I would be seeing in twenty-four hours.

My mother became uncharacteristically silent the day before my departure. "I don't like to think about it," she said. "I can't help it," she said. "I get depressed." And I thought how awful the feeling of being left behind is: of those bright blue afternoons in Aruba when the plane bearing my sister or aunt or uncle to Miami finally disappeared in the cloudless sky, and we drove back to a bungalow made deathly still by their absence. Yet there was nothing to do. "I know you have your own life to live," she said as she sat there blinking damp eyes, citing one of those rules governing family life which are as clear-cut as any property law, even if the property is freedom. But these words had an effect opposite to what she intended: They made me think how trivial, how selfish the life I planned to live was. I wanted to turn to her and say, "Oh, Mother, I'm not going back to anything so important." Whose life was?

She refused to come to the plane. My father and I drove mostly in silence to the new solar-powered airport in Gainesville. That hour, too, had a dignity out of proportion to what was actually said between us as we drove through the lakes and pecan farms, the flat fields on which immobile cattle grazed, my heart lightening with each landmark put behind us. It seemed like a moment for final words: serious thoughts, the laying on of hands. But he only asked me, as he always did, if I had my ticket and enough money for a cab when I arrived. "Your mother hates to see you go— I do too—but she'll get over it," he said. And with that we entered the airport. I disliked displays of emotion in public (real tenderness was private, I thought) and was glad my father and I shook hands before I melted into the crowd of passengers beyond the glass waiting to be called for boarding.

The airport was strange to us; it did not belong to Jasper. Crowded with basketball teams and professors on the way to metallurgists' conferences in Bulgaria, it was part of that bustling, busy, bourgeois world which my parents (in old age) and I (in the black, Hispanic, homosexual milieu of New York) had nothing to do with anymore. I was by now a kind of bag lady, walking across the blazing tarmac with a shopping bag from Astor Wines and Spirits filled with the few items I was taking back to my apartment in New York. The three hours between Gainesville and Newark in the company of those who fly (the ambitious, energetic, money-making, progressive America I had little to do with) made me feel like a visitor from outer space. I finished my Act of Contrition just as the wheels of the plane left the ground, and as I murmured, ". . . and I detest all my sins," I began wondering if the handsome dark-haired student on the aisle two seats from mine could possibly be homosexual. This thought made me nervous, however, and I put down the copy of *In Flight Magazine* and told myself that I was traveling north not only on jet fuel, money, the centuries of science, the work of men which made this flight possible, not only on the stream of air beneath this Boeing 737's wings, but on the love my parents bore for me. I was filled with a sense of disloyal selfishness as I flew north. I turned to the window and said to its scratched glass, "My parents are dying. They've done nothing wrong, they've been generous and good and loving, and they're sitting in a house in Florida turning old. Soon they'll be as brittle as those pieces of brain coral on the shelf on the porch."

At that moment the attractive stewardess beside the cart in the aisle called to me: "Would you like anything to drink?"

"Club soda," I said.

And when I got my drink I began reading an article in the magazine about the churches of Prague, and then another on the wines of Sonoma County, in order to forget the morbid and pointless fact. High in the sky I calmed down. By the time I arrived in Atlanta the self individualized by the love of my parents was beginning to disappear in the oblivion of public life, and I felt myself shrink to insignificance in the crowd, hoping to be rescued from the ghostlike nullity induced by large airports by locking eyes with some handsome Cuban flight attendant. Sitting in the lounge in Atlanta I was already free of Jasper: pleasantly no one. By the time the second plane began its descent above Newark I began to tremble with impatience to resume the life that—despite its dangers and tedium—was the only one I loved.

No one met me at the airport. I was accustomed by now to preparing a face to pass the crowd of strangers waiting for husbands, wives, children, grandparents—braced like panthers to throw their arms around some family member—and merged quickly into the mob of passengers looking for other gates. I bought an automatic radio alarm clock to replace the one I assumed had been taken by the thieves who broke into the apartment every winter despite the presence of my roommate, and boarded the bus to Manhattan. I was absurdly happy. The city rose above the golden marshes, the rotting piers, the empty railroad yards of the Jersey shore, like Camelot. Yet I was still part of Jasper, and when I saw my first homosexuals on the subway in the city, they seemed to me—having been away nine months—as exotic as gazelles on a plain in Africa, creatures of a species I did not belong to. They seemed so odd I felt sorry for them: locked in their little uniforms (short hair, moustaches, Air Force bomber jackets), as sad as middle-aged women who no longer dress smartly and who go out to their clotheslines in their robes during the day.

I got to the apartment—made even more chaotic by the thieves who had indeed broken in that winter—and stood there for a moment agape. I was able for a moment to view it with both sets of eyes: those of Jasper, and those of New York. The first saw it as a dark, filthy jail cell whose light was shattered by the window gates which the thieves had bent with pliers. The second viewed the rooms as the temple of so many lovers, nights, dreams, that the candles I lighted whenever I had a guest, and which now sat stubby and half-melted on the kitchen table, might well have been candles used for some religious rite—and I was surprised that the white walls were not blackened, like the glass interiors of hurricane lamps, with the residue of those men, those nights. And I stood for a few moments in the late August dusk before I turned on the lights to savor this atmosphere. Then I turned on the light and dialed my mother to say I'd arrived safely. Her voice sounded shrunken on the telephone: the voice of a lady in a small town down south. I thanked her for her hospitality and assured her that I was in for the night.

"You're sure?" she said. "You're not going anywhere?"

"No, no," I said, "I'm in for the night," because I knew she would worry if I told the truth.

The moment I said good-bye I dashed out the door into the streets of this city to which I was addicted. I was still between selves those first hours after my return from Jasper, and when a woman stopped me on the sidewalk and said, "Where is Stuyvesant Street, please?" I told her with the pleasant knowledge that I was a man who looked reassuring enough for strangers to ask directions of him. In fact I was becoming something else and I merely wondered when my second nature would, like Mr. Hyde, assert itself. Jasper was nothing if not the kingdom of the aged—a kind of enchanted village in whose dining rooms I sat, thirty-five and celibate, listening to men eighty years old flirt with widows they wished to marry now that their first wife was dead. Men courted women on our patio in the moonlight. Octogenarians placed personal advertisements in the newspaper. This only made me sit up in bed as I lay waiting for sleep in Jasper and say, "I'm going to make love every night of my life when I return to New York!" This vow was not so easily kept as it seemed in my room in Jasper, but when I returned to New York its pressure made me wonder not if, but when, I would break my erotic fast.

One arrives in New York at various times of the day in different seasons. It is possible to find a city as quiet, as empty as a village, depending on the hour your plane lands; people are sleeping, or at work, or away on a summer weekend. Sometimes I went out to Fire Island because it was a Sunday in August—but when I got there I was still not my northern self yet, and the crowd of two thousand bronzed men on the beach before the Pines unnerved me. So I took a walk. If I turned left I walked past the Pines and the men who went there to display the physiques they fashioned all week in the city's gymnasiums, and then to Barrett Beach, the haunt of teen-agers from the shore towns of Long Island, and then Water Island, a collection of houses before Davis Park. If I turned right on the beach I walked through Cherry Grove to the Sunken Forest and then Point O' Woods, a town restricted to members of a corporation which the more raffish citizens of the Grove said excluded not only homosexuals but Jews. Strolling on the beach at Point O' Woods I imagined myself being taken for just what my father no doubt wanted me to be: a lawyer, accountant, or stockbroker relaxing from a proxy fight that week downtown. Sometimes I saw a man and a woman supervising their children who reminded me of my parents when they were younger, teaching their offspring to be unafraid of the water. Among all those towns containing more life, and more varieties of life, in one afternoon than I had seen in six months in Jasper, Point O' Woods was a great relief: a fantasy as extreme as any I encountered at the baths. As I walked in my suspension between personalities I speculated what it would be like to be the head of a family, as if with that all my problems would drop away, when in fact they would have merely been replaced by another set. I would not have worried about the size of my penis, the restrictions of age, the difficulty of finding love; I would have worried about mortgages, tuition, my youngest daughter's asthma, my competition at Shearson Loeb Rhoades. And death would still preside over everything. When I came back from Jasper I more often came to a stop midway on the beach between Cherry Grove and Point O' Woods (as in the woods above Heidelberg) to watch the sky turn gold at dusk.

As I sat on the beach in the no-man's-land between the orthodox Protestant community of financiers and the towns in which beauty was paramount—as if between my father and mother—I began that examination of conscience which I often underwent on arriving at the baths, before surrendering myself to sexual life. I thought of the family I left behind each time I came to New York: the aunt in Chicago who said, "I'd love to see you," and who could not live too many more years, she was so old now; of Inez, who wrote to ask if I were married; of people who had already died. And I began to suspect that the world a man occupies is a tiny sphere after all, that as the people who love that individual die, one by one, he is erased gradually like a drawing, limb by limb, till he hardly feels he exists, or the world is real, occupied as it is by hordes of strangers he has never loved and who have not loved him. Each time I returned to Jasper the father who met me at the airport shocked me in the same way the portrait Dorian Gray kept in his closet made him gasp. For me to worry about passing time, when he was facing death, seemed as petulant as those young homosexuals I sat behind on the train returning to the city whom I overheard saying things like "I thought he was twenty-seven. But he's *thirty*-seven!" Or, "I'll never be thirty. I'll never have hair on my back." Or, "I was insulted last night at dinner—a man asked me what I taught at college, and I said, 'I don't teach, I'm still a student!'" If I felt angry at the changes in my neighborhood—if when I went downstairs now I found St. Mark's Place in 1981 thronged with people whose style and attitudes were not my own—how must my father feel about the world itself?

On my return from Fire Island that same day, spent in self-criticism and despair over my stunted life, I was walking from the train station to Central Park, not even aware of the honey locust trees still blossoming above the sidewalk at which I was staring. Something made me look up. A tall shirtless man was looking at me as he guided his bicycle past me. His chest was the white of flesh which has never seen the sun, and filmed with sweat. His eyes were dark. He promised the kind of sexual abandonment possible only with strangers. I looked back to find him still staring at me. At that moment I passed a window from which the fragrance of roasted coffee issued. My heart expanded and I said to myself, *This* is happiness! *This* is what it means to live—a summer afternoon, a man who wants to sleep with you, the odor of coffee through a window! How can you be sad? You are alive! And though I kept walking and did not pursue the stranger—because I realized suddenly it was only the cook, who did not recognize me bearded, and whose beauty I had seen anew because in my brown study I did not identify him immediately—all the possibilities of life were once more present before me, and I was so happy when I sat down on a bench in the park that my joy bathed the newspaper I had bought to read. Its articles only informed me of the countries I still had to visit, the cuisines I had not tasted, the existence of a way to cook chicken I had never known about till now. On finishing it I got up and walked over to the Rambles—not to find someone whose life I wished to share, but to roam among the men I still felt not part of. By this time I was wary of disease, aware keenly of the limitations of these brief encounters, and considered homosexual love affairs as likely to survive as a kamikaze pilot. Yet I went in and found myself locked in an embrace with someone I had not even spoken with. The hug was all I needed. For that moment, as when I embraced my mother in Jasper, I felt a strength, a warmth stealing into my bones. In that instant I reached a truce with men: the secret embrace at the end of the day. And I could walk off afterward restored and confirmed in my existence as a human being.

This human being had habits, however, which seemed even more compelling following his release from the town in which the autumn of life was evident. I knew I must visit the baths. But when I chose the Fifth Avenue bus, rather than my usual subway—which always contained at least one extraordinary face—I was shocked to see a world of people who only confirmed morbid fixations. On Sunday afternoons in August the city was almost deserted and those who remained were very old. A quartet of gray-haired women leaning on canes saw one of their group onto the bus and waved good-bye like schoolgirls as we accelerated; only they were near death. The bus driver was talking to a man in the front seat about the weather. It was a Sunday in late August but a cold air mass had come to town and it was only sixty-five degrees; autumn was in the air, like a song the *discaire* introduces pieces of before he gives it to you whole, like the consciousness of mortality that strikes us every five years or so and then vanishes after we have wrestled with it and decided, of course, to go on living, thank you. The sun at six o'clock was a gold blur beneath a pale gray skein of wintry clouds. "I like autumn," the bus driver was saying.

"You like autumn?" said the old Jewish man.

"Yes," said the bus driver. "Autumn is an emotional time. You think of, you know, *death.*"

An old woman hoping to shop at Sloan's on Eighth Street before it closed got on and argued querulously about a transfer. An older man with a cane helped his wife up at the next stop. She had no chin and came into the bus with the visage of a blank, gasping fish, staring at the passengers before her, and gasped for breath after her husband had seated her. A trio of Japanese businessmen got on but could not understand the requirement of exact change and got off. A Pakistani and his wife in a sari got on; then a man and a woman with a picnic basket who could not stop kissing each other. And as the bus halted—haughtily ignored by people standing at the stops who wanted a different one but refused, to the driver's fury, to wave it by—accelerated, stopped, began again, it bore this little kingdom of the aged down Fifth Avenue in the crisp twilight.

A vast sense of loneliness pervaded me. How easy it was to be proud when one was young, and strong, like the man walking up Fifth Avenue whom I eyed through the window. I began to feel men were merely ghosts brought into the light by the passion of two human beings, and that in the atmosphere around me countless more ghosts pressed against the thin line dividing the present from the future, the visible from the invisible, begging to be made flesh. And like a ghost, a vampire, I had to find the look in the eyes of a stranger that certified I was still alive, or at least wanted by someone on the street. I needed this as much as my mother required a denial when she looked at me in Aruba and said ironically, "You don't love me and you never have." We were surrounded in New York—as if in a city at war—by the dead and dying. They got on and off the bus as we went down Fifth Avenue in the autumnal dusk; they read their newspapers and looked for bargains on iceberg lettuce and suede coats.

As I went to the baths after getting off the bus at Union Square—deserted on a summer Sunday afternoon—I was eager to see who would be there sharing this knowledge with me. When I saw in the darkness of its long halls a naked man lying in his room breathlessly masturbating, he constituted a bright and vivid tableau in the artificial night. At six o'clock on Sunday he was as improbable as a martyr in the catacombs, or a man in outer space whom one encounters after floating through the primordial void for ten thousand years, a man whose orbit grazes yours and then keeps drifting on into intergalatic oblivion. I stared at him, afraid of disease but absolutely convinced that the unique antidote to the daily massacres of Time was located at that point on the vault of the Sistine Chapel at which God's finger nearly meets the extended hand of man—who in this case was probably the manager of a radio station in New Jersey, or a city employee sick of Jones Beach.

6

When later that night I finally walked down the narrow, fluorescent-lighted hallway to my apartment in New York, I could hear noises within: The water was running and Stuart was talking to someone. He was quite alone when I opened the door, however. He was talking to himself, the way my mother talked to herself when she walked through the garden in Jasper and passed my window. My roommate no more liked living alone than she did. "How's Helen?" he said when I opened the door and came inside, as if I had been gone only five minutes to get the newspaper. "How're Helen and Bob?" he said. "Look!" he said to the cat. "Daddy's home!"

"Fine," I said.

"Why *do* you go down there," he said as he stood at the sink turning over three spoons in the torrent of water issuing from the faucet. (Out of loneliness, or a desire for luxury in otherwise depressing surroundings, this man who remained incommunicado with his own family always left the lights on and ran the water full force.) "Why *do* you?" he said.

"Because they're my parents," I said. "And they ask to see me. Is that so strange?"

"I *guess* not," he said in a theatrically whimsical tone which let me know he thought it surpassing strange indeed. "But then why do you stay so long?"

"For various reasons," I said. "Tell me," I added, to change the subject, "are you in love?"

He turned to me—the difficulties of my return behind us, my desertion forgiven me—and said in a solemn voice, "There's this guy from L.A. at the gym who made us feel *flat*-chested."

"That's impossible."

"You should have seen his forearms!"

"What about his forearms?"

"His forearms," he said, "make mine look like those of a twelve-year-old *girl*! Who's ano*rex*ic."

And he took off his white pumps, put them in the closet where the cat could not get them, and left for the gymnasium murmuring, "No, my forearms aren't ready." I went to the telephone and called Jasper to assure my mother I had arrived safely. Within hours life had assumed its patterns as if I had not been away at all. That evening Stuart returned from the gymnasium rhapsodizing over an Italian-American clothing salesman with whom he lifted weights and was in love. This man was replaced by a new one a few days later. On a piece of paper taped to the kitchen wall, I wrote down his vow: "I'm going to sleep with Frank Petrocelli before Christmas. This is going to be a major winter affair." At the end of the week I inquired about the progress of his plan and I learned Frank was no longer admired.

"Why?" I said.

"He has bad politics," Stuart replied. And, "He's terribly stupid." And, "He likes skinny young blonds." My roommate—as devoted to the search for a lover as anyone in New York—had high standards: a bearded, muscular, older man, intelligent, Italian or Jewish, connubial, politically liberal, nonsmoking, and bored by the social circuit in which my roommate found himself. A palm reader on St. Mark's Place—seated among her children and her cats, watching, with wide eyes and a perpetually startled expression on her face, the obsessed citizenry who passed her window—told him he would meet his lover in 1986.

"What will you do till then?" I asked him.

"Work on my forearms and legs," he said.

And when he saw me write *Cancelled* across Frank Petrocelli's entries, he asked me not to do this—it was too final a repudiation of the hope that characterized not only his days but my life, too (which began anew each time I went downstairs wondering what faces would appear in the street this time). We were all living on hope—the ultimate gasoline. We were all convinced, like my mother, that the next roll of the dice would be in our favor.

Her ignorance of just what game I was playing in New York, however, was such that she could only express her frustration in concern over my physical safety. The city was the world into which I had disappeared. News from New York on the television she took personally because I lived there, just as she always looked up the temperature listed for Manhattan in the newspaper. And once a week she waited for my call. We spoke each Saturday on the telephone. This call gave her such pleasure (long-distance was somehow a part of her Saturday, just as taking a swim was part of mine) it seemed all she required of me. I was relieved that so little brought her happiness. Eventually making this call seemed as annoying a duty as visiting Jasper once a year—there was little to tell on my end—but each time I hung up, I heard the same regret in her voice that turned her melancholy when I left Florida. One year a man was killed by debris falling from a skyscraper being constructed on Fifty-third Street, and she called to say, "You'd better come home."

"That was in midtown," I said, "and I haven't been in midtown in years. I just don't go there anymore." My life in New York was more reclusive than hers in Jasper; I seldom went above Twenty-third Street.

"Well, I think you should come home. Things falling off buildings!" she said.

The year that people in a Chicago suburb died of poison inserted in Tylenol capsules, I remarked one Saturday that I was about to catch a train up the Hudson to walk on the Appalachian Trail and see the autumn foliage. "Be careful!" she said. "Another person just died from Tylenol."

"But, Mother," I said, regaining my voice, "there's no Tylenol in the forest. I'm going to the woods."

"Well," she said, "be careful. Because you never know. Some maniac's on the loose and they haven't caught him yet."

By now I was used to her concern—subways, skyscrapers, expressways, mass murderers, were part of the general menace—but I no longer wanted to conceal all my movements. Indeed I foresaw the day when I would stop lying simply out of fatigue with it. There was so much I did not tell her, I leapt at the chance to say I was going up the Hudson to see the leaves: That was something I could talk about. As it was, I did not tell her about the crazy black Muslim who shot up a bar I frequented on West Street because God told him homosexuals were trying to steal his soul. I did not tell her about my friend stabbed on Tenth Street, while I ran ahead of him because I did not want to be late for *The Mary Tyler Moore Show*. I did not discuss the trial I had attended of an art dealer murdered by two youths who could not read or write and attracted him for that reason. The telephone made it possible to manipulate reality, to claim whatever one wished to. And I began to create excuses—medical, social—which precluded my arriving in Jasper in time for Christmas, excuses my parents always took at face value so that when I hung up the phone, my relief at having my departure postponed was mixed with the horror of learning how easy it is to lie to people who love you.

Indeed, Vittorio confided in my mother—whose sense of fairness made her the confidante of more than one resident of Jasper—far more than I did. When I went home I had little to tell her beyond descriptions of the parties I worked as a bartender. She enjoyed these—but they were all I described.

Our lives in New York and Jasper were utterly dissimilar. In Jasper I found trees, gardens, blackbirds, clean sheets, order and calm. The town park was bordered with beds of petunias and crossed by paths strewn with fragrant pine needles. In New York the park I lived near was a dust bowl in which old men played checkers while drug addicts slept on benches around them. I crossed it only to visit the dancer who lived in a tenement missing most of its windows and doors. In New York I was not conscious of time at all; in Jasper I was. In New York I lived purely in the present; in Jasper, immured in the past. In New York no one died. The only cemetery I saw was that vast necropolis off the Long Island Expressway on my way to Fire Island. Each time I went to Jasper someone we knew was dying, or there had just been another funeral. In New York worries over the fate of the world were forgotten in the insults of the city itself. In Jasper one lost sleep over the Russians. In New York I lived on a block with Pakistanis, Poles, Puerto Ricans, Chinese, Jews, Brazilians, and Africans. In Jasper the sole exotic citizen was a Cuban doctor. In New York I felt perfectly safe walking down the street if only because its dangers were familiar to me. In Jasper I viewed every stranger who came down the road as a possible lunatic or criminal on the loose from Monroe; and when a Jehovah's Witness began to come by and mumble in the driveway after learning there was no yard work, I was worried he would one day arrive with a rifle and shoot my parents while I was away.

Still, my mother viewed New York with a certain affection produced by her visits there years ago. In this city she was once young and good-looking, and had walked me to Times Square to see the billboard advertising Camel cigarettes on which the man puffed real smoke through his wooden lips, and taken me shopping on Fifth Avenue. Now I went to Times Square to see the hustlers and walked Fifth Avenue only on Sunday when it was empty. When she mused one Saturday morning on the telephone that it would be nice to see New York again, to visit Rockefeller Center and see a Broadway show, I said, "Mother, I would never allow you to come here now. First, God knows some Marielito would hijack the plane. Second, even if you got here in one piece, you wouldn't recognize it. That New York doesn't exist anymore. It's an almost completely black and Hispanic city. It's been colonized by people from San Juan. I would be petrified to have you come here, especially now that you've become a woman living in a small town down south, hanging her clothes on a line between two pine trees, feeding cardinals. You'd be mincemeat in New York, mugged within an *in*stant of leaving your hotel! You're not used to this anymore!" I said, pulling on my shoes because I was late for a dinner party in exactly the kind of neighborhood I was describing. "They dump mental patients here from asylums upstate. New York is a trash heap of human garbage. It's as civilized as Dodge City. I live here only because I can break into a run. If you can't break into a run, forget it. I would never let you loose in the Atlanta airport, that mass of morons, much less New York!" I was warming to my subject so that as I stood there holding the phone I was scowling fiercely, regarding through the window the dome of the Ukrainian church, the water towers silhouetted against the white evening sky, the lights of Wall Street honey-gold and sparkling at that magical hour of dusk which thrilled me every time it arrived and made me feel like an actor about to go onstage.

"Well," she sighed, "I didn't think it was as bad as all that. When I was your age, the saying was you shouldn't live in New York unless you could afford to take a taxi. Not break into a run."

"Well, it's changed," I said.

In fact the city was calm and empty because the parts of it I visited and the hours I went there were both deserted. After dinner that night, I found myself on the sidewalk at three in the morning with a few drunks and shopping-bag ladies sleeping next to baby carriages filled with balled-up copies of the *National Enquirer.* I no longer searched in the places of my youth for the person with whom to share my life. My companions were men talking out loud on the street.

By this time I went to the baths on weekday afternoons in hopes of finding the odd exception to the rules of homosexual society, which I now knew was as disappointing as any other. What I really wanted, I concluded, was a skinny Oriental accountant who wore glasses. I now saw sex as simply a brief athletic encounter similar to a game of handball or a swim. It seemed to make no difference. It was something one had in the evening; if I didn't pick up someone in my neighborhood park, I went to the delicatessen and bought a pint of Breyer's Dutch chocolate almond ice cream. I had reached that middle period when life—any life: surgeons or housewives, homosexuals or cops—goes stale for a while and one is prisoner of habits that no longer bring happiness, or even pleasure. I became angry and heard myself talking out loud as I walked down the street like the men I had considered maniacs when I first arrived in town. I began to hate my own tribe. One day in the gymnasium, the doctors, attorneys, cab drivers, and cooks arguing around me whether it was proper to attend a pre-Saint party if one did not intend to go dancing at The Saint afterward suddenly sounded like sophomores in a sorority at a southern college chattering in their bedrooms. When I went to The Saint it seemed filled with two thousand men who were twenty-eight, dark, bearded, and distinguishable only by the shape of their noses. They all had hungry mouths, nervous faces, smoked cigarettes, wanted penises of a certain description. "It's got to be uncut," one man said to his companion as I rested on a banquette between songs one night, "but what I really like—are *big balls*."

I went to Fire Island in late September thinking I would not see many people there at that time. Yet I was still so sentimental that when I saw someone ahead of me on the beach, no matter how far from my point of origin, I kept walking till I passed him—simply on the hunch that this could be my next lover. It usually turned out to be an off-duty policeman fishing in the surf, or two local children building a sand castle in the crepuscular light. Once it was the Clam. He began to cackle.

"This can't go on," I said.

"Oh, yes it can," he said.

Yet when I had to leave for Jasper, I was furious, and I left my arrival date vague and undetermined so I would not have to leave the city until I absolutely had to. I stopped in Atlanta to change planes, got off and took a bus through the city wondering if some face on its streets would be the receptive one. Where was this skinny Oriental accountant who wore glasses—or some other version of him? It was only in transit between the two places, New York and Jasper, that I felt hope. It was only suspended between the two lives that I felt any calm at all, or possibility, as if in going from one cell to another, I might spy a means of escape.

The means of escape appeared on the runway in Newark one evening under the wing of my airplane transferring luggage into its hold: It wore a stained gray jump suit and a baseball cap and stared at me as I stood in line waiting to board the plane. I turned and went back into the terminal. The lounge was empty. Dolly Parton sang "Here You Come Again" as I stood there waiting. Crystal Gayle sang "Don't It Make My Brown Eyes Blue." He came into the lounge and walked to the men's room. Linda Ronstadt sang "Blue Bayou." I went in and found him washing his hands. He looked at me. He had green eyes, a long nose, unruly moustache, and shaggy golden-brown hair. He had an expression one would have said was blank, or sweet, except for the fact that his eyes shone with an enigmatic but calm radiance, as if he had a secret he was merely waiting for me to discover. He said: "I have my break now. I live in Parsippany. Come home with me." He turned and I followed him out. We walked down the long corridor.

We got into a van filled with sheets of plywood, an electric drill, cartons of nails, and a metal tool box. A plastic monkey and a plastic clown dangled on strings from the rearview mirror. He looked at me as he shifted gears, and smiled. He drove fast, through a parking lot filled with the cars of people in Florida, onto a highway that led through a snowy landscape of parking lots, Howard Johnson restaurants, along Route 46 until we reached an apartment complex between a shabby line of stores connected by a veranda and a vast new shopping mall in a wilderness of parking spaces ringed by a gas station, a doughnut shop, and a carpet barn. It was late afternoon. Just beyond a gas station whose sign rose over one hundred feet into the air on two white poles, the countryside began: soft hills whose pale green grass was visible between patches of snow, dark stands of naked trees, the blue outline of hills on the horizon. Women were walking their snowsuited babies across the pale gray slush to a play area adjacent to an empty swimming pool surrounded by a chickenwire fence.

We entered an apartment furnished with a yellow-green shag carpet, a chrome coffee table, and an aquarium whose single Siamese fighting fish hung suspended in the silver water as still and quiet as the room itself. We sat on a green modular sofa and drank beer. Then we went into a dim plush bedroom whose chandelier was connected to a rheostat which my host lowered so that it cast a light simultaneously golden and gray. Our figures were reflected, as we undressed, in the smoked-glass mirror that covered the wall above a large bed. To my astonishment my host was far more handsome than I had judged him in the Newark airport. And afterward, as I lay beside him—thinking, I have no idea who sent this person to me—I could hardly speak.

My host looked at me with the same mysterious smile, the same tender eyes, he had on the runway. "I said to myself before I went in to work today," he said quietly, "I just have a feeling."

"A feeling?" I said, turning to him.

"Yup!" he said, and he began to laugh.

"What is it?" I said, raising myself up on my elbow.

"I'll tell you later," he said, with that air of having a secret; then he reached up and twisted the tip of my nose between his thumb and forefinger. He smiled. I smiled back.

We ate two TV dinners: ravioli and lasagna. It was dark. We drove back to the airport. We spoke of our former lovers, hometowns, families. We exchanged opinions of the baths, bars, beach towns; we addressed the question Which is more important in choosing a partner—face or body? The wilderness of gas stations, motorcycle dealerships, restaurants, slipped past, brilliant white lights that were no longer ugly.

When we got to the airport he said, "Where were you going?"

I said, "It's not important. I'll see you in two weeks." When we parted at the ticket counter, I was so discouraged by the insignificance of erotic life that his appearance seemed to me as drastic as that of a seraph intervening in human affairs when they are at their lowest point.

The absurdity of his being there when I returned acted as an insulation around my heart at first. "I didn't know if you'd want to see me when you came back," he said as we drove down Route 46, "so I said to myself, 'If he does, great. If he doesn't, then at least we had one time together.'" The stoic good sense of this remark was even more unsettling. In my mailbox in New York I found cards that said *Thinking of You* above wicker baskets filled with puppies, kittens, chicks: one mailed each day I was gone.

I took the bus from the Port Authority to New Jersey that Friday in the spirit of a man pursuing a path in the forest just to see where it goes. During dinner Sal asked quietly if I recognized the records we were listening to. I paused and drew a blank. "They're the songs that were playing when we met," he said. As we ate spaghetti I listened to everything Sal said about his former job managing a pet shop in a nearby shopping mall, about the man who bought him white silk pajamas and wanted him to move upstate, about his shyness in high school in a small town on Lake Champlain. I then went into the kitchen and dried the dishes he washed. Through the window above the sink I could see the fenders of the cars in the parking lot gleaming in the light of the sodium vapor lamps. Half of them were still covered with snow. The kitchen was warm and clean. When we put the last plate away, Sal turned to me and said: "Is there anything about me you don't like? Is there anything you want different?" I only smiled, embarrassed by the question, but to my own astonishment as I enfolded him in my arms, I thought, Not really. "Because you're perfect," he said. I thought, It's as if I've been struck by a car. We went into the living room and turned the television on. As we lay on the sofa together, our heads on a pillow, I watched the film of tenements burning, criminals being handcuffed, police searching woods, bombs exploding in Afghanistan, the mob of Iranian zealots screaming "Death to America!" outside the American Embassy, as if all these events were occurring on a planet far from my own—far, far below me on another more angry and ugly sphere. In Jasper the news horrified us. Here it was of no importance. "They're turkeys!" Sal said, jumping up. And we went into that silent room bathed in a faint gold light and went to bed, while the branch of a small tree tapped against the window in the wind outside. As I lay there, I thought, This is the center of the world, the peace beside which everything else is nonsense and babies screaming for their mothers.

The fine layer of snow was blowing across the asphalt of the parking lot when I woke in the middle of the night and went to the kitchen to get a glass of water. I stood at the kitchen sink looking out the window. It was absolutely silent. The snow blew across the dark pavement like sand or sugar, forming crescents until a new gust of wind drew them into another shape. As I watched, they gradually became miniature versions of the crested dunes seen from the window of an airplane or in photographs of Arabia. The windshields of the cars were crusted with ice, and the parking lot was bathed in the orange radiance of the arc lights. Outside it looked bitter cold and dead, as the wind tilted the sign that said COLONIAL OAKS APARTMENTS. I leaned forward to put my face beside the window and feel the chill night on the glass. Finally I was in one of those kitchens encyclopedia salesmen visit. Everything around me was warm, neat, and gleaming: counters, cabinets, boxes of cereal and crackers lined up beside a tiny marijuana plant in a plastic pot. The snow was still blowing against the tires of the cars whose owners, lovers too, were all sleeping in the apartments around this one—and after staring at this eerie courtyard of cold cars, I went back to bed and lay awake beside Sal's warm body, and savored the profound peace of a house in which one's lover is sleeping.

But on Sunday when I packed my shaving kit to catch the bus back to the city, Sal saw me take my toothbrush out of the ceramic holder and said in an alarmed voice, "Leave that here! Why take it with you? You're comin' back, ain't you?"

"But I need it in the city," I said. "Of course I'm coming back," I said. "I'll just bring it with me." And as I embraced Sal, I reminded myself that in this world such things loom large where other ceremonies, rites, certificates, are lacking. Riding back to the city in the dark chilly bus shared with one other sleeping passenger, I savored with a faint smile the power the little yellow toothbrush represented. I looked out the window and vowed: I will never, ever hurt this person. I will never hurt him in any way. Yet as I watched the white lights, the snowy median strip tinged amber by the radiance of gas stations, I reflected that I had no certainty Sal loved me. It might have been anyone he met that day in the airport, I thought.

That winter I made excuses to my friends each weekend; I kept Sal a secret (too delicate to expose to their critical faculties) and went to him. We did many things together—skied, danced, drove to Cape Cod—but my favorite moment occurred simply when I went on Friday night to the Port Authority Bus Terminal to catch the bus to Parsippany because we had decided to do nothing. It was often snowing. The other passengers—suburban teen-agers in high-school jackets, girl friends laughing over the day spent shopping, men doing paperwork on their knees as they went home to their house in the woods—became familiar to me. The industrial plain of New Jersey, the twinkling lights and refineries, lay beneath us as we waited for the bus, watching dusk settle through the fluttering snowflakes. From the moment the doors of the bus closed behind me, I felt I was in Sal's apartment. I felt a comradeship with everyone in the bus, and when the driver stopped opposite the House of Pancakes solely for me, I thanked him with the sudden conviction that despite the horrors of the twentieth century, men were fundamentally good, and stepped down onto the frozen snow and watched the bus accelerate again with an excitement that imbued every aspect of my surroundings with beauty. The carpet barn, the Kawasaki dealership, the doughnut shop, the slender spires of the Mobil Oil sign rising into the air at the blood-red intersection glowing with traffic- and taillights, made me smile as I waited for a break in the line of passing cars and trucks. Running across the frozen snow of the median strip, I scraped my ankles each time I broke through the ice. I ran past the bakery managed by a married couple just shutting up the cash register, blessing them in my heart because Sal and I bought doughnuts there, and went up the stairs to the Colonial Oaks Apartments. The courtyard was deserted. A single tricycle was abandoned in the snow, tilted onto its side. The wind whispered in the small naked oak trees. Above the roofs a pale blue band of air glowed, and high above that the icy stars glittered in a very dark clear sky. I stopped and thought, This is it. No one is more alive than someone on his way to meet a lover. And I went up the path to Sal's apartment and turned the key in the door—not knowing if Sal was still at work or had come home—and tiptoed into the bedroom, where I found him sleeping. I stood in the doorway looking at him, the final object in a series of Chinese boxes I had been opening since I left the city, each one more precious than the last. There at the base of the immense pane of smoked glass, in the dim gold light of the chandelier, my lover lay: this prince on his pallet waiting to be awakened with a kiss—which once given, stirred him to open his eyes, smile, and say, "Hey, shithead. What time is it?"

"Ten-fifteen," I said, climbing into bed with him.

"I worked late," said Sal as he stretched his arms and yawned. "This guy didn't show up and I had to work three flights." He reached over and twisted my nose between his thumb and forefinger. "Why didn't you wake me up?"

And I said, "I did." And then we fell silent and wrapped our arms around each other and lay wordless in the perfect still peace, so very different from the milieu of Saturday nights in New York. But the usual milieu was just what I was sick of. And when Sal wanted to drive into the city to dance I discouraged him. I wanted to keep the two worlds separate: my prince in the thorn thicket, and the freedom of Manhattan—which no longer pained me in any way when I returned each Sunday evening, knowing, as I did, that at the end of the week I would be with someone who loved me and whom I loved.

The sting of the crowds, the challenge of faces, the demands of bodies, the thousand pricks of desire which the briefest stroll through the streets of Manhattan engenders, held no power over me now; the city whose conversations I overheard seemed filled with disappointed moviegoers finding fault with films they had just seen. Phone calls to Jasper were serene. Sal came to town on his day off—a Thursday, in lieu of the Saturdays he had to work—and I was brought to a halt when, on entering Central Park on a warm February afternoon, Sal looked at the sun shining on the silvery branches of the wooded hills around us and said, "What's this?"

I whispered, "Central Park." My heart expanded. The thought that I had the entire city—the city I refused to allow my mother to visit, the city whose pleasures I was sick of—to show him made me dizzy for a moment. We went into the Metropolitan Museum and again Sal stopped and said, "What's this?" And I, biting my lip to disguise a smile, was delighted that I had the treasures of thirty centuries around me to offer this man—who told me when asked why there was only one *Road and Track* magazine in the house, "I never read. It makes me fall asleep."

I said, "The Metropolitan Museum. Come, let's see if the Christmas tree is up." And I led him back to show him the Neapolitan crèche, past the medieval armor which, like the news of fires, riots, drownings that seemed to have occurred on another planet distant from the sofa on which I lay with Sal watching the news in New Jersey, seemed to exist now solely for our pleasure and interest. The purpose of the world was finally clear: It existed for the delectation of lovers.

All that winter I seemed to be an actor taking a part that had been given him for no reason he could discern: I was happy. I kept searching for explanations but in the end there weren't any.

On one of the evenings we spent apart, I came home after a night of dancing and came to an astonished halt when I got to my tenement. Sal sat on the steps, his head and coat dusted with the snow falling at that hour, dozing slumped against the railing like some figure in a tale by Hans Christian Andersen. I shook him. "Hey, shithead," Sal said.

"What are you doing?" I said.

"Waiting for you. Don't be mad. I missed you, so I said, I'll go in and wait for him. I knew you'd probably be out, but now you're here!" And he stood up and wrapped his arms around me. The collar of his coat was crusted with snow. As we stood there in the hush, I marveled at a devotion I felt I had not earned. The snow accumulated on the tops of the garbage cans, and I fell a little bit more in love.

"You never complain," I said as we walked up the stairs to my apartment.

"Why should I?" said Sal. "What's the point?"

"Well," I said, "to some people, complaining is a way of life. Our dearest possession: our critical faculties."

And I took Sal back to the scrofulous apartment which

always quietly horrified boys from New Jersey, who woke in the middle of the night to find roaches crawling over their chests. But Sal did not complain. He only wanted me to confirm the fact that we were lovers. He wanted this with the stubborn pertinacity of a woman who wishes to get married in a church. I summoned all my critical faculties to avoid making this pronouncement. Whatever love meant to me, I could not promise it in a Chinese restaurant in the east Thirties. I expatiated upon the meaning of the word *lovers* with the care and detail of a lawyer analyzing the terms of a contract between tenants in common. I never knew if Sal was really listening to what I said—it was like talking to a dog sometimes—and I was often surprised when Sal recalled a remark I myself had forgotten making. That night as I lay beside Sal in my apartment, I felt a strange stillness around me. I turned and saw, in the neon light reflected on the brick wall outside the bedroom window, Sal staring at the ceiling. His face glistened with tears. I did not ask "What's wrong?" I turned away and stared into the darkness myself.

Afterward I conceived this moment in romantic terms: I told myself the god—in Greek myth or the Bible—often appeared among men in ordinary guise, and tested them, and having done so, withdrew, back to Heaven. Just so Sal, on learning I refused to call him lover, changed. He began to see other people, just as I (nervous at being the sole object of this man's intense desires) had urged him to. At first I enjoyed hearing of Sal's adventures when we met to sit on a pier on the Hudson River to watch the sunset. Then I realized Sal had found another candidate: a Colombian fabric-cutter who lived in Asbury Park. I listened to Sal describe his shortcomings with a smile. I took Sal to parties at which I introduced him to other men. But I was happy when he left with me and we ended the evening at our favorite restaurant. Yet whenever I embraced him now his body was heavy as lead. He went limp in my grip. He would not even raise his arms, and when I lifted them anyway and wrapped them around my neck to reproduce physically the embrace I now missed more than anything else in life, I felt I was practicing the dead-man carry in a first aid class with a perfect stranger. The patience with which Sal submitted chilled my heart. The amazing love offered me on our first meeting was now just as astonishingly absent. He was abruptly very embarrassed by the cards he'd sent, the records he'd bought, the phone calls, the nicknames, the professions of love—as if, not being lovers, we had nothing in common as people whatsoever: a fact I had to acknowledge to myself was true. That was all we had shared: love. Yet I was now convinced—like my mother on passing a motel she had not told my father to stop at—that this was the real love of my life and I would never have another like it.

For my breaking with Sal coincided with my ceasing to believe in general in romantic love between two men—a belief which, if illusive, at least makes love possible while it is held. Now Sal was detached and I bereft. I found myself saying good-bye to him in tears on the cement island of Herald Square, the pier at Morton Street. I became one of those people I saw emerging from the subway in stylish clothes, briefcase in hand, tears streaming down their face, borne along by the oblivious crowd like a dead leaf on a stream. Flocks of pigeons rose at my feet as a great blur. Sal told me he was tired of New Jersey, and that spring he obtained a transfer to the new Dallas-Fort Worth airport. He met his next lover his first night there in a bar. They bought a house in the suburbs with two pecan trees in the backyard and its own gazebo. And the love I felt for him began to intensify implacably, like a burn that flushes the skin after the sun has set. I was more attached to him than I had ever been while going to Parsippany, and a winter's

day when there was snow on the ground was all I needed
to believe the best days of my life were behind me now.

In fact—as if all experience produces delayed reactions
—I began to live the winter I'd spent with him over again
each succeeding year, in memories triggered by insignificant things: the hiss of tires on the pavement, the smell of
snow in the air, the sound of bare tree branches scraping
each other. Winter in New York became only the presence
of this person I did not even see again for several years.

This melancholy surprise I tried to convey to Vittorio
the night I met him at the airport in Gainesville not long
after Sal's move to Texas. Vittorio only nodded. "It's like
that," he said as we drove home through the profoundly
tranquil darkness, past the post office and the closed gas
station, their white frame facades gleaming ghoulishly in
the streetlight. There was, when we came to a stop at the
intersection just outside Jasper where the yellow traffic
light blinked in the vast, empty night, a moment of silence
that finally made Vittorio sigh.

"I'd just like to fly to Fort Worth," I said. "Rent a car and
drive past the house and see them, I don't know, washing
the dog, if they have a dog. Just see them. But I can't," I
said. "I'll never do it. I might as well book a seat on Pan
Am's first flight to the moon. Imagine," I said as we entered
town and drove the last long curve along the lake, "that out
of all these years in New York, the person who finally gives
me the love I'm supposedly searching for is a crazy kid who
worked at the airport in Newark and doesn't read because
it makes him fall asleep. And who can fall asleep in discotheques! As he used to do. And who only wants one thing
in life—a lover. Someone he can buy presents for and be
utterly faithful to. Nothing in life is ever where you look
for it!" I said as Vittorio got out in his driveway. "Nothing!"

The next time Vittorio returned he wanted to know if

we could drive first to the bar in Gainesville before heading to Jasper. He didn't want a drink; he just wanted to postpone the inevitable abandonment of a personality which was becoming more and more based on the proximity of available lovers. He saw Jasper in a detached, objective way now. "You must admit this town is so pretty. Just the way a town should be." But it got harder to come to Jasper direct. He began flying via San Juan (it was cheaper, so odd were the air fares when the industry was deregulated) and a little hotel there where no one asked questions. He stopped in Miami and lived for a week at the Club Baths.

There were many pleasures in life in Jasper which I seldom enjoyed during my increasingly long sojourns there because I did not have anyone to taste them with; and when Vittorio came, I insisted—despite his certainty that two men at our age, together, were suspicious—that he go with me to Cumberland Island, the Ocala Forest, Crescent Beach. In winter I took Vittorio down the Itchetucknee River in a canoe; the mosses, lilies, and grasses, the strange flowers growing beside the water had recovered from the jostling of three thousand people in inner tubes each day of summer, and we had the whole stream to ourselves. The river was so clear one could see thirty feet down to the scales of limestone shale and mica, glinting like silver ingots on the white sand bottom, and large catfish suspended in the transparent water, their whiskers and fins undulating in the current. Blackbirds and crows called in the woods, rafts of water hyacinths bumped our canoe, and the sound of waterfalls led us up still inlets to the springs themselves, gushing over a mossy fallen pine. It was the original forest untouched, in which I found surcease of the melancholy afflicting me since Sal's disappearance—but even there, as we floated effortlessly over the platinum-and-turquoise depths, Vittorio rested his paddle, his back to me, and said, "You know, I used to love all this, but I've changed so much."

He gave me news of the little band as we drove from the airport another night: The cook had married a childhood girl friend who now worked in New York, and they bought a house and moved to New Jersey. The Clam was in Arabia again and Wheatworth had just been operated on for a rectal fissure. Stone had moved to San Francisco. "Sex *is* better in San Francisco," Vittorio sighed as we turned left in Monroe at the filling station and began the last stretch through the woods to Jasper: a formerly empty forest in which subdivisions were sprouting as unexpectedly as toadstools on our lawn in the morning.

"Look, that's new, that steak restaurant," Vittorio said. "Aerobic dance classes at the high school!" he said, when we stopped beside a bulletin board at the city hall. "How eighties!" When he returned to Jasper, Vittorio expected everything to be just as he left it: a rural dream. He disliked signs of sophistication in the woods. He said, "I imagine there's everything in Gainesville now but sushi."

I said, "You know, I think of Sal almost every day and I haven't spoken to him in over three years. You'd think that if you once loved someone, you love them a little for the rest of your life. You'd think the person would call. But then, I haven't either," I said. My voice grew hoarse, and the profound silence waiting like a deep cold pool at every intersection at which we came to a stop began to affect Vittorio. He yawned, and in a few moments was dozing on the seat beside me.

His father drove with me on one occasion in their large, complicated car. He was growing deaf, and on our way home left his seat belt unfastened. This caused a buzzer to sound. Vittorio was embarrassed to draw attention to the fact that his father could not hear it, so we drove home with his seat belt unfastened and an angry buzz. "This car tolerates *no* imperfection," he said. And he added, "Nor do they." But his conception of his parents' judgment was his own—he was attributing to them the stern standard he judged himself by, which might very well not have been theirs. He would never know if it was, however. There was, after a certain point, an arrangement one reached with one's family. In my case it was so comfortable that when my sister came to visit with her children, it seemed as if they were a storm which would soon pass, so that we could return to our communal slumber. My father had his habits; my mother had hers. If there was anything to mar the tranquillity it was only the fact that my father began to worry her.

In fact their positions were now completely reversed: He was idle, she occupied with her work as an officer of the local Senior Citizens Center. In this new phase I watched their relationship unfold. He drank with the judicious consideration of a retired doctor sedating himself at intervals throughout the day. She lay awake before dawn listening for the telltale noises in the kitchen. When she heard them, she got up and went into the hall. He saw her and pretended to be doing something else: mixing a jar of orange juice, removing frozen meat to thaw. This became a game of theirs, as crazy as any of mine on the streets of Manhattan, and one I witnessed for once as a spectator.

One afternoon I walked up and down outside our house while my father sat on the porch playing a peculiar game of solitaire (taught him by a fellow passenger on a ship to the Far East in 1950), telling myself I should go in and talk to him. Don't stand in the cemetery rebuking yourself that you never had an intimate conversation with him, I thought. Do it now, while you still have the chance. Ask him what's wrong.

But I could not—no more than I could visit Sal in Fort Worth. The respect, the distance between us, was so immense, I could no more go inside, sit down and tell him my thoughts than I could throw myself off a cliff. We talked briefly that afternoon about the various provisions of the tax law and he advised me on my Form 1040. Then he finished his card game, sat back in his chair, and stared at the curlicues of cigarette smoke hanging in the air before him. I could not sit down and ask him what he thought of life, why he was surreptitiously drinking, or what he felt about us. I suspected I already knew. He did not particularly like life now that he was this old, he was probably unamused by the prospect of death, and he loved us in his way. He was playing solitaire again when I finally mustered the courage to go onto the porch, sit down across the table from him, and ask about his youth. He did not even interrupt his card game. He told me as he moved his jacks and queens about that his own father died when he was a young man, that he worked in the farms around the small Ohio town in which he was raised until he got tired of it, went to Chicago, took a job with an accounting firm, and lived very happily in the city until he decided to go to Aruba. He drew no moral, no lesson, from any of this. He finally gathered the cards together, sat back in his chair with his cigarette held up in one hand and looked at me as if wondering what my real question was. I did not know what the real question was—and when later in the afternoon, he called me into the kitchen, I was relieved to find a problem with a practical solution. He held out a jar of peanut butter and said, "Will you open this?" And I realized—as he, my mother, and I burst out laughing—that the central fact about our relationship was this: When I was a child he opened jars for me.

"Well of course he did!" said Vittorio when I saw him uptown. "So did mine." Vittorio was more relaxed about these matters. He was more relaxed about everything—even Jasper. And he tried to lift me out of this depression. "I've been to two funerals this week," he said. "I've decided to live."

Vittorio was planting cherry laurels himself along the

side of his yard that was exposed to the windows of their neighbors. He wanted absolute privacy when he inherited the property. "I want to *fill* the yard with naked boys after they've gone. I'm going to have everyone down from New York!" But this scheme did not ring true; it was one of those dreams he used to relieve the pressure of reality. He would be, after their death, as conservative a citizen of Jasper as he was now. He was, at the end of a decade in New York, something of a homosexual emeritus. Each year he stayed a bit longer in Jasper—and his compulsion to return to the erotic life in Manhattan waned. For one thing: "I think I've slept with everyone," he said. He now found beauty in youths fishing offshore, or harvesting blackberries in the marsh. This new idealism—after years of carnal episodes—found its most surprising expression in the person of a new altar boy he noticed in February, one Saturday afternoon when he was standing in a shaft of sunlight coming through one of the narrow windows of the new, energy-efficient church, holding the wine till the priest turned to take it from him. Winter was cold in Jasper in 1981, so cold that when I took the walk before bedtime which was my habit in the country, I found myself wearing the same clothes I wore in New York in February. The days were short and when we left Mass it was pitch-dark. The sun set very low behind a stand of turkey oaks in a sandy field behind the church, and the light coming in as Mass began was more golden for the gloom surrounding it. It was like autumn. In the spring the altar boys were sunburnt and the light bounced off the brass patens they held beneath each communicant's lips and veined their faces like leaves; but now the altar boy's visage was pale, and the light less fierce. He stood out in the dusky shadows of the nave like the face in a portrait; like a soldier at the foot of the Cross in a canvas of Mantegna.

The sky was gray more often than not when we came to

church at five-thirty on Saturday afternoon. The dried
brown and brittle leaves of the oak trees blew up around
me in a cloud as I walked from the car, and the wind—so
strong in north Florida sometimes—seemed to be blowing
the silvery clouds across the sky as I watched. I went into
church. There was no guarantee that the altar boy we
found beautiful would be serving Mass; sometimes two
youths with almost-white hair stood in their red robes in
his place—future jet pilots, or professional golfers. But
most Saturdays he served the Mass at five-thirty. The red
and white robes were already too small for him. When he
sat down at the side of the altar during the priest's sermon,
he tugged at the sleeves to pull them down over his wrists.
He was the last child of parents whose other offspring were
married and living elsewhere. When he paused at the head
of the sloping aisle at the threshhold of the church, his face
half-shadowed, half-lighted, holding the Cross as he waited
for the priest to start the procession, one could look at him
frankly—because the whole congregation was staring at
him as they waited for the procession to begin. One Saturday, Vittorio said, *"He is made of ivory."* He said no more,
but I knew just what he meant: There was a fineness to the
proportions of his face, the moulding of the chin beneath
the long straight nose, the delicate lips, that recalled a
Roman head carved in ivory, or—as he stood under the
light with his staff, serious, still, impassive—a young
Roman soldier in one of those novels by Thomas B. Costain
or Lloyd C. Douglas that I read at his age. Vittorio would
not allow himself to stare, however, and when I asked him
casually what penance he planned, what sacrifices he intended to make, during Lent, he replied, "Why, simply to
listen to Father Bob's sermons and *not* look at Patrick Mor-
dino."

This lasted till the middle of March—and then the altar
boy took a job as a bagger at the supermarket and Vittorio

decided that his enthusiasm for him was due to the religious context in which we saw him. In the light of day he turned out to have bad skin, like a man one sees for the first time outside the red glow within a bar. He was busy packing bags under fluorescent lights while the loudspeakers played "The Girl From Ipanema." He wore a white plastic boater which the supermarket workers were forced to wear that year to celebrate the chain's anniversary. He joked with his fellow baggers, dropped packages of instant mashed potatoes, told women where the pickle relish was as Vittorio stood in line at the check-out counter. He ceased serving Mass. He came late and sat with his parents and yawned during the sermon. He was succeeded by a nondescript child of nine. But when we emerged from the church, throughout these regimes of altar boys, one thing was always there: the immense and beautiful sky, its cumulus clouds scudding before the wind, a flock of red-winged blackbirds rising from the top of a pine tree at the slamming of a car door and flying off as the parishioners went home to supper.

By the time Easter arrived, a disillusioned Vittorio was working outdoors in the garden his father no longer took an interest in: He planted the row of cherry laurels that transformed one end of their circular drive into an alcove in which he could sit reading unobserved between a bank of azaleas and a neighbor's hedge. Even this was not private enough for Vittorio, however. When he wanted to read pornographic magazines or *Glamour* or *Vogue* he went to a state park five miles outside Jasper in the middle of a weekday afternoon, when the place was deserted, and read them there. He went in his own car because he did not want to be seen with another bachelor. Once in the safety of the empty parking lot in the state park, however, he read aloud to me the articles written by psychologists advising people to avoid neurotic behavior in love affairs. "I'm Number

Five," he said. And he quoted: "You refuse people who pursue you, and pursue people the moment they run off on being rejected." He looked up. "That's exactly what I did with Tom! How sick!" And he got out of the car to walk the central feature of the park: a ravine.

The ravine was unique in that drab countryside: The trees which everywhere else were stunted grew here to heights four times their usual size. Their leaves were a dark, northern green and glinted in the sunlight they were trying to reach. They lined the banks of a shallow stream so transparent one could see the imprint of the current on its white-sand bed. Only the sound of a crow croaking in the top of a nearby pine tree impinged on our solitude—until we rounded a scrub oak and looked up to see a family of three staring at us. Their shocked faces mirrored ours. We eyed one another as if the opposite party were a rattlesnake. Then Vittorio delivered a curt nod, and they mumbled "Hello" and moved past us with downcast eyes.

"I should wear a sign around my neck," Vittorio sighed when they were well behind us. "*Unmarried man visiting his mother for a few weeks. Will not rape wife or molest children.* Everyone down here thinks you're an escaped convict." We walked another hour down the ravine to the ruins of an old mill which was the focal point of the trail and worthy of a small wooden bench overlooking a clear pool. "Well!" Vittorio said under his breath. "The whole world is here!" We came to a halt; two women sat on the bench.

The husky woman with short black hair and blue denim skirt stood up and greeted us. The plump blond woman in a blue sweater smiled and did not rise, but sat there looking at us with bovine blue eyes. Within five minutes Vittorio was talking to them with the candor of Americans who tell their life stories to strangers on airplanes. They had moved here from Miami and both worked in a hospital in Gainesville. I finally excused myself to return to the car. When

Vittorio appeared he was pale and wide-eyed. "Lesbians!" he said. "We found two lesbians in the forest! On a Tuesday afternoon in Jasper! It makes sense, doesn't it? They too wanted to be alone, so they went to the woods. They both left their husbands in Miami for each other and are now settled in Fort Green. Amazing!" he said. "The wounded in their sex meet in the forest primeval." And he got into his car. He was still excited as he turned on the engine and called, "I am so jealous of lesbians! I think it's the only solution. I always have," he said, and drove off around the curve.

On the first of May, Vittorio was still in Jasper, and when I saw him next he was raking leaves into a pile on the beach in front of their house for burning. "I was on the phone last night with William Friel!" he said when I came up to him.

"What's the news?" I said.

"His mother died in November," Vittorio said. "He went out to Brooklyn and stayed with her. Cancer in the bloodstream. They just watched TV in her hospital room all day, and he read to her. At night he went to the baths. He said it was the only way he got through it. He was supposed to go to San Francisco, and his mother insisted he not change his plans, and he knew he would probably never see her again, but she wanted him to go. So the last thing he said to her was, 'Is there anything I can do for you?' And she said, 'Turn on the *Today* show.' That was it. The next day she died, and when he came back for the funeral, his four older brothers—those louts who give money to the I.R.A.—wouldn't let him carry the casket. He asked why and the one he hates replied, 'Because you're a fruit.' And William was left there on the church steps."

Vittorio tilted the wheelbarrow and watched the leaves cascade onto the pile. The gardens behind us were turning dark, the trees to silhouettes, and finally all that remained golden in the world was the crescent of grass, as isolated as it was when a thunderstorm approached, radiant and glowing against an ashen sky and lake. Egrets converging from other parts of the lake flew low across the water into the wind, allowing it to lift them up when they arrived over a pond invisible to us within the weeds. There, beating their great white wings, they descended into the marsh and vanished from sight.

It was so still we could hear Vittorio's neighbor Mrs. Hall calling out to her daughter (an elderly widow herself), in a voice that allegedly frightened the nurses at the hospital in Starke, to help her go to the bathroom. Her daughter continued talking to a man who lived down the road—a man who fixed cars, washing machines, and televisions, and was so useful to several widows they all said the moment he left Jasper they would too—about the costs of installing a roof over her back patio. No one knew whether Mrs. Henry would last the spring. Everything about her was decaying except her indefatigable heart. "She'll live to be a hundred," said Vittorio. "And her daughter will be canonized. That's what Mother said this morning. Mother says we're put on earth for a brief time and only as a test."

"A test of what?" I said.

"A test to see if we use our talents in the service of God," he said. He began raking leaves the wind had scattered into a new pile protected by the large one. "You know, I used to wonder which was real. This. Or that," he said, moving his head in the direction of what I took to be New York City. "I still don't know," he said. He threw his rake onto the wheelbarrow. It was nearly dark now; a single star burned ice-white in the pale green band of air above the trees on the opposite shore. A blue heron stood at the edge of the marsh, as motionless as the bird on an Egyptian funeral frieze, and the chill began rising up from the damp earth as we walked up the long lawn to the house in which his parents sat waiting for him to begin dinner.

When we reached the patio he picked up the newspaper

214 · Andrew Holleran

he had been reading that afternoon and shook it in the
gloom. "It's Rape Awareness Week in Gainesville," he said.
"Do you suppose it means balls and dinners and things?"
And: "Belk-Lindsey is advertising *spirited* and *sassy* shoes.
Shall we go over and have a look at them? What could a
sassy shoe be—one that talks back to you?"

We drove to Gainesville the next day. The mall was
nearly empty and the sight of the bored clerks entombed
in the fluorescent depths of record stores and shoe salons
reminded me of age, death, and the struggle to make a
living. By the time we left the mall Vittorio could not be
tempted with films, bookstores, the nursery, or state museum. Gainesville stretched before us as a vast parking lot,
its acres of automobiles gleaming dully under the overcast
spring sky while plastic pennants flapped in the breeze
outside a Pontiac showroom. People were making money.

"What's wrong?" I said to my uncharacteristically silent
passenger as we drove through the flat green fields, the
grazing cattle immobile in the distance, the pecan groves in
new leaf.

"I miss New York," he said.

"What about it?" I said.

"Everything," he said. "The gossip, the filth, the soot and
venereal disease. Doesn't it bother you? Don't you feel as
if you're in a morgue down here? How can you stay as long
as you do?"

"It's peaceful. It's quiet," I said.

"But peace and quiet are not life!" he said.

"I'm happy," I said.

"Happiness is not life!" he said. "If you haven't noticed,
time is passing. You've only this summer, and the next one,
and a few more. And then it's over! You can't sit life out
on the sidelines. You can't withdraw from the world. None
of these people would be here if they weren't retired. You
must get out of here!" He fell silent and then he said, "It

is wonderful to sleep under one roof with people you love, but you should realize this is your only life. And the older I get the more precious life is to me. How stupid to quibble over the terms it's offered on. To think how much I've flagellated myself for this and that. When all one has to do is live," he said. "Live. The whole thing is an accident; it goes very quickly."

And so Vittorio flew the coop one hot June afternoon— but only because a friend of his was flying a dozen people to Paris for dinner to celebrate his birthday. The invitation came while his parents were fishing in the Ocala National Forest and it was I who drove him to the airport. "Tell them I'll call tonight. Don't tell the details, of course. *Ciao!*" he said, and waved as I watched him walk across the tarmac to the plane.

And Vittorio was gone for another year and I drove home from the airport through the cattle ranches and pecan groves and tiny towns so well represented by the watercolors local artists painted: splash of dark green for the live oaks, pink for the crepe myrtle, gray and white for the weathered gas station or post office which stood at two dirt roads disappearing in opposite directions into the woods. All the towns there looked pretty much like one another. When I got home I found tasks awaited me: my mother wanted me to type a letter to a congressman, about milk prices in Florida, and then check the moles on her back to make sure they were not changing dramatically. At eight o'clock my father went to bed. At eleven o'clock my mother and I followed suit. Although the most remarkable thing about Jasper to my mind was that I fell asleep almost immediately after lying down, my mother slept fitfully, if at all, having little need for it in her old age, and waking up occasionally at dawn because in her sleep she thought she heard the sound of bottles being taken down from the liquor cabinet. She got out of bed and went into the hall;

there was my father at its opposite end, standing at the counter in the kitchen with a glass of orange juice in his hand. He looked at her. She looked at him. The wind scattered the dead leaves across the roof as if squirrels were running over it. And she retreated from this portion of the day which for all these years my father had occupied independent of the rest of us, while I lay in the darkness in my room marveling at the fate which kept us three together.

7

There always came a moment when I began to think of leaving Jasper—on a given day, that is; the general idea was with me from the moment I left New York. Sometimes I vowed to get a job in a bank which would leave me only weekends free, so that—as in the army—my inability to visit would be out of my hands. The reluctance to leave, my fear of hurting my parents' feelings, was so peculiar that my remaining resembled some penance, or a spell a traveling knight falls under at a castle. In reality I was simply afraid to take leave of my mother. This was a craziness so bizarre I searched for reasons—but I could not find one that explained the paralysis engendered by my reluctance to say good-bye. I knew no one my age need feel guilty about leaving home. And it may be a mere metaphor to say an unmarried child is an unstable molecule that has not formed a bond with another, and is therefore subject to the nearest field of force. Yet when I left Jasper for New York, or vice versa, I felt as if I were leaving one magnetism and entering another. Hence my reluctance to tear myself away from each, and my inability to return once I had done so.

My sister found this silly, and told me flatly, "You stay there because of Mother! Pure guilt!" Yet my sister was not immune to craziness. Shortly before Thanksgiving of 1982, my father—who, with his cards, newspaper, habits, had no desire to leave Jasper anymore—declined to come to Pennsylvania with my mother for our annual reunion. When I (in New York at the time) also said I wasn't coming, my sister called me one evening and said, "You are *just* like Daddy! *Just* as stubborn! I *knew* you wouldn't come! You're horrible, all of you!"

I said it was no surprise our father had decided to stay home; he was quite old. And as for myself, I had a deadline and must stay in New York and work.

"What kind of a family is this?" she said excitedly. "What kind of a family? You all stink!"

"But it's only *you* who set this great significance on Thanksgiving," I said. "If you don't see your family at the table, you think we don't love you," I said, realizing suddenly that her departure from our family was no more complete than mine. "Of course we love you. Family is for all year round, not just one day. I'll come out next week when we can be more relaxed, and talk."

"Listen!" she said fiercely. "I said I wasn't going to lay a guilt trip on you, but I am! If you don't come out here for Thanksgiving, that's it! I never want you here again! You go down to Jasper but you won't come here!"

"But that's different," I said.

"It is not!" she said. "You go down *there* because of guilt."

"Well, what about your own children?" I said, citing the return of my niece and nephew from college for the holidays. "Why do you think they come home?"

"Guilt," she said. "I don't know."

"Why don't you ask them?" I said.

"Because they'd lie," she said. "Oh, Nancy might tell me the truth," she said, naming her defiant daughter, "but not John."

"Why not?" I said.

"Because," she said, "he pleases his mother."

"What a thing to say! How cynical!" I said.

"Why?" she said. "Look what he gets away with."

And when I hung up the phone and told my roommate —who, having not spoken to his family in nine years, loved to hear news of anyone else's and had always watched the television show called *Family* without fail—he said, "You know what the *Times* says—Thanksgiving and Christmas, families go berserk. Everyone is depressed and anxious because they're supposed to love each other."

"That's true," I said. "I think of sitting down to turkey as sitting in a mine field. There's always a scene, and if there isn't, you feel when you leave the table that something's missing. How odd!"

But that year our households remained apart: We celebrated Thanksgiving separated by thousands of miles. I spent the day with friends who were by now a kind of family. Holidays were emotional crises that vanished anyway the next day. When I went to Jasper, I preferred to arrive after Christmas for that reason. But I began to look forward to being there. Each year our life together was simpler. As they got older my parents grew less critical— or rather, their interest in judging a world they had already played a part in waned—and we got on well. We were now three people reading in a house in the country. We took turns cooking for one another, and as if I could make my mother happy now simply by washing windows, I performed chores they could not or did not want to do themselves. And because the life we led together was close-knit —and so serene I sometimes poked myself—the day I chose to leave Jasper was difficult. It was a parting; because they were old, it seemed more a desertion. Physically they no longer resembled the people going out at night in Aruba. Nor did their lives resemble their former ones: They were very quiet.

By now every foursome with whom my father had played golf had died off. One winter, his pride offended by the fact he could no longer play as well as he once had, he decided to stay home and play solitaire. My mother goaded him to get out on the golf course. It did no good. He remained at his table on the porch, facing the wall, his back to the garden, the sky, the birds flying low across the golden crescent of marsh grass, the lake which was never used by any swimmer except myself—and continued to turn the cards over for hours each day.

Eventually my mother decided there was no point in renewing their membership in the golf club—but this was like saying there was no point in participating in life anymore; and I was not surprised to see her fall into an odd depression over the fact that they were letting the membership lapse. It was the first time in forty years they had not belonged to a golf club—and while it seemed a trivial fact to me, to her it was but recognition of the fact of life's finitude; and my disposal to view this as a comic event in suburban life was stayed by the sight of her at seventy-five rushing out to play with women younger than she every day of the last week of her membership. She returned home one afternoon so pale and dizzy she had to lie down, and I ran back and forth with glasses of water, fans, bowls of food, urging her to unbutton her blouse, loosen her brassiere, put her feet up, lie down. She became sad as the day their membership lapsed came closer; together she and my father composed a letter thanking the club and notifying its president they would not be renewing their membership. It was a solemn, gentle document. They sold the golf cart at an absurdly low price, as they sold everything; they disliked making a profit, much less taking advantage of people. The week after they ceased to play golf my mother's sadness vanished—and she declared she was happy not to have to debate whether to play golf or not; one fewer choice, more freedom. A couple down the road came by to say they felt a similar feeling of relief after recently deciding to have themselves cremated by a funeral parlor in Gainesville which provided for cold storage of the bodies while relatives were notified; they did not want to burden their children with having to make decisions under the pressure of their demise. The man and his son from the funeral parlor came by to talk to my parents the following Monday and enrolled them too. By chance I went to the beach that day and when I returned it was all settled; and I was grateful yet one more time to them.

And so they dwindled to two mice living in a house in the country; whole days passed in absolute silence, broken only by the thunderstorms that came to Jasper every summer afternoon around three o'clock and discharged with violent lightning bolts the moisture that had made the air unbearable and soggy all day. My father went onto the back porch and sat in a folding chair to watch the lightning whiten the garden through the dense rain blowing past him. Rain in Jasper in midsummer was never gentle—it was no place to plant delicate borders, or flowers that could not withstand the most intense monsoons. But my mother, livid that Florida had the highest incidence of cancer and lightning in the nation, would hang behind in the foyer and call to him through the louvered door, "Come in here, you fool! How can you do this to me?" During the course of the storm she ran around the house unplugging the television sets and lamps, wearing tiny gold tennis sneakers so she was grounded, and finally sitting in a dark room till it passed. I was glad my father remained on the back porch watching the spectacle; I was sorry that the storms scared my mother so. But this was not the only way in which he tortured her: The surreptitious drinking made her so upset she rose one morning and went out in her nightgown to my father reading the newspaper in his chair and told him if he did not stop, she would leave for good.

This proof that no relationship—not even theirs—was

secure until death so astonished me I felt nothing in the world could last. And when she apologized for discussing her troubles with me, I saw anew how courteous she was. Yet her apology was merely formal. My mother and I discussed my father at length as he sat playing solitaire on the porch; we argued whether we should take a trip to North Carolina, Alaska, or the east coast of Florida. She felt it would enliven him but I said, "What happens when we get there, though? Won't we just be changing the table he plays solitaire on? What if we do take a motel room at Crescent Beach—will he take a walk on the beach, or just sit down and deal the cards again? If he does that, why bother?" And as I told myself I should simply go with them, in their old age, on the journey they took us on as children, out west, I realized in my reluctance to do so a selfishness that was by no means pleasant to admit—but I did not want to spend a month conducting a man who had decided life was over through the Rockies; it seemed beside the point. So that left us with the alternative theory: He was actually happy. He was content with his daily journey to the post office, his game of solitaire, his cocktails and sleep. "Hasn't he always done what he wanted?" I said. My mother nodded. And four hours later we found ourselves just where we began: he playing solitaire and she sitting in the den saying, "A mind is a terrible thing to waste."

My mother did not care to go anywhere, but she was aware of what went on in the neighborhood and when I came in from my walk each evening, she would ask, "Who's still up? Is anyone up?" And I would tell her whose windows were still lighted, and what I had encountered on my walk. The nights in spring in Jasper were extraordinary: The moon was so bright the dogwoods in flower stood out in the silvery woods, and the air so soft the dogs sprawled silent when I walked by. When I turned onto our lawn the trees stood in dark circular shadows on the bright grass, and the sky was crusted with stars from horizon to horizon. I no longer imagined lovers with whom I would share this beauty here; the sight made me simply think I should return to New York. Some nights I walked uptown to the post office. The town was quiet. Jasper had about it a picturesque order that made one think, This is just how a town should be. The orange groves were sweet with blossoms; the gardenias exuded pools of scent as distinctly marked as shafts of cool water welling up from the bottom of the lake on hot days when the rest of the water was uncomfortably warm. An old woman sat in her chair before a television set in the front room of a tiny house I passed, so close I might have reached in through the window and jostled her awake. Water sprinklers revolved in the darkness, with a sexual throb, throwing bright drops over the perfect lawns. On the back porch of a somewhat dilapidated house two adolescents were lifting weights under a bare ceiling bulb. They huffed and puffed, and dropped the weights with a clank. Across from them in the second-story bedroom of a more prosperous house two girls were testing each other on the history of the Panama Canal. In the kitchen of another house I passed behind on a dark dirt lane, a shirtless young man stood before an open refrigerator, suspended in indecision before its shelves, wondering what to take out. I imagined him living alone, a solitary homosexual, the only one in town, and the love affair we would have right there in Jasper. Save for the man at the refrigerator—whom I never saw again—and the two girls studying for their history test, this tableau never changed. Each night I took the walk the old lady dozed before her television, and the friends lifted weights on the screened porch, and the pale lavender bug lights around the roof of a house near the public beach went *Zap! zap! zap!* in the perfect stillness.

One evening I encountered Vittorio on the road transfixed before the sight of the two boys lifting weights. "*Re-*

gardez," he said, turning to me. "Isn't that what it's all about? Pumping up at sixteen, to look good for the girls at the beach. What wonderful things one sees here at night!" He did not like to walk because he had bad luck with dogs, and asked me what routes I took. "I simply had to leave the house tonight," he said. "So much television—a man in the newspaper said that if you watch more than sixteen hours a week, your life is boring. This got us all upset. Years ago my mother wanted me to be President. Now all she wants me to do is sit with her when she watches *Love Boat.*" He stubbed his cigarette out on the road and said, "Tomorrow we have a big project, however, which will provide a break in the routine. Tomorrow," he said, waving his arms in the air as he walked off into the gloom of a grove of live oaks to resume his nocturnal stroll, "we are going to organize her shoes!"

The next day my own mother seemed tired of television herself. She came into my room in the middle of the afternoon to say, "You could have been a professional golfer. You had such a nice swing!" As for herself, she felt life was pointless now that she no longer had her looks. She came into my room an hour later with her two hands pulling back the folded skin beneath her neck and said, "How do I look? Should I have a face lift?" In fact her skin now bore the brown spots that even Porcelana could not remove, and her shoulders had both caved in and bunched up. Now when I embraced her—still finding in this contact some immense warm strength, as if I were Ajax and she the earth —she felt extremely fragile, as if her bones were hollow now, like those of the mockingbirds talking outside the window.

She returned from her walk that evening to tell us that the woman who lived three houses away from ours had a brain tumor. Gloom descended on the entire neighborhood. My father—whose seclusion did not prevent him from being so liked he was perhaps the most popular pall-bearer in town—made custards and sent them to her in the hospital. By the time she died, and we attended her funeral Mass, I was so depressed myself by the death of a woman I hardly knew—who apologized to the neighbors visiting her in the hospital for spending so much time in her house —I dared not forecast my reactions when this event befell my own family. At the funeral Mass I was surprised that Father Bob's cheerfulness, which usually made me clench my teeth, was the perfect note. He gave his most convincing sermon. His cheer no longer seemed shallow, bromidic, but muted, brave in the face of Death. I sat astonished at the beauty and dignity of the rites and his performance of them, while my father, who had suffered so many funerals, looked at his watch frequently throughout the Mass, sighing noisily through drawn lips and playing with his false teeth, impatient over his incarceration in church. At the Kiss of Peace I turned to my father. He looked at me and held his watch up, thinking I wished to know the time.

A moment later as I leaned over to whisper in his ear that the Mass was drawing to a close, he said in a voice that rang out in the utterly silent church, as clear as could be, "When's this damn thing over?" My mother did not move. Nor did anyone else; people are always polite.

As we walked from church afterward, she said, "You have to look at it humorously. Remember the deaf geezer at the Cooper wedding who sat down in front of us and started talking in a loud voice about all the daughters' divorces and former husbands, till his niece shut him up? Lose your sense of humor and you're finished," she said, as we got into our car under a bright blue, hot sky and assured my father we did not have to go to the cemetery.

Age was eroding them, like wind or water, leaving the barest elements of their personalities: They became silent for long stretches of the day, had no desire to visit or be visited even by their friends in town. I began to screen telephone calls. Whole days passed in absolute silence— broken sometimes by my mother coming into my room to ask me if I thought she should visit the hairdresser, or, prodded by some memory, to tell me a story. The past spilled out of her, new tales added to the repertoire familiar to me in Aruba. It occurred to me that I might ask her anything about her life—except the one thing I was most curious about: how she married my father. These questions about their romance I could not bring myself to ask, feeling, somehow, they were vulgar, even though as we sat together through those long, quiet afternoons, it seemed she was willing to answer any question at all, even about her feelings on that porch as we sat up nights in Aruba.

My mother in fact professed a new indifference to the things she once worried about—the general release of old age—but I did not believe this when I saw her rage over items on the evening news we watched together during dinner. She got so furious at reporters, or the Speaker of the House, that I would finally yell to calm her down: "Mother, they *want* you to react this way! That is the point of the news—to stir you up. That's what Schopenhauer said—journalists are professional alarmists. Relax!" But she would not. She would not drive with us because she thought my father and I steered too close to the edge of the highway. She would not help me decide which plane to take when I returned to New York, because she did not want to be responsible if it crashed. Yet when one Saturday morning she received word her favorite sister had died of an aneurism in Chicago during the night and she made reservations to fly there, she was not nervous at all.

At the Mass we attended together that evening, she stood beside me with her invisible sadness, dignified, calm, stoical, quiet, recalling her own memories of a childhood I was ignorant of, shaking hands with the person at her side and murmuring, "Peace be with you." As she left the church and moved through the crowd trading pleasantries with people she knew, her calm was all the more moving to me because there was not the slightest outward sign of its costing any effort.

I did not go to Chicago. It was decided I should stay home to be with my father: an assignment that was no doubt unnecessary and spared me from attending a funeral I could not imagine going to. I could not imagine entering the house we had spent so many Julys in on furlough from Aruba, going up the narrow staircase into my aunt's familiar kitchen, the formal living room where she often played the little Hammond organ for us, tossing wisecracks over her shoulder at the audience, and not finding her at home. I dreamt that while everyone was at the wake, or the cemetery, she was preparing dinner for them, and when they all came back from her funeral, she stood at the head of the stairs, wiping her hands, and said, "Sit down! What do you want to drink?" Such was the force of her personality, her love of life. My conclusion was: If it can happen to her, it can happen to anyone. My feeling was: This great and happy family, this prosperous, cheerful, numerous family's defense has now been breached; the enemy has landed, and it is only a matter of time before he works his way to the capital city.

Mother returned from Chicago with the same calm evident at her departure—she who was so nervous at the prospect of flying had returned in a thunderstorm and not been frightened at all, I learned on inquiring—and told us about the funeral. "They do things differently now," she said. "We went to a Mass and didn't even go to the cemetery. That was the last we saw of her, in the chapel. The funeral home takes care of the burial." And I was surprised to learn that funerals reflect the styles of the day as much as haircuts. As she removed her shoes and sat down with the drink

228 · Andrew Holleran

my father mixed for her, she told us of the past four days.
My mother could not stop praising the suits my sister wore,
and the compliments she received on her daughter's
beauty. So hopelessly bound up was my family with looks;
toward the end of our conversation my mother complained
that the last time she was in Chicago, men turned around
on the street to look at her, but this time she was ignored.
"The worst part of being old," she said as she sipped her
welcoming cocktail, "is that you're invisible!"

The journey, or the four days in a northern climate, or
the thoughts a funeral inevitably gives rise to, stirred the
flame of life in my mother's soul for a while after her return
to Jasper. She came into my room later that evening—
bored with television, as I knew she would be, unable to
resume life in her prison quite yet—and said, "Whatever
you're going to do, do it now."

I looked up at her standing just within the door and said,
"What?"

"Whatever you're going to do," she said, "*do it now.*" And
she turned around and went back to the den, hearing the
theme music for the program she liked. The words seemed
to me to belong to that same category as those addressed to
Vittorio when he left business school: "We only want you
to be happy." They were admirable and generous advice
and so general that like Saint Augustine's summation of
morality, "Love God, and do as you will," they left it completely up to me to choose my action. Only what it was I
still had no idea.

My mother was unsure of what to do with the newfound
energy induced by her trip north; we discussed a trip across
Canada by train, a cruise up the Alaskan coast, but nothing
came of these plans. Each evening found us instead in front
of the television attempting to answer the questions on
Joker's Wild. On Wednesday, Mother went to the beauty
parlor and came into my room afterward and stood in the

doorway waiting for my appraisal. Each time I tried to discern some new aspect to praise or criticize. Each Saturday she argued with herself whether she could afford long-distance calls. (Whenever the stock market fell more than ten points, she would turn from the television set and announce, "We're wiped out.") I convinced her that she could. But then I passed her doorway and saw her sitting with her hand on the telephone staring into space.

"What's wrong?" I said.

She said, "I can't call Chicago." The fact that she could no longer talk to her favorite sister momentarily stopped me too. We looked at each other. Then she got up and put the phone back on the little table beside her bed.

Occasionally at night my uncle called and began to sob on the telephone to Mother that my aunt was his whole life, and his own life was over now that she was gone. My mother wished to invite him to Florida but could not, because on a previous visit he and my father did not get along —two Germans who had stubborn ideas about how things should be done.

It looked as if my father thought his life was over, too, despite the fact that his wife still breathed. When we drove to the airport one day toward the end of April, while the woods and gardens were still laced with white dogwoods and pink azaleas, and I said, "Look! The azaleas are still blooming—isn't that amazing?" He replied, "Yes, they're just about finished, now the hot weather is here." And I realized—as I had when I turned to shake his hand in church, and he had held up his watch—that we regarded the world with fundamentally different biases, due simply to our positions in time; and where a young man saw a forest still filled with color, an old one saw spring expiring in devastation around him.

I often thought of seeing Savannah, the barrier islands, Charleston, on my way back to New York—these beautiful places I was always flying over—but never did. I got onto the plane and was home in three hours. The city I returned to was always as unexpected as the mother I found on the porch when returning from school in Aruba. It was surely not the one I had found when I arrived in 1971. The city I kept coming back to long after the romantic hopefulness of youth was exhausted did not resemble the one I had lived in at the start of the decade. For just as Jasper was no longer the rustic little backwater we found on settling there—just as its drab woods held new suburban ranch houses, its main street an art gallery, boutique, jewelry store, its airport drug-smugglers, its lake the effluence of septic tanks owned by citizens who refused to invest in a modern waste-disposal system because they had retired to Florida, after all, to escape taxes—so the small sliver of New York in which I lived was altered. And the changes were perhaps more striking to someone who has been away for a while, who returns to town, not like Rip Van Winkle but like someone who hasn't seen a particular friend in several years and is surprised to find gray hair at his temples. For the one thing I had been unconscious of till recently, the single element I had utterly ignored in my anxious worry about the nature of my life and relationships with other people, was time. And I now saw that my conclusions, or lack of them, were beside the point: Whether one played the game or stood on the sidelines watching, the afternoon waned.

There were changes visible to me on the street as I walked east to St. Mark's Place from the subway, in that curious mood of detachment and relief, estrangement and joy, that I always felt on returning to New York from Jasper before I told anyone I was back. It was more crowded for one thing. The neighborhood in which I lived was now popular with young people because rents everywhere else were absurdly high. There were more homosexual men than ever before living south of Fourteenth Street for another, and many of them belonged to a new generation whose style was different from my own when I was twenty-six. The style which was so masculine in my youthful eyes (the short hair, beard, plaid shirts, an ensemble so evocative that when I thought of the cold evenings on Fire Island in late September which brought men into the Sandpiper in woolen shirts, I wanted to go there again) was now discredited: a cliché in which many of my generation were immured, so that when one passed me he simply seemed like a worn veteran of a war that was now over. It was a style we disdained if we still saw it on another man who had neither the taste nor intelligence to realize it was meaningless now, unless it was some homosexual Spaniard or Frenchman vacationing in New York for whom the getup was still *au courant*. On the sidewalk west of Astor Place on which New Wave groups stenciled the names of their bands (with that passion for advertisement which made one think they spent every night pasting posters on the walls and mail bins of St. Mark's Place), I noticed as I walked east the words CLONES GO HOME. I peered closer and saw that the author was a collective called "Fags Against Facial Hair." Moustaches and beards were now as unpopular among young homosexuals as the Gang of Four was with the current regime in Peking.

Yet even these figures I viewed coolly; not only was erotomania something which finally had loosened its grip on me, but everyone was suspect now. Celebrities of our sexual demimonde were dying of bizarre cancers, and an epidemic of intestinal parasites had subverted the pleasures of promiscuous sex as abruptly as OPEC ended the era of cheap energy. But more important, I was no longer compelled by desire. It was apt that the cockring I encountered on the most jaded homosexuals at the Everard baths when I first went there was now worn as a bracelet by the New Wave check-out girl in the grocery I stopped in for a carton

232 · *Andrew Holleran*

of eggs, the beautiful mulatto with green hair. Truly, another style, another generation had moved into my dear streets like a vast, shallow tide while I was sleeping.

Yet I should no more be surprised by this fact than I was to enter my building and remember that there were still five flights to climb to my apartment. The stairs were exactly as I remembered them—including Mister Friel at the top of them, sitting in his apartment when I knocked on the door, reading *Interview*. "Oh, *bravo*! Oh, my dear, how good to see you!" he said, getting up. "Welcome back! I'm waiting for a phone call from a man who's going to teach us to unite love and sex. I know it's hard to believe anyone in New York—anyone on earth—knows how to do that, but I met him at Sullivan's last night at dinner and he says he can. And how were your parents? You know, I have not had a good winter."

"I'm sorry," I said. "I heard your mother died."

"She did. It was hell. Someday I will de*scribe* to you the scene at the funeral home. Imagine a farce by Racine," he said. "Yet you know? I still feel she is with me. I can't explain it, but you can't be that close to someone and have it end. Do you understand? We are still together," he said.

"Still together?"

"Yes," he said, wiping his forehead and sitting down on a stack of newspapers, flushed and excited. "I think of her every day, and when I go to sleep—oh, God, I won't tell you what I think then! Black thoughts, black thoughts, the blackest. But *she* was the world for me, and the world without her is not quite real, if you know what I mean. *She* is more real."

"The woman on the plane was reading one of those books about how horrid our mothers are," I said. "I don't think we can blame it on our mothers, do you?"

"Why not?" he said.

"Well, it's not their fault," I said.

"It's not anyone's fault," he said. "Except His." He looked up to the ceiling.

"Then you think people are unique," I said, sitting down. "And irreplaceable. You don't think love is just something that comes out of us, and it doesn't matter who the object is; anyone will do. Which is what I sometimes think."

"Well, of course they are unique, and certain relationships are never replaced! Especially those, as Kierkegaard says, rich in time. So cling to the ones you have, my dear, cling to the ones you have! And yet in clinging to the old ones, we must not forget that life consists in making new ones. Like the young man who is going to teach me to unite love and sex," he said. "Was it Scott Fitzgerald who said, 'Life has little more than youth, or the love of youth in others'? Romantic, John used to say, but so true, my dear. So true. To be with this young man from Ohio was to bask in the warmth of life itself. I came home last night so exhilarated. I wanted to write his parents and say: My compliments. Thank you for producing so admirable a human being. I wanted to write the governor of Ohio. I wanted to say: Thank you, Ohio. I think we are entering a new age," he said. "The cancer has everyone so frightened now that they won't just sleep with anyone that moves. As they did five years ago. No, they are terrified. Out of this dreadful disease, perhaps something good will come. We are treating each other like human beings again. Not like hamburgers. This young man is interested in knowing a person before he sleeps with him. He told me so! He wants to put sex after intimacy, rather than the other way around." He waved his hands in the air. "So be as cheerful as you can, my dear, despite—because of—all the reasons not to be!" The telephone rang and he jumped up. "There he is!" He picked up the receiver. "Hello? Oh, no, John, I cannot talk now, I must keep the line open for a very important call. I tell you I have to go, the bank is closing, my hair is on fire! Call me later!" he said. I left his apartment quietly while he was still trying to persuade his caller to end a conversation he could not. Mister Friel could not hang up on anyone. He rose each morning and said "No" twenty times before getting his coffee in order to instill in himself an ability to refuse people which was not his naturally. And I thought as I returned to my own apartment: Nothing changes. Not even the voice of my mother when I telephoned her to assure her I was safe.

On this first call we were people who had just parted and might be said to be in different rooms of the same house—one that contained both New York and Jasper. On the second she began to sound like a separate person. On the third and fourth she reverted to an old woman living in a small town down south, who told me about my father's visit to an ear doctor the previous Monday.

We always pretended I was returning to Jasper after a brief visit to New York to pay my bills and collect my mail. As the spring wore on this lost its force. She said, "When are you coming home?" and added quickly, with a laugh, "You don't have to answer that," in the shy voice of a girl of seventeen hoping not to be rejected. This voice was so peculiar it reminded me of her saying, "I may look like Death, but I feel seventeen inside." Or she would say, "Be careful going out, Paul," and in using my name shock me even further, for it implied she conceived of me as a separate person. I still did not think I was—I was still traveling on the passport the two of us shared when I was young, with its photograph of me on her lap, and she in her prime. The thought of her came to me at odd times that summer: at the beach, watching a young woman dip her baby in and out of a tidal pool, or even while swimming, when I was grateful to her for having introduced me to the ocean early in life so that I felt confident in the surf. In the middle of the sea I reflected that I owed her and my father this day, and all the others. It was when I was happiest that I felt worst. A person is after all not the son of God but rather of two people in Florida. On such ordinary days—in the ocean—I thought of them with surprise. They entered my mind at odd times (in the way Sal did): like ghosts. Thinking of these former loves convinced me the freshest part of life was behind me, that everything else would refer to the past. I felt stuck in self-pity. What had happened was simply that I'd arrived in middle life. I was middle-aged. I no longer regarded the strange man looking at me as we stood a few feet from each other in the surf with the excitement I felt ten years earlier, when love and desire were inseparable. This unifying lust—this spark that leapt the space between two beings with utterly different pasts, and in their union produced a future—no longer impelled me to do things I couldn't do without it. Under the gaze of this young man, I felt helpless—for I had too much of a past at this point to leap the space between us. I was obdurate, crusted over with the past—and knowing this, I turned away and walked back down the beach to the house of friends with whom I had now been familiar for a decade.

It seemed to me there was no point except pleasure in further love affairs; and to a puritan that can never be the point of anything.

And the nights I used to spend dancing or walking the streets, I now spent in bed reading *The New York Times*—with which I postponed the moment when I finally turned the light off. I read the article on the the deployment of missiles in Europe, the withdrawal of troops from Beirut, the robbery of a bank in Queens. I read the temperatures of cities around the world, and the fishing forecast for Long Island Sound. I read a review of two restaurants, a piece on moisturizing lotions. I read an article on a man who sold Milanese food in Soho—and then realized he was someone

I and several others had fallen in love with when I first came to New York. Then I read the tiny paragraphs which told—on an obscure page—of stabbings, holdups, the robbery of a man in a wheelchair by thieves who took the wheelchair too. When I turned off the light I could not sleep at all; so I turned it on and read an article on politics in Chad and then retired again.

Sometimes I fell asleep only to waken in the depths of the winter night at the sound of the steam hissing from the pipe. My thoughts were always clear: Whatever I had been thinking of during the day—traveling to Rio de Janeiro, for instance—now seemed stark and dreary. I could not go to Brazil; what a stupid idea; I must tell Mister Friel the trip was off; what was I thinking of, trying to escape? What will you find in Brazil? What can you possibly believe in now? And I thought of the poem by Cavafy which tells us in ruining one city for ourselves, we ruin all cities, and so it is pointless to change residences. At night one could not fool oneself. Thoughts were so different then, the events and people who moved you during the day were stripped of their urgency and glamour.

One night I awoke with a violent start, as if someone had touched my shoulder—an angel, summoning me for an interview with God. And when I recovered my sense, I wondered: What if this ever happened? Would I have a cold, as I did now? Would I enter His presence having to piss, as I do now? And I realized no angel had awakened me; only my bladder. Or rather, my conscience.

And I turned over on my side and began to imagine making love with someone—the only comfort at that hour; allowing the two of us to be perfect lovers, because it was a dream. Then I told myself this was stupid. Why in New York should I content myself with an imaginary lover? So I threw back the covers, dressed, and ran downstairs. The street was always empty at that hour. A youth in a leather coat was putting up a poster for the Dead Kennedys on the wall of the St. Mark's theater as I broke into a run up the avenue—simultaneously exhausted and delighted to be awake at three in the morning, racing to reach the park at Fifteenth Street and learn who was standing beneath the trees. Most nights I found no one—it was too cold—and I returned home with the consolation that I had at least not missed anyone. And as I undressed I realized that all these clothes Sal had given me: a pair of boots, a green shirt, a blue parka with a yellow lift ticket—from a ski resort we had visited one Sunday as cold as this one—still attached to the zipper. I refused to throw the lift ticket away. It was proof of his kindness, the winter I thought of each November I remained in this city, unable to leave it.

And as I lay there I thought I would have to get out of this room; I could no longer lie in it at night, and I began to imagine other rooms, larger, in the country, with high ceilings, a fireplace, windows against which tree branches tapped at night.

And in the darkness I began to see that I was now, for better or worse, truly in the middle of the night, in the middle of life, the point at which my parents were when I entered their lives. And I began to think of them with curiosity and awe. I had no more seen all of their lives than they would see of mine. On Easter Sunday my conception of them was even more confusing. Holidays annoyed me for the most part—Thanksgiving and Christmas visits to Pennsylvania or Jasper seemed like journeys I made under duress. I wanted to be free of the family and their judgment and expectations. The summons to a reunion was like the summons to a funeral. I wanted to stay in the city instead and eschew the obligatory and tedious customs. Easter was quite different. It was not a holiday one had to visit one's family on, nor a holiday one dreaded or resented because of the commercial hoopla. No, Easter was a minor festival unclaimed by the major department stores, and when it occurred, the nostalgia I felt was even more disturbing because it was unexpected.

Sometimes after returning to New York from Jasper I continued to attend Mass at a cavernous church on Eleventh Street where the crowd was so sparse at the five-thirty service that during the Kiss of Peace the bums, students, widows, and tourists nodded at each other across a space of six empty pews like duchesses at a garden party. I even persuaded Vittorio to go one Saturday evening, but when we came out and I inquired how he felt, he said, "I spent the whole time thinking about that lousy shit Eddie Schlageter and how he owes me three hundred bucks but keeps telling me about the coat he bought at Bloomingdale's or his trip to Paris, as if he doesn't owe me a cent! That's what I thought about during Mass." And eventually I stopped going myself, for without my mother, away from Jasper, it seemed a pointless exercise. On Easter Sunday, however, I awoke in my apartment and thought, Who can I call who would go to church with me? For I did not want to go alone.

It was not out of any religious impulse that I felt I had to attend Mass that morning. Certainly I no longer believed in that event whose sudden banishment of the somber gravity of Lent struck me as odd, abrupt, arbitrary, even as a child: the Resurrection. Sometimes, because it was still early to call my friends for fear of waking them after the debauch of Saturday night, I took the Bible down and read the account of Mary Magdalen's discovery of the stone rolled back from the Tomb. Like everything in the Gospels it had a powerful effect. I believed in the events narrated in the New Testament not so much because I believed in God but because its accumulation of detail rang true. I might doubt the divinity of Jesus but I believed absolutely in the naked youth who appears while Christ is being arrested and then runs off into the night. Why would he be mentioned, except that he did appear and run away in just that manner? Yet little else was certain. I no longer believed when I awoke in the morning that I could, by lying still in my dark room, balance past, present, and future, or figure everything out. I was certain that even death would provide no illumination—that we died ignorant, confused, like novelists who cannot bring an aesthetic shape to their material. There was no point in settling accounts with my parents. How could it help? We knew everything—and nothing—about each other now. We might be joined beyond the grave, and we might not. There might or might not be some moment of forgiveness for everything. But surely we had been together once on a morning just like this—and the memory of those Sundays began to replace, with the sensual realities of the past, my religious doubts.

When I awoke on a hot Easter Sunday in Manhattan with no one to attend church with—Mister Friel was in Brooklyn, escorting his father—I remembered those Easters in Aruba when my mother, in short gloves and a hat, the apotheosis of the mother of my dreams, would take us to Sint Nicolaas for Mass, and then back home to our garden to hunt for colored eggs hidden on the lawn. So sentimental did I turn that I reached for the telephone and called Jasper instead. How proud I was to be a Catholic on those Sundays in Aruba; how beautiful the island seemed with its gardenias, temple lilies, flower-filled church! But the woman who answered I did not even recognize at first —her mouth was full of salad. She was having lunch with the Farrells and wondered why I was calling. I could not tell her. I wished her a happy Easter, said nothing about her gloves, or perfume, or colored eggs, and hung up. As I sat there in my silent room I saw these memories would be with me forever, that wherever they were, I was: some part of me. But the life I must begin was my own—a separate person's. This was difficult. For I realized that so much memory and desire swirl about in the hearts of men on this planet that, just as we can look at Neptune and say it is covered with liquid nitrogen, or Venus and see a mantle of hydrochloric acid, so it seemed to me that were one to look at Earth from afar one would say it is covered completely in Ignorance.